WATER STREET

JP MAXWELL

Published in 2023 by BK Fiction, an imprint of Bennion Kearny Limited.

ISBN: 978-1-7393062-3-6

Published by BK Fiction, an imprint of Bennion Kearny Ltd
6 Woodside
Churnet View Road
Oakamoor
Staffordshire
ST10 3AE

www.BennionKearny.com

It might seem too much to thank the ancestors, but it was their voices that I heard calling me from across decades and centuries. Their immigrant song lilts away in my noggin and they speak to me in old photos and letters. They are in the oral tradition of the Maxwells, Burkes, Howards, et al, more profound than any archive. Thanks to my beloved and much-missed parents Mary and Don for passing me this torch, at the top of this legend with their place in eternity.

To Clare Coombes at The Liverpool Literary Agency for her guidance and boundless energy. Also, to James Lumsden-Cook at BK for his willingness to take on a new voice and gumption to the task of getting this up to its best scratch.

To Khurram Shabir and Christian Murray-Smith for believing in this yarn and their boundless faith and encouragement when it was nothing. To Jeff Young and Caroline Smailes for making me believe. And to my amazing wife Katy as an inspiration behind the creation of strong and smart women. Water Street is the sum of all their parts.

- JP Maxwell, April 2023

PREFACE – FROM A GAOL TO A COFFEE HOUSE SERAGLIO

Late in the evening, June 2nd 1863

Nib on paper, scratching out an exquisite cursive hand, the first words of *The African Leviathan, a novel by Mr Payton Ake.*

'Bah.'

Alas. He screws the folio up and tosses it into the fire. The problem? It is too quiet in here tonight. Too quiet to read or write. Too quiet to do anything but expect trouble.

Mr Ake runs the busiest bridewell gaol in the entire city. This is on account of the proximity to the docks and Landing Stage, where all manner of seafarers, warehousemen, thieves, prostitutes and racketeers ply their trade in an endless cycle of victims and perpetrators, playing out nightly hard luck stories. The worst offenders are usually corralled into this dense, red brick pen, prior to court, prison, the rope or going back on the streets. Never is there a dearth of customers, day or night.

The Campbell Square Bridewell is a small but impregnable bastion of correction, the vital first staging post of crime and punishment and the West African leviathan that is Ake values that principle like no other. He has known the fear of death in battle, on the high seas, in thick, corroded iron chains, in the dark alleys between warehouses. He knows where he prefers to be, for the future of his children, if not so much for his own sake. To be on the right side.

Law is protection.

Law is certainty.

Mr Ake is the law.

What else is there to do? Mop the floor? Wash the walls? The sweet aroma of his sandalwood and ether solution clings to everything, sanitising and masking. He only coated the place minutes ago, and it isn't even dry yet. So what else? Write a novel? Tried it. The problem with having too much to say is where to start.

Some evenings, when he gets too much time to think, he doubts all of his high principles and attempts to better himself, this being one of those particular nights. Because it is quiet. Damn it. Damn that quiet. It is a cacophony. It is an echo chamber of madness.

That's good. He should write that down. He picks up his quill.

The iron door reverberates with the clanging groan of the knocker. Is this the devil come to claim him? Has Old Nick stopped time and arranged for this still evening, just so he can feast on Payton Ake's rich, delicious Igbo soul without interruption or distraction? If so, at least it is salvation from this dreadful inertia.

He unbolts the door and pulls it open.

'Captain Frank?' he says. 'This is highly unusual for you to come here…'

A gloved finger is pressed to a trimmed and moustachioed lip. It belongs to a diminutive man in an immaculate cape and top hat ensemble. He is Captain John Frank, Commander and Chief Constable of the Liverpool Watch and Mr Ake is quite correct. He never comes here, or goes anywhere in this city, these days. So then, why tonight? Mr Ake quickly gathers that the empty gaol really is no coincidence. Captain Frank remains on horseback in the shadows of the narrow yard, keeping at eye level with his old, old friend.

'Payton,' he rasps. His eyes are bloodshot, his manner shaken, discombobulated. Something is very wrong. Mr Ake knows this man like no other.

'John? What is the matter?'

'I can count on you. Can I not?'

'Always and forever.'

This relieves just a pinch of his troubled temper. 'That is all I wanted to know.'

'John, what vexes you so?'

'Awful trouble, Payton. A disturbance to this fair city like we have never seen before. A rift in the ranks, a deep and sudden schism. I must warn you, but I must also count upon you.'

'John, please tell me what…'

He presses his finger to his lips again, giddies his horse and canters out of the yard before galloping away, hooves thundering. Mr Ake is left with a riddle, as he always is when he meets this man.

'John?'

Half a mile across town and another world away, there is drinking, gaming and cavorting above a coffee house on Castle Street. Discreet, worldly gentlemen clientele call it *The Seraglio*, although there is precious little discretion on display tonight.

The Commander has done this in every port worth its salt, from Savannah, Georgia to New Orleans to Cherbourg and Rotterdam. A life as a senior Naval officer takes you to some places, but this – here – is the zenith of drinking, gaming and cavorting. This here is hog heaven; this here is Liverpool. Real Ottoman stylings, sweet hashish and opium aromas, exclusively reserved, the finest of gentlemanly pleasures from all over the Empire under one roof. Do they ever serve coffee here?

The cooze, his favourite, whazhername, Nancy that's it, blonde ringlets, porcelain skin, sits on his knee, grinding her purrrfect lil derrière into him. She's probably Irish, but he'll disregard that on the grounds that she is so good at what she does. The Mayor himself recommended her to him, offering up nothing but the finest of everything to his guest in the city. The Commander sups rum, none of that rough Navy swill but a rare and expensive molasses distillation. His fingers go walking upon Fancy Nancy and his hands follow, like he's playing a bass fiddle. She can handle his roughest touches, unlike all the others.

A fulsome win on the tables tonight, though he'd swear that the powers that be make it happen that way, for he never loses in this town. Rather takes the fun out of it. It mirrors all his other business in Liverpool and Great Britain, and man does he have some other business, but this slinky trollop reminds him fast that he's done with all that for tonight. She grabs the bottle and swills rum in that pretty little mouth of hers before kissing it back to him, long and deep. She looks like she is actually enjoying the whole act, all sassy 'n' slinky, tireless in her work. This gal really knows what she's doing. She'd give them New Orleans coozes a run for their money.

Click. He hears that tiny sound from across the room, attuned to it from his long years of bushwhacking and river piracy on the old Mississippi, unmistakable and deadly. Nancy yelps as he pulls his Smith & Wesson and shoots instantly into a red curtain at the far end of this long room.

His slug catches the ingrate sniper with a whomp, and the would-be assassin falls out from behind the fabric and onto the wooden floor, thudding down stone-twitching dead as he strikes the wooden deck, an expression of surprise on his mug. Caught him square in the moustache, a neat hole in the front, brains spattered out of the back. Too bad he got killed rather than maimed as, inevitably and immediately, there are questions to be raised about this incident. The Browning pistol remains clutched tight in his hand, an inferior weapon held by an inferior fellow.

Commander Banastre Xavier Dunwoody delicately removes the gasping Nancy from his lap and gets to his feet, groaning and too full of rum to have to deal with this bullshit. He goes over to inspect his failed nemesis closer. Everything and everyone has stopped in this room, all eyes on either him or the corpse, depending upon which sight takes their fancy in this den of sin and iniquity. Reckon this fella had not one iota who he'd been commissioned to shoot, else he wouldn't have dared set foot in this place. Reckon too he can't talk much now with that slug in his face and his grey matter dripping off the crushed velvet drapes.

'Damn.'

Well, that's a mighty fine evening ruined, then.

#1 THE STINK

About town, June 3rd 1863

Rotten eggs and fish. All about every estate, whether in the gentrified streets of Toxteth where they live in their townhouses on 101 Canning Street, or further down the hill to the sprawling, endless docks, the court slums, the sloppy slurry at the riverside. The stink is angry; the stink is relentless. It annexes the nostrils, only escaping down into the palate to coat the tastebuds with the most horrid of lavatorial tangs.

There she is, unrecognisable in a stove pipe hat and dark blue great coat several sizes too large for her distinctive shape. Astride a sturdy filly, cantering down the hill from Canning Street towards the grand but ominous Customs House before passing the United States Consul on Paradise Street. It is not a route they had to take, but they have special reasons to.

Harriet Dunwoody, a glowing, pregnant Southern Belle who has somehow found herself displaced to this maggot hill of a Northern clime, hard sniffs a handkerchief laced with pungent, Parisian cologne to cover the malodourous imposition, but it permeates and overwhelms everything else and, in all those months since their arrival, she still hasn't adjusted. Her condition doesn't help much either, with every sensation that much more febrile, especially pain and smell. Ugh.

Some whiff about this here Liverpool.

Her nag's hooves clack and scrape the cobbles in a steady rhythm, and she considers what must presently be called home, the townhouse back up there on the hill and the man she left in bed, snoring like a spent boar. She has his every movement mapped and logged. Commander Banastre Xavier Dunwoody, her beloved husband and pappy to her baby, won't rise until midday, and that is as surefire a bet as you'll ever get.

Then he will demand a hearty breakfast and admonish the staff for something non-existent or trivial. Then he will, perchance, maybe head to what he calls 'The Consulate' on Rumford Place to begin his day's business of snorting and swearing and cursing the Yankee Yoke and all its hideous insidiousness. Perchance, probably, definitely, maybe, *certainly* drinks to follow with those Denizens of the Cotton Exchange, nouveau riche merchants frothing with rage at the Union for causing a confounded cotton drought in the port and mills of Lancashire. How dare their gains be attacked and withdrawn so. How much her Southern gentleman husband knows their chagrin, milks it, harnesses its angry potential and distils it into his own power; the furnaces of hell. How now Master and Commander Banastre Xavier Dunwoody, friend of the businessman, fervent ally of The Chamber of Commerce. Now there's a *real* American. A gentleman blessed with purview, a messiah of the Mississippi, arrived to the Mersey with a chest full of promises. Bravo Banastre, tell us another of your roister-doister seafaring tales while we ply you with rum, cigars and tarts. Harriet knows all of it, every tired line and every drunken tryst. It is her business to know, on pain of death.

Conté Marie-Louise Louverture, the one member of staff that Harriet was able to bring with her from the Creole house detail in Baton Rouge, accompanies her on Rosalinda, her favourite steed. Well, 'staff' is a term reserved for those who can only observe the pair at a distance, for they are first among equals and have been for a lifetime. Only the accident of birth dictates what they must show the world in regular circumstances. This morning though, the circumstances are far from regular. They are both clad head to toe in Peeler outfits 'borrowed' from the Constabulary laundry, baggy enough to hide their womanhood and identities at a glance from any chattering classes in the street.

They pass the official American Consulate, the huge golden eagle above the doors indicating this city's long and intractable links with what is now a troubled land, a place on the edge of doom, fighting for its survival from the likes of Banastre X. Dunwoody. There he is, the bald eagle himself, United States Consul Thomas Haines Dudley, on his hands and knees scrubbing faeces off his patio doors as his long-suffering staff tackle the obscene graffiti on the whitewash. Banastre pays local gangs to perform this mischief often thrice daily, and every morning, noon and night Dudley is there with a bucket of suds, setting a pious example to all. Bless him, but he cannot know about the two figures gliding past him on a particular business of their own. If he represents the fair means of winning the war,

Harriet and Conté are the foul. Their commanding officer has seen to that.

Boarding the paddle steamer Cheshire still mounted on their horses, they sail across the Mersey river, taking in all the contrasts of industry, maritime trade, poverty and opulence in one vista, before landing at Woodside Ferry. The Bayou, it ain't. Landing up, they traverse the seawall track in the direction of the Cammell Laird shipyard in Birkenhead, the fastest-growing part of the city. Just a pair of Watchmen watching; nothing to see here.

And how the other side of the river really, really goddamn reeks, even worse than across the water. Necrotic and sooty, choking and acrid. The coal black death, mined from deep underground and delivered to the lungs via the burners of industry, mingling with the stench of a river that is an open sewer, a fiesta of cholera. Praise be for the Mississippi, how Harriet laments it.

Conté says nothing on the ride, quiet in public places as usual. She is as far from knowing her place as she will ever get, more that she retains her own counsel to stay covered and alert to a long tariff of dangers that follow the pair everywhere they go in this city. A pregnant lady and her maid shouldn't be seen out at all, never mind riding in disguise. Conté has adopted the stiff-backed countenance of a Peeler, and she knows how to carry herself just right to evade anything but the closest of inspections. It is an easy role for her.

At the grand, cast-iron gates, they espy the tangle of looming masts belonging to vessels of every variety of size, commission, construction and repair. This is only matched by a ragged cacophony of metal and woodwork, created by thousands of yard workers regimented to the beat of foremen and supervisors with their blueprints and their commissions and their ambitions to dominate the seas with their smoke stacks and paddle wheels, to which there is no ceiling. This place is richer than a goldmine; Harriet has seen the accounts liberated from Banastre's records. Hidden in plain sight, some 53% of the builds carried out here are for the Confederate Navy in direct violation of the British Government policy of neutrality – a fast and loose statute if ever there was one. This city does what it wants, for better or worse, because it has the money, scandalous to say so, but more than even London at the current rate of growth. There is not even a token attempt to hide this magnificent maleficence here at Cammell Laird.

Conté grabs her shoulder and reads from her notes. 'The Confederate State Ship Banshee, stage name HMS Serendipity, natch. 533 tons. 68-pound guns. 5-inch iron-plated armour. A 15-foot spiked ram. Damn.'

She jabs a finger at the vessel, but it is impossible to miss it.

'Damn,' mutters Harriet, 'Some ram.'

'That big fucker will rip our fleet to driftwood.'

'Yup.'

Harriet had heard about this, but it hasn't prepared her for the sight. A huge, looming, ironclad, side paddle-steamer, lurking in dry dock just beyond the schooner builds dwarfed by its majesty, awaiting launch amongst a trove of smaller gunboats destined themselves for The War. It is a giant floating buttress and visual proof that the limeys are very much part of it all, as much as The British Government feigns to demur from such accusations.

It is the *CSS Banshee* and Harriet can already hear it screaming.

'You've gone a worrying shade of puce, Harry. Are you quite woozy?'

'I'm fine. Don't start fussing again.'

'Liar. You're having collywobbles. Plain as day.'

'Indigestion.'

Conté cracks her jaw. 'We don't have to do this.'

'We don't have to do anything. We're women. Sorry, we're ladies.'

'Speak for yourself. I'll rephrase. You don't have to do this.' Harriet shakes her head. In what world would that statement ever be correct? Her companion is content to persist with her line. 'I'm gonna keep saying it, whether you like it or you don't, Harry.'

As they get up close to the ironclad beast and stalk the quay, Harriet is mindful of their manager in this enterprise, all of 4,500

miles away from this spot. Is it Major General Butler's fault, or is he just restricted by the whims and follies of his own superiors? Do they actually want to win this goddamn War? Conté scribbles notes into her notebook and then artfully sketches what she sees. More numbers than words go down on paper, and she scratches her head again, baffling herself with logistics.

Harriet stares at her upright, uptight friend, who speaks back at her without taking her eyes off her notes. 'And I'm gonna *keep* saying it, Harry.'

'Your mouth will stick fast that way one day. Don't say I didn't warn you.' Harriet knows how to stand her ground with Conté, where few would. She's had nearly a lifetime of practice. 'This isn't a one-woman job, Conté.'

'That's right. It's a one-army job. So if anyone is getting killed, it should be me. There are two of you. At least that sum is simple.'

Harriet strokes her friend's arm, rebuffing her attempts to protect her from what is coming for the umpteenth time this morning. 'How much dynamite are we going to require?'

Conté sucks air through her front teeth and wedges the pencil behind her ear, checking her figures again.

'I'd say a ton,' says a voice behind them. 'But I'd also say that youse are stark-raving fuckin' mad. A right pair of wagons so.'

The voice is gravelly, pickled in sarcasm and deep as the bottomless pit. The face is wide, bent, pocked and scarred with a thousand brawls. The eyes are wide and cute, full of Donegal devilment. He almost sings his words rather than speaks them.

'Then what are you doing here wasting your time with us?' growls Conté without even looking at him.

Royston Chubb chuckles and prods a meaty thumb in Conté's direction.

'Listen to this one. Because I like gold, you cheeky sweat. That makes a man mad too. I heard stories about your Wild West.'

'Harriet, I don't trust this common, scabrous turd, and I don't care if he hears it.'

Chubb's wide mouth gapes like a fish at the brazen insult, voice raising a couple of octaves. 'Listen to her. She's a cheeky one above her station, isn't she? Go fetch me somethin' or other.'

Harriet says, 'We're all on the same side, Mr Chubb. Both of you, wind it back.'

Conté continues to seethe and shirk eye contact with Chubb. 'Butler can go whistle from a thousand leagues away. Setting us up with local criminals. This is not a fit enterprise, Harry. Let me act alone.'

Chubb is missing several of his front teeth, and the rest are brown stumps. 'Harry, is it so? That's a chappy's name. Ye don't look too much like a chappy with that babbee belly of yours. I can see it under that big coat of yours. No flies on me. You must be sweating like a geebag.'

'What?'

Conté finally brings herself to glare at the man, which is hardly an upgrade from ignoring him. 'We can manage just fine without your help, sir. You'll still get paid. So off with you, clamber back under your stone.'

Several of the Irishman's chins wobble as he shakes his head, red and silver tufts of his receding hair dotted around his glistening pate, which he mops with his tweed cap.

'Fucking maddening hot, so it is, for a morning.'

Conté bristles again. 'Mind your language.'

Chubb hold his hands up. 'What? Ladies present, is it? Ha, right you are, Duchess.'

'If we can get back to business?' intercedes Harriet. These two have taken an instant dislike to one another. Like it or not, Chubb is all they have.

His glance darts between the two of them, doing some working out of his own. 'So who's the boss of this operation betwixt the two of youse, eh? Mistress Round Belly or The Louisiana Lip?' He eyes Conté up and down. 'Genuine, no offence Missy but I've never met the likes of you, and I've met every type in my puff, tall and short. You are a curiosity.'

'Plenty of offence,' snorts Conté, keen to be out of the man's company, 'You'll find more of me across the river if you care to look. Living with the rats, crawling off the boats half-dead. You Irish cuss and complain about maltreatment, then you look down upon us. You have no idea.'

'What do ye know about rats, girl? Come on now. In your nice house up on the hill. Ye don't fool old Royston. Cutting me with that snarky gob on yers.'

'You fucking idiot.'

'Language.'

Harriet steps between them again, this time having to push them apart. Chubb's a big man, but she knows all about Conté's artfulness with a fist and blade. Now is not the time. 'We just need to know, Mr Chubb. Are we still on?'

Chubb and Conté continue to eyeball each other. 'I know who's boss – who will always be boss – and I did the deal with him, not ye… girls. General Butler must be awful desperate, so he must, if he's got a plump porcelain chick with child and her indentured flunky to do his bombing. If you ask me.'

Conté emits a sour little smile from the corner of her mouth. 'We didn't. Ask you.'

'Funny. Look, that's no slight, like. It's just the way it is. Animals, vegetables and minerals, birds and bees. God's order of things.' Chubb's jabs a thick thumb out to sea, then at Harriet and lastly at Conté. 'Him before you. And then you before you.'

Conté looks fair ready to knock Chubb into next week. That might appear ridiculous to a stranger, but Harriet's seen her take down bigger, quicker, stronger and younger men than him in an instant. 'What the hell are you talking about?'

'Still, we're all in this together, so let's get about the business, eh?'

Chubb spits on his palm and offers it to Conté, who sneers. Harriet intervenes by accepting his handshake. His giant paw closes around her wrist.

'So we're all set, Mister Chubb.'

'Aye. Provided you get me my gold, none of them Yankee dollars. They won't be worth the paper to wipe me arse with if your lot lose the war. I'll have to vanish myself, so this is vanishing money.'

Conté persists in bristling. 'We won't lose the war.'

She's met with a low chuckle from Chubb, as if he's just heard a dirty joke. '*Her* beloved husband and the father of that bun in her oven is cocksure to disagree, chicken. I won't tell, though, provided you're both as good as your word.'

Conté draws to Harriet's side, but she doesn't need her protection from Mr Chubb's words or from his teasing manner. 'Uh huh.'

Harriet follows a more pragmatic line. 'Question. Your Fenian friends won't be happy if you vanish on them, will they?'

Chubb spits. 'I'll be happy. Nelly will be happy. Everyone else can go and shite. I've no loyalty to this city. You've not been here long enough to see why, but hang around and you'll see.'

'I'm sure we will,' answers Harriet. She can feel Conté's hot, needling eyes without even looking at her.

'Midnight tomorrow. It launches the following day, so you'll have no other chance. They're already stoking the furnaces for the launch. What with the amount of ammo on board… whoo-whee. It'll make for one fuckin' almighty bang, so it will. They'll hear it in fucking Virginia.'

Conté remains still. Harriet nods. 'Acceptable.'

'Nightwatchmen and the boilermen crew are paid off; they think my boys are just thieving some tools and such. Still think ye can do this by yourself, dear?'

Conté casts him a sideways glance. Harriet knows that this is exactly what she wants to do.

Chubb hacks up some mucous and deposits it on the cobbles. 'Pay me by noon tomorrow and Butler will have his great exhibition. That's provided youse two grand fillies are halfway competent in your bid to stir up so much. No offence.'

He stuffs his hands in his pockets and saunters off, blissfully unaware that he nearly ended up wearing his balls as earrings a moment ago, goading her friend in that manner.

Conté sneers at his back, still mighty irked. 'People who say 'no offence' always mean some offence, and that's not even a pinch of the damage that imbecile can cause to us. Butler is as much an oaf for employing him. Now he has our trust in his hands. What if he sells us out? He's a cheap bastard from head to toe; you can tell that just by looking at him.'

'Now, now.'

'Sorry, but I'm not sorry.'

'Butler is our commanding officer. And Chubb's all we've got. We must go with it.'

'I don't like this, Harry. Any of it. The plan, the place. The people.'

Harriet stuffs a pipe and lights it. 'You've made that plain.'

'You smoke like Banastre. You know that?'

'Suppose I do pick up some of his mannerisms.'

'Be careful with that. He's a charming man. For a devil.'

'What is this, an interrogation? Conté, I have to look the part.'

'But you don't have to like it.'

'What's really vexing you? Spit it out.'

Conté shakes her head. 'Does Butler actually want us to succeed?'

'Not this again, Conté.'

'Yes, this again.'

'We got our orders. Mister Chubb is right, unfortunately. Who are we to question?'

'Which part of you is talking now? The Irish? The Choctaw? The gentle Southern Lady? You play so many roles that you forget who you are.'

'The part that wants to win this war. Like you, I'd hope.'

Conté sneers. 'I come from a long line of people who did question. Toussaint Louverture, leader of the Hispañola revolt.'

'Right. You have not mentioned your hero Granddaddy for at least five minutes. Why don't you tell me again? I'm sure I've forgotten.'

Harriet starts walking towards their horses. Conté stalks her. 'First ruler of free Haiti. Defeated Napoleon Bonaparte no less. And sarcasm is the lowest form of wit.'

'Please, tell this to someone else for the first time, Conté. I don't mean to reduce it, but we need to live in the present. You are the hero now.'

'Who will listen here apart from you? It bears repeating.'

'Oh God.'

'Don't you patronise me too, Harry. I've read more books than you. Who taught you to read?'

Harriet stops in her tracks and looks to the heavens. 'Look, Conté…'

'You are in no condition. I said so. Listen to me for once. I won't see the death of you. You mean too much to me.'

'And you to I. So…'

'If that were true, you would let me go alone. I'll blow that crate alright; I've got it figured. Let me do it. For the love of God, let me.'

'So you can be the great Toussaint? The legend? And who will Butler tell about you? Or me?'

Conté's face sours. 'This all stinks. This place, this deal. I believe we've entered hell on earth and you do so willingly for a snake of a lawyer from Massachusetts. And you open your legs for that other horror of a man.'

Harriet reins in her impulse to retort and permits herself to pause, to let her friend simmer down as much to salve her own conscience. It is difficult. What kind of choice do they have in Butler or Banastre? Has there been a moment this morning when she hasn't considered returning both of them to Canning Street to be the obedient wife and servant, to let that weird Bostonian oaf go hang and just live their lives out peacefully? To welcome Banastre in having his way with her, with Conté, with the world? No, but that is an idle folly that would become a living hell. There would be no peace, ever.

That is fear invading her sensibility, just like the stench around here. Harriet Dunwoody just has to live with both, and do it with a steely eye on victory. She knows why they are in Liverpool, and so does Conté. Stand firm.

'We have our orders. Our commanding officer…'

'Oh, you going to do this now? Pull rank?'

'There are no ranks between us, Conté. Don't make this awkward.'

Conté nods, fully dialled up from furious to hurt now.

'Have it your way. No, not your way. His way.' She mounts and gallops off.

'Conté, hold up. Wait.'

Harriet is suddenly mindful of anyone in the yards who has been watching this little festival of bickering. Conté Louverture most certainly won't hold up, for man nor beast. Her friend and erstwhile Mistress mounts and gallops after her.

#2 THE ATHENAEUM

June 3rd, 1863

Banastre Xavier Dunwoody's head aches like some randy mule just gone kicked it. The throbbing in his temple and sinuses just won't abate, while the churning in his belly and foul, silage taste in his mouth make being a popular fellow in The Athenaeum Club a difficult act to deliver. Suffer as he might, though, he is determined to succeed today and every other day, striking deals big and small for Dixie.

The club is his haven, a place to make subtle enquiries, a hub to influence hearts, minds and pockets, as much as the Cotton Exchange does across town in the more bellicose and frenetic fashion typical of men rising from lower backgrounds to quick, vast fortunes. It is one of a handful of establishments worth being seen in, in this city, if one can be assured of the right company.

And so to some luncheon business with Mayor Lord James Russell Harrison, a fellow Mason and veteran Admiral of the incursion on the Crimea Peninsula, a spent war that he has dined out on ever since. Ginger, as they call him in the club (his nickname from his time as a senior commissioned tar in the Royal Navy), is a jovial fellow of 56, florid of face, hair and beard and a bit gouty, but cheerful as they come as long as you agree with him or line his coffers, which amounts to the same thing. You only need to know five men in Liverpool, and Ginger Harrison is worth all of them.

He shovels roast pork medallions into his face and washes them down with a thick and fruity red as Banastre chuffs on his pipe, mewing about his woes from last night.

'The foul little rat caught some of my lead in his face. Just wish I could have put him on the rack and questioned him about his sneaky antics.'

'Ah, the perils of being a dead-eye shot, old boy.'

Banastre shakes his head, not interested in flattery. 'I can't fathom it. Then those bloody leeches in the Infirmary invoiced me an arm and a leg for treating a corpse. Sheer gall of it. All I wanted was an identification. Is that too much to ask?'

Ginger stabs pork with his fork and smothers it in English Mustard and apple sauce.

'I'll see to it that you are remunerated for that.'

'Ginger, I need to know who put this commission out on me. Had they succeeded, it would bode negatively on your relations with Richmond. A deceased Consul doesn't look too mighty fine.'

Ginger prods the air with a forefinger. '*Unofficial* consul, old boy. Don't want to upset Whitehall just yet. Not while Westminster is sitting on the fence. Bigger picture. Discretion, what what.'

'Sure. But it wouldn't look good, pal. That's all I'm sayin'.'

Ginger finishes his plate, wipes his furry mouth, crosses his cutlery and massages his round and spongey midriff. 'Banastre, I would see it as a personal grief above anything else. Our deals are our deals, but I believe we have become firm friends since you arrived on our shore. Just how is Harriet?'

Banastre shrugs, in no mood for domestic tittle-tattle. 'Harriet is Harriet.'

'Ah, the Southern Belle. Not long until your first born, eh? Heir to the empire, eh? Chip off the old block, eh? Relish the embellishment, what.'

'Something like that, Ginger.'

What a crashing bore, forever preoccupied with small talk and banalities. Still, he holds all the keys to the city, so patronise his soft soak of an ass. Ginger knows how to tell him what he wants to hear, as much as the other way around. He stacks his pipe.

'Look here. We'll dangle whoever ordered this abomination from a heavy rope, rest assured. The chappy-me-lad behind it…'

'Some pond life,' mutters Banastre, mighty keen to go after the scoundrel himself.

'Yes indeed, pond life is how I say it, sir. Bound to be some Paddy Whack, I'd venture. Don't let my appetite fool you. I'm furious, Banastre. Every Peeler, lookout and snitch from the docks to Dovecot is making a search right now, root and branch. I'll get you some answers and some thick Irish heads on pikes. Expressly.'

Banastre nods, comforted a touch. Ginger says and Ginger does. Or at least that's what he promises. 'I thank you, Ginger.'

'You are most welcome, Brother Dixie. Always welcome. Ah, Thomas! Dear young Captain of Industry!'

A rangy, awkward-looking chap in his mid-twenties hovers over them. Banastre is a bit perplexed until he figures out the identity. Again, Ginger tells him what he already knows.

'This is Tom Ismay. Freshly established in the city himself, aren't you m'lad?'

Ismay shuffles on his feet. Banastre shakes his hand without bothering to get up. 'Well, I've been here for a while now, Ginger.'

Ginger says, 'Tom is a whizz with shipping liners. The new… White Cross Line?'

'White Star Line, Ginger.'

'Silly me. White Star, yes. Tom's quite the engineer and fortune maker, aren't you, Tom?'

'If it ain't cotton, baccy or molasses, where's the money to be made?' Say it how it is, Banastre Xavier Dunwoody. The boy's powder just got pissed on.

A stony, choked silence. Ismay shuffles on his feet, clearly unsure whether or not to defend his business or bow to the rank and protocol of the club and say nothing. But as much as there might be some game to getting a rise out of this boy, Banastre reminds himself that young Ismay's got money and keen money at that. 'Easy pal, I'm just getting a rise from you. Seems to be this Liverpool way. Man, I love entrepreneurship; it is the backbone of civilisation. Why don't you join us, Mr Ismay?'

'What what! Sit your tidy young rump down with us, Ismay! Be a sport, me-lad!' grunts Ginger, affably stupid and randy as per his wont. He's not averse to a bit of boy sport, on the quiet.

Ismay remains flustered by the backhandedness, but this is quickly washed away in the flattery of being invited into such company. Banastre is delighted to have another prospective investor in his web, one so readily charmed into putty. Everyone wins this evening, even if the attempt on his life last night adds a slight aftertaste. Never mind, he'll get to the culprit his own way, not Ginger's. He has his methods, tried and tested.

Once the baby comes, then the pressure to consort with other wives of the great and good of this city will swell, possibly to unmanageable, intolerable levels. Then, any sense of independence will vanish, which will rather stick in the craw. Banastre took Harriet straight into the top tier of civic society when they landed here, and this brings formalities and expectations, social niceties that she always slalomed back in Baton Rouge in favour of a more rural existence, but there are fewer hiding places in Liverpool, especially for a lady with sabotage of this scale on her mind. Is she too ambitious? Are there smaller victories to be had? Yes and yes, but the need is too great to step back now and smaller victories just won't do.

Banastre has opted for a quiet night at home for once. Harriet offered him gin rummy and a cuddle, but her husband declined, quiet and morose as he has increasingly become in sober moments. It is preposterous that she should worry about a man who she is trying to usurp and undermine, let alone offer to cuddle him, but these are preposterous times.

What vexes her more again is that someone tried to kill him last night, and that person wasn't her or Conté. Banastre may have enemies the world over, but his mission is greater than the man and making him vanish is not part of the brief, as much as she would love to. Otherwise, this whole trip and charade would have been saved with a single slug to the back of his head a long, long time before they landed upon these shores.

He reads and smokes in the library while Harriet joins him in front of the fireplace with her crochet. Conté serves a selection of sweet treats and Demerara coffee and Harriet watches him studying her hind quarters as she leaves the room, dismissed for the night. No, never worry about him.

'Darling?'

Banastre has returned to his book. Some mercantile tome that he probably isn't even reading properly. No answer.

'Darling?'

He lowers the book, dead behind the eyes.

'Sweetness?'

She smiles at him.

'Never mind.'

Banastre grunts and returns to his fake reading.

'Darling?'

He slaps the book on the side table, annoyance riding across his brow.

'Yes, dear Harriet?'

'Conté told me that there were flecks of blood on your shirt and you were in a state of distress last night when you returned home.'

Playing dumb is an art.

'A dutiful wife that had waited up for her husband would have been able to determine that for herself.'

'I am carrying a child, Banastre. I get tired at night. Like most normal people and especially like a lady growing your offspring.'

Banastre sniffs and pours himself a single malt.

'Same excuse what I always hear from you, woman.'

'Sorry, Banastre.'

Harriet is not sorry. Conté is never sorry.

'Huh.'

'What happened? Please tell me. I am worried about you.'

There she is, treading the boards on Broadway again.

'Hrmph. Okay. I'll tell you, I suppose, but don't you breathe a word to a soul, y'hear?'

Harriet nods.

Banastre says, 'Damn Yankee agents, out to maim and murder your husband. Out to plot, agitate and spoil our good relationship with the fine city of Liverpool. This is what I have to deal with, day in, day out. Does that satisfy you?'

Harriet does her best to look shocked.

'To kill you? Really? Oh my.'

Banastre nods and sips more whisky. He draws his Smith & Wesson and she gasps. He cocks and aims at a portrait of Harriet's old Grand-maman as a slip of a girl, next to the river in what was New France. Another concocted fake, another part of the ruse. He mouths 'pow'.

'But lemme tell ya, they didn't reckon upon who they was dealin' with, sweetness.'

Harriet lets some tears fall. Timing is everything in these situations. It melts Banastre, who places his gun and glass down and approaches his wife, kneeling at her side.

'Aw, Belle. I'm sorry if I get a little rough and cussing in my tone. It comes with my job.'

He kisses her whitened knuckles and produces his pocket square, wiping her cheeks down.

'Oh Banastre…'

'Now then. Nothing for your gentle heart to worry about, angel face. I've got every manjack in this town looking for the scoundrel or scoundrels. Won't be long before someone squeals for money or from sufferin'. Banastre Dunwoody is on the watch now. You're safe. Commander Daddy always prevails.'

More tears from Harriet, inspired by the harsh smelling salts in her cuff that she had prepared earlier.

'You must tell me everything you know, darling. Have you any names? I must know it, or I might go insane with worry.'

Oh the melodrama. She rubs her belly bump and he buys right into it. It is exactly what Banastre wants, all neatly compacted within his world view and his consideration of the roles of women and men. As long as she flutters and faints like this, she'll always have him. Harriet despises herself a little more every time she has to do it, but the greater good wins again.

'Rest easy, sweetness. I will tell you forthwith, as soon as I am certain. I'll even let you pull the lever on the gallows when the time comes.'

Harriet gulps and squeezes his hand.

'Will you? I'd like that, darling. Very much.'

'Good show, sweetness. Petite chou-teau. Good show.'

#3 BUSINESS BANKING

June 4th, 1863

Number 4 Water Street, the district office and central branch of
Martin's Bank. Conté takes a sturdy pony down the hill of
Parliament Street and traverses the hotchpotch cobbles of the
Strand towards Goree Piazza, taking in slums, curiosity shops
and wharves, before returning herself up Water Street in the
direction of the Town Hall. She never fails to notice the African
figures carved into the ornate pillars of the edifice, like gargoyles
on a church except with enhanced meaning; this city is propped
up on African shoulders. It says everything she would need to
know about Liverpool and reminds her of the need for haste in
her operations this morning, ahead of what she hopes will come
after nightfall.

'Anything to report from the Master of my house?'

The bank manager, Mr Rollo, a neat man with a straight
countenance, has become a firm friend and loyal servant of the
two ladies since they first entrusted him with their 'delicate'
business, not long after Banastre did likewise. He has invited
Conté into his private office in order to complete her transaction
this morning, assured of a very generous commission as usual.
He must rub his hands every time he gets wind that Conté has a
pending visit.

Rollo hands over coded, meticulously written-out copies of
missives sent by Banastre back to Richmond. He may as well be
telling her the information himself.

'Received with thanks. I shall inspect. Now to the main order
of business.'

Conté leaves the bank replete with an assignment for £3,000
sterling in gold coins, received last week by special transfer via
Pony Express from the Federal Reserve to the Anglo-American
Sugar and Tobacco Company in New York a shell for Union
funds. It arrives here in Liverpool upon the order of a certain

Maj. Gen. F.B. Butler's private office, 1448 Fourth Street, New Orleans, Louisiana.

She feels the weight of a nation in those saddle bags and even the short ride around the corner from Martin's to the back of the Slaughterhouse Pub on Fenwick Street is fraught with a monstrous, creeping, cumbersome anxiety. There is a crook and a Watchman Peeler on every corner, and within every cranny of these streets, and only one needs their curiosity arousing to blow her cover. She knows that she is a curious sight above many other curious sights in this vicinity. Conté is ready to defend her cargo, but she'd rather not have to, given the stakes.

The things she does for this cause. For Butler? No, never. Rather, for the greater good of those who are not permitted a voice.

She picks her horse through the slurry in a spot of dressage. Sure enough, Chubb is waiting for her by some stray kegs, cellar doors open, anticipating a special delivery. His countenance is altogether more serious today and he stands alone, which can only be a good thing because the fewer who know what they are up to, the better.

'Well?' he mutters, approaching, chuffing on a corn pipe.

Conté nods and brushes her heel against a saddle bag. If he thinks that she's dismounting here, he has another thing coming. If trouble visits, she cannot hang around.

Chubb unhooks the strap and shoves his hand inside, going for the lucky dip. A paw emerges with a fistful of gleaming sovereigns. He bites one and smiles, doing another of his trademark jigs. This is his moment. Things are looking up for Royston Chubb. Bully for him.

He tightens the strap and unhooks the bag, feeling the satisfying weight in his arms.

'Ooh, you're a good un, y'are.'

Conté stares through him.

Chubb tosses the bag into the cellar and it lands with a satisfying clunk. He walks around the back of her horse and makes to do likewise with the other bag. Conté jams her heel against the leather.

'You'll get that when the job is done. Back off.'

Chubb shakes his head and pulls at the bag. Conté has a pistol trained on him.

'Whoa. Not much trust going on here, chicken,' he grunts, stepping back but not far enough for Conté's liking.

'As per our agreement and to keep you honest. There's much more where that came from.'

'Even I won't need any more than that. I'm not a greedy man, love. One of the things that keeps me breathing in this shithole of a place. Spend enough time here and you'll see I'm the best of them.'

'If you're not greedy, then you'll honour our agreement.'

'And what if you blow yourselves to smithereens, eh chicken? What will I do then?'

'You'll find a note in a safety deposit box at Martin's Bank with your name on it and the location of the balancing amount. In that event.'

'How can I trust that?'

'You have the bond of the United States Government. There is no greater assurance.'

Chubb has no audience and nothing to prove. He remains all about the business. He spits his hand and offers it to Conté. She spurs her horse and rides away, leaving him with half his fortune and a wet palm.

The Irishman watches her go and stuffs his hands in his pockets, glancing down into the cellar. It's a tidy sum alright, more than the fat of the land. But he calculates that he will need the rest in order to pay off his debts and skedaddle out of town. After all, he has people who depend upon him.

Crispin Starkey, a squat and thickset lad of 19 who looks twice his age, clambers up from the hatch, grinning at his boss. Following is Pat McCartney, a few years older than Starkey but altogether more sinewy, diminutive and lynx-eyed. He hangs back, not trusting his own shadow.

'Pat?'

'Yes?'

'I need you to go to Wales. Tonight. Be ready to pick up the goods in the morning first thing as scheduled.'

'Ah what? I've two babies with typhus. Why can't he go?'

'Because you're my best man.'

'I'm your best man for climbing up drainpipes and picking locks, so. I'm not your best man for going to Wales.'

'You're going.'

'Why me, Royston? What about this fella?'

Starkey lights his pipe and scratches his chest. He grins back at Pat. Starkey never stops grinning, it seems.

'Because I asked you, you little bollocks,' grunts Chubb. 'You know the plan.'

'Shite.'

'You know the plan. Right?'

'Right. I know the plan.'

'Good.'

'No, not good. Shite.'

'Off with you. Watch your back and your gob.'

Pat shuffles off and Starkey slaps him on his backside.

'Oi.'

Chubb chuckles as his boy leaves the yard. Starkey drinks up his approval.

'Little bollocks.'

#4 BAILEY HILL COLLIERY, NORTH WALES

June 5th 1863

'Mae'r idiot Gwyddeleg yn meddwl ei fod yn well na ni, Gethan.'

'Nid wyf yn ymddiried ynddo, Ieuan.'

There's nothing else to see here but a huge, black slag heap and rusting ironwork, yet the birds still tweet among the deep, Welsh voices and crunching mechanism of the pit head. This dawn chorus echoes around the satanic arena that backs onto a huge pit wheel at the gates of Bailey Hill Colliery in Mold. Streams of miners traipse through iron gates towards another day's work, like damned souls heading down into the depths of hell. Ieuan, a brawny, no-nonsense miner and his equally rough pal, Gethan, tower over Pat, clearly out of place in the daylight, never mind at the gates of a coal mine. Like most fellas that he comes into contact with these days, they're having fun at Pat's expense.

'Mae'n debyg y bydd yn chwythu ei hun i fyny beth bynnag.'

Pat is trying and failing not to show his annoyance. He has a job to do, and these two big, burly bastards are wasting his time.

'Oi.'

'Ei geffyl yn edrych yn farw.'

'Speak English willya. Flinty fucks.'

The two Welsh flatcaps look at one another and back at Pat, amused at his muttering impudence.

Ieuan, the slightly bigger and denser of the two, steps up to Pat, towering over him. 'Steady boyo. Got to have a laugh, have you.'

Gethan steps up, forming twin towers. 'Right and straight. You don't speak English either, by the sounds of you, isn't it.'

Pat is eager to get this done. He taps a tatty briefcase with his foot and watches the droves of miners as they pass.

'You sure we should do this here?'

Ieuan shrugs. 'Do what?'

Pat twitches, adjusts his braces and nods. 'Yeah well. Yeah. That's right. Do what.'

'Slide it over then, boyo. Standing there, picking your bum.'

'Scratch and sniff, isn't it.'

More laughs.

Pat grabs the case and plonks it at Ieuan's feet before carefully backing off. Gethan scoops it up, opens it, and they both observe the bundles of cash within.

Ieuan nods, places two fingers in the corner of his mouth and whistles. Another miner leads a half-dead pit pony out from behind the stope cabin, pulling along the world's most ramshackle cart. The cargo lies beneath a dirty, canvas cover.

Pat rolls his eyes and mutters to himself. 'Taffy bollocks. I can't fucking believe it.'

'What you saying, boyo? Speak English do you?'

Pat takes over the bridle and offers a weak smile back at Ieuan.

'Best be on me way, then.'

'Best you had, laddie boy.'

He tips his cap to the men and trails off with the horse and cart.

'For fuck's sake.'

Pat struggles to lead the ancient nag along a muddy hedgerow as it pisses down with rain. He grinds his jaw as the animal feeds on some kerbside vegetation and he tries to yank its head back into the task. Pit ponies, even ancient knackers like this one, have awful strong necks.

Exhausted, he stops and leans against the cart. It creaks.

He peeks under the tarpaulin to see neat stacks of industrial dynamite. Then he holds a hand out as water splashes on his palm. He pats the pony's neck.

'At least the sticks won't go off in this, eh Ned? Small mercies.'

The sun beats down, baking the cinder path, pony and the contents of the cart. Pat sweats like a pig and stops Ned, tying him up to a milestone that says: *Birkenhead 10 miles.*

He scrambles down the riverbank and scoops fresh water into his mouth. It tastes like ambrosia, but that does little for his current temper.

'Fuckin' pathetic it is. Fuckin' bollocks, Royston. Twatty Welsh boyo this, laddie boy that.'

Up above, Ned brays and wobbles. Pat dips his cap into the water and scoops up some of it. He carefully heads back up the embankment. 'Don't you worry, old Ned of the Hill. I've got something for you.'

But Ned is past worrying. The pony's legs buckle and he starts dragging the cart with him, loping closer to the edge like a drunk. There isn't much of a wall to stop him and he drags the trap right over. With one hand clenching the driver seat, Pat gets there just about quick enough to pull on the reins with the other, but his straining efforts are futile as the pony reels over the edge.

'Oh God, no.'

The horse's weight brings the trap crashing into the wall and over. Ned dangles in his bridle, tongue flapping, already dead. Pat tries to use his own weight to counterbalance the trap and stop it falling over the side, but it is starting to lurch and he doesn't have any options. If that trap goes over the edge, he might as well not survive.

He strains with everything he has. 'Tight-arsed taffies!'

He scrambles over the tarpaulin, boxes of sweating sticks beneath – rattling and digging into his shins. He pulls his apple knife, used for scrumping normally, but now a potential lifesaver.

He slashes at the leather harness connecting Ned to the trap. The first one whiplashes and nearly takes his eye out, slapping and burning his cheek. Ned drops and the fall causes the remaining strap to fray and snap. It recoils and whacks Pat across the chops, sending him down, down, down.

Groan, crunch, crack, splat. Black.

Pat comes to. The corpse of Ned is further downstream. The cart creaks as it hangs off the edge of the bridge.

He climbs to his feet and splashes his way back up the embankment, panting and spitting.

'Royston Chubb. I do so wish with all my puff that you'd go and have a terrible shite. A curse upon you.'

He springs up to the dry stone wall, climbing it like a spider up a drainpipe, grabs the cart and begins the long pull to Birkenhead.

Chubb sits by the gates, swigging from a hipflask and chuffing on his corn pipe. He consults his pocket watch and hisses.

Pat emerges around a corner, tugging the cart along.

'Oh, fine time, isn't it. Did you go on the piss or summat?'

'You have no idea, Royston. Fuck off with it.'

'Oh, ratty are we? I'll tell you who's proper ratty and that's me, Padraig. Aye, your generous benefactor and don't you forget it. Ye were supposed to be here two hours ago, maggot.' Pat groans as he stops, so exhausted he's almost in tears. 'And what happened to the horse? I'm charging ye for it. Them Welsh boyos will want it back. Tight they are.'

Pat can't summon the energy to sneer. He releases the straps and staggers off into the gloom.

'Oh, that's charming, isn't it. Little bollocks.'

#5 THE BIG BANG

June 5ᵗʰ 1863

Chubb has fulfilled his end of the bargain. It sits in the back of an abandoned shipwright's cart, just within the grand gates of the Cammell Laird shipyard of Birkenhead, under the cover of a tarpaulin and the blanket of night. Banastre is out 'playing cards' this evening in The Athenaeum, so he won't return home until the early hours, if at all should he decide to go over to the Seraglio with his friends from the club. If all goes well, his evening will be cut short by the tremorous sound of a huge explosion emanating from across the river; he might even be able to work out the rest, depending upon his level of stupor.

They hook the cart up to Conté's horse, using all of her delicate dressage skills to ensure as smooth a passage as possible for the contents, given their volatility under vibration. It occurs to Harriet how on earth Chubb managed to get them here without leaving a crater the size of Birkenhead. One full ton of sweaty nitroglycerin-silica or 'dynamite', patent pending by Mr Alfred Nobel of Stockholm, freshly liberated from Bailey Hill Colliery. It is among the finest inventions of the 19ᵗʰ Century. Small wonder Conté ensures that her horse is sauntering steady, in spite of the pressure for haste.

The series of recces conducted in recent weeks has told them all they need to know about this shipyard and the plan is complete. Any collateral damage to the infrastructure or other boats can only be a good thing, as Cammell Laird and the Board of Trustees will certainly want to keep the details of what is being constructed here away from Fleet Street. The furnaces of the *CSS Banshee* are lit and it is primed for launch tomorrow. It's now or never.

If they die in the process, then never would there be a stronger blow by any individual in this war or a nobler sacrifice. At least, that is what the coded messages from their commander say.

Up to the spectacular hull of the Banshee, not a soul in sight as Peelers are not permitted upon private land and the security detail is either drunk or asleep from drink after Chubb ensured several cases of strong port were delivered to them earlier in the evening.

Conté swings a hook on the end of a rope and scales the hull, leaping over the side like a cat on an alley wall. Harriet loads the first box of explosives and steers it up the side, slow and steady in spite of the biting need for alacrity this evening. What if it starts raining? What if the sticks are dud? What if they explode prematurely? How many assurances are possible?

Once the sticks are loaded up into the main deck, Conté will crowbar her way into the hold via a small door at the back of the mess hall, which they know about having procured copies of the blueprints for the vessel. Then she will locate a trolley and carefully place all the explosives within the belly of the ship, in the engine room, which is right next to fuel tanks that have already been bunkered to the brim with coal, ready to power this beast all the way to the Eastern Seaboard for its first engagements. As if that isn't enough, the cache will be right next to the ammunition store and ordinance bay. With the grace of God, the maiden voyage of the *CSS Banshee* will never happen. If all goes well, they might indeed hear the bang in Virginia, but over the water in the environs of the Town Hall will suffice.

This will take some time, and then Conté will need to hook up a long fuse. Harriet stews in her helplessness, retreating to the shadows of the quayside to keep lookout, itching for something to do. They've gone way past the point of explaining this one away as a jape or jackanape.

Do or die time.

Pat rows a small boat with Starkey as Chubb clutches a boatswain's telescope. They look like the worst pirates in the world. They're in an adjacent dock to the shipyard, as close as they can get to the action to call a safe distance. Pat isn't amused, as per usual.

'I know I said this before, like, but do we really have to be here? I've nice, warm stew waiting for me at home.'

Starkey chuckles. 'A nice, warm fanny you mean.' He pushes the heels of his palms into his cheeks and makes obscene squelching noises.

'That's my Sarah you're talking about. A good, pious woman. Royston, tell him will you. I do not like the company you're keeping these days.'

'Quit bellyaching, Padraig. I won't tell ye again. And ye call me boss in front of others.'

Starkey prods Pat in the side and issues a toothy grin. 'Yeah, Cavan culchie.'

Pat ignores him and they climb onto the shore. Chubb checks his pocket watch. 'Something's off about all of this, lads, but I can't quite fathom what. We want to see it go off smoothly, like. Don't we, boys?'

'If summat's off, I wanna be several miles away, Royston. That's some firecracker they've got there. Can't believe you got us into this. Just can't, I can't.'

'What did I say to you? Mardy little gobshite y'are. These girls need someone to watch their backs.'

Pat squints and tries to see what Chubb is looking at through his scope. 'I didn't know you cared.'

'I'm just protecting me investment.'

'Their boss' investment you mean.'

'My. Fuckin'. Investment.'

Pat shivers and shakes his head. 'Sorry, but they're dead already. Why don't we just go home?'

Starkey clips Pat. 'Ah shut up, yer mardy little gobshite.'

'I swear to God, Royston. Tell him to back off. He's been five fucking minutes off the clipper from Cork and he's already lording it over me, goading me so. I've been at your side for fifteen years. Where's your loyalty, eh?'

Chubb continues to peruse via the telescope, chewing his bottom lip. 'Moan, moan, moan. One last time, son. Quit with ye gurning or I'll push ye in the drink myself and have done with it.'

Ah, back in the Ottoman Seraglio, a sure-fire sign of a good evening and a better night to follow. Banastre cradles his winnings, rictus grin all over his face and drunk as a skunk.

'Whitehall better get their wise asses into Whitehall. S'all am saying.'

Ismay gets up, wobbling himself. Ginger snorts and laughs. 'And where are you off to, fellow-m'lad?'

'Wife. Home. Something.' Ginger snaps his fingers and Banastre's favourite Fancy Nancy appears. Just as Ismay tries to put his coat on, she peels it back. 'I can't be doing her. That. No sir. I say, sir. No thrice no.'

Ginger wags a finger. Banastre guffaws as the Mayor leans in, eyes wide. 'Thrice yay, you can. You will. You must. For Queen and Country. For The Athenaeum.'

'But my Isobel, Mathilda, little girls I have to home to bedtime them a read story…'

Nancy makes a grab for his nether regions. Banastre falls about laughing.

'No I … Ooh.'

Ginger grins. 'If you want to be in our club, you have to stir our porridge, chappy me lad.'

Ismay smiles at Nancy. Nancy smiles at Ismay. Banastre lights a thick cigar and sucks on it like His Satanic Majesty. 'Whitehall Willie wanna watch.' Banastre's eyes light up as she pulls down his breeches. 'Maybe more than watch.'

Banastre's glass is topped up with more wine as he whips himself into a stoned lather. Yeah, it's a mighty good night when anything goes.

Panting, Conté scales a rope down to the side of the dry dock. Harriet is nowhere to be seen.

'Where in hell has she gotten to?'

'Conté dear. Psst. Up here.' She notices Harriet sitting cross-legged atop the launching platform, clutching a jemmy. She tosses the wooden plaque for *HMS Serendipity* to Conté's feet. 'A souvenir. Serendipity, my ass.'

Another plaque for the *CSS Banshee* adorns the spot on the hull beneath where the original was mounted.

Conté continues to unravel the coil and humourlessly kicks the plaque away in one movement. 'Oh. Very good, Harry. But not strictly necessary, is it?'

Harriet climbs down. 'You're no fun tonight.'

They've disembarked to the river bank now. Chubb squints to spot Conté through his telescope as Harriet helps her feed fuse wire across the wharf. Starkey slips away, behind some large rocks.

'They'll get ripped to pieces so close to it. The shockwave alone will devastate them. This is a cruel business so.'

'Don't you think they know that, Royston? Maybe they want to die. Part of the point?' Chubb leers at Pat. 'I mean boss. Boss man.'

'Aye. Suppose. We don't have to sit and watch though. Something not right, I say.'

'So someone has to save them from themselves? Come off it. Let them take their chances. We got paid, man. Well, *you* got paid. Leave it. Sorry to be harsh, but we've got families, you and I. Not him, like.' Pat jabs a thumb in the direction of where Starkey was standing, but he's not there. 'Where is he?' Pat was hoping he was getting somewhere with this line, but even in his absence, Starkey finds a way to banjax him.

Chubb's conscience is having a shit-throwing party, but then the same thing dawns upon him. 'Where the fuck's Starkey?'

A Limerick drawl echoes out from behind the rocks, the voice of Crispin Starkey, replete with a new level of bravado. 'Well then, the Cavan culchie and his fat eejit of a boss.' He holds his hands together and rolls his eyes, cooing and falsetto, 'Aw, I've come over all sentimental over the pregnant tart. Do you fancy her, you dirty old bastard? Or the other one?'

Starkey is king of the hill atop a boulder, pointing a shooter at them, full view of the Landing Stage where he came in but weeks ago behind him. The boy grins, jams a whistle between his teeth and blows hard.

Pat nods. 'Royston, I so knew you couldn't trust that mangy little dog.'

Peelers emerge from every direction. Pat stays rooted, hands aloft. Chubb darts behind another rock and Starkey takes a potshot, missing him.

Pat snarls at Starkey. 'Jackeen, y'are.'

Conté lowers the cable wheel to Harriet and scales an iron ladder down into the empty dry dock adjacent to the quay where the *Banshee* sits, hull secured, ready to slide into her working life as a crushing menace to Union ships. They've packed cotton wool plugs for their ears and scarves to wrap around their heads to protect them from the cataclysmic detonation, but – in all truth – there is no telling whether or not they will perish in the pending boom. If they do, then the job will be done well and their mission will be complete.

Harriet cuts the end of the wire from the wheel, connects it to the detonation box and pulls up the hammer. She hugs Conté, who kisses her cheek. They squeeze hands. Harriet rubs her bump and whispers a prayer for a child she probably will never have, but this is war. Total war.

They have been ready for this moment since long before setting foot on these peculiar shores, long before even clapping eyes on Banastre Xavier Dunwoody.

'You do it,' says Harriet.

Conté nods, eyes steely in resolve. She kisses her fingers and places her free hand upon Harriet's bump. 'God bless you, Harry.'

'God bless you, Conté.'

Conté pumps the hammer down.

Nothing. What?

Panic. Harriet checks the wire. Going all the way back to Louisiana, they've rehearsed this moment, picking out the grade of explosive and even the appropriate supplier this side of the Atlantic, one of a tiny number offering this specific, experimental grade. The conditions are perfect, so unless someone else has sabotaged them...

Crunching footsteps from above. Their hearts quicken. The jig is up!

Chubb's round, stern face leers down at them from above, a bowie knife and severed wire in his hands. His crooked jaw grinds, his eyes blaze fury and he jabs a thick sausage of a finger behind him. 'This was altogether a very bad idea, girls.'

Harriet is finally at Conté's level of anger toward him. 'We had an agreement, Mr Chubb. Re-attach that wire, immediately.'

Chubb's hand are aloft. 'Now ladies. Permit me to explain, like. This right scabby little shithouse who I thought was a loyal boy has …' Harriet raises a pistol and aims it at Chubb's face. 'Oh. Right, then,' continues Chubb, 'Just hear us out now. Please, I'll beg youse.'

Conté steps up to him and points to the end of the wire. 'You heard what she said. You made an agreement with the United States Government, sir. Do it or she'll put a hole in your stupid goddamn head.'

Distant shouts, getting closer. Conté notices the lanterns starting to encircle the perimeter dock wall. Chubb nods and shrugs. 'Do what ye must, but I'd say your boss, commander, whoever he fuckin' is, is playing the both of youse. Yer man, whazzizname. Butler. Yes, Butler.'

Conté studies his every twitch and move. Harriet is fair ready to pull the trigger. 'Do you now?'

Harriet pulls back the hammer. Conté urges her to lower the gun and she frowns. 'We haven't got time for this.'

Chubb seizes the moment. 'Look, someone wants your husband dead, dear. It's not me. And it's not even you.'

'Oh I want him dead alright.'

'Blow that ship and ye'll lose your War. I've sniffed enough bullshit in my time.'

'You expect us to just buy that, Mr Chubb? How do we know you haven't sold us out?'

'For fuckin' fuck's sake, dearie. Why would I be standing here with me thumb up me jacksy if that were the case?'

Conté's eye dart about this arena of death, back and forth to Chubb. Lights and whistles, bearing down from every direction. Why would he indeed? But here he is, his very presence indicating his loyalty. Chubb stands to lose a fortune and his skin tonight.

Harriet looks bowled over, awkward. A rare sight. Conté steps in between her aim. 'Hate to say it, but I think he's right. Man's got wits. Something stinks and I've known it all along.' She cranes her neck to Chubb. 'Go! And try not to get yourself caught, Mr Chubb.'

Incandescent, Harriet still trains her pistol on him, but Conté eases her trigger arm down and persuades it away, shaking her head. Chubb doesn't need a second invitation. He's off into the shadows; agile for a big man.

Harriet seethes. 'We're disobeying orders. Why did you do that?'

'We'll think of something. And I did it because he wasn't lying. We were set up to fail.'

'How do you know, Conté?'

'I know. I always know. It's a talent in my blood.'

Conté replaces the hammer and tosses the piece into the river.

'Hey, that's mine,' exclaims Harriet.

'For all the good it'll do us, Harry. And just so you don't go harbouring any ideas when we get caught.' Conté nods and watches the shapes move closer and close. She looks out to the expanse; the Mersey lapping against the dock shore, silhouettes of huge buildings across the river embossed in relief against a bruised, purple sky, endless smokestacks.

What to do? Fall on the mercy of the US Consul? Use diplomacy to save them from the clutches of Banastre? Hope for a miracle?

Harriet is stripping off. 'Way I see it then, there's only one way out, smart ass.'

Conté flinches as she sees the moving sentinels of gas lamps closing in on them from across the dry docks and shipyards, Peelers' whistles echoing, promising death.

'No, Harry. Come on.'

'What do you mean 'no'?'

Conté brushes her hand in the water. 'Freezing. And if that won't kill you, the savage current will. Or the poison or slurry in the filthy water.'

'Big ol' river don't scare me. We've done the Mississippi. I beat you then, and I'll beat you now.'

Conté grabs her shoulder. 'This ain't home, Harry. You have a chance with the baby. Banastre will show mercy on you long enough for you to plot an escape. Please.'

'I doubt all that. I can't let you go to the wolves, Conté. I will not.'

'You never listen to me.'

'I do. Most of the time. Sometimes. Well, occasionally.'

'Never.'

Harriet is now down to her one piece and wading into the river.

'Ooh, that's a bit brisk, mademoiselle. Last one to the other side's a horse's ass.'

'This is madness. Dudley will advocate for you. We'll be deported but no court will convict us. Butler will be pissed but... Harry? Wait.'

Harriet is swimming out now in an able and quick stroke. 'Shake a leg, slow coach. Or are you chickenshit?'

Conté gurns in derision and pulls off her shoes. Damn you, Harriet Farrell. Damn you and your brave face to hell. Show some fear for once, goddammit. 'Everything has to be a competition with you, doesn't it?'

Harriet has swum into the night but her voice travels back across the swell. 'Thaddagirl, Conté Louverture.'

Conté dives in and her skin tightens in shock immediately in the cold flow, which belies the warm night air. She can sense voices and dogs behind her, but much as the cover of night protects her from the men on the river bank, so does it impede her from spotting Harriet in the water ahead. Harriet would tell her to look after herself, but this is an instinct that goes back to the very first day they met. Conté Louverture saved her friend's life on that day and – ever since – it has been her duty to protect her.

She briefly espies an arm, craning out of the water in a familiar stroke. Hope.

Back by the rocks, Starkey smokes and watches on as Pat is bundled into the back of a black carriage.

Pat spits and snarls as he is manhandled like a stray dog towards the Black Maria. 'Your mother would be ashamed of you. Jackeen.'

'Good job I've never met her then. Little bollocks.'

'I'll tell everyone about you, I will. Your name is shite in this town.'

Starkey holds his palms up in mock surrender. 'Hey boys, you all listening to your man here? He's going to tell everyone something or another.'

Laughs. What a popular lad Starkey is among the constabulary. Pat is shoved hard into the back of the carriage and the door is padlocked. What about Sarah? What about the babies?'

What the hell just happened?

'We should really call a physician,' says Ismay, gone a shade of boiled shit. Banastre takes a napkin and picks up the wine glass, sniffing it. That bull's blood vino was meant for him, but Nancy did her party trick of swilling it down and emptying it over her bare front. Now she is convulsing and bleeding from every orifice. His money's on arsenic, but young Ismay here doesn't look too up for a wager.

'Dang. Pah. Nancy's no longer fancy.'

Ginger continues to swill brandy, regardless. He wobbles into Banastre's hazy stream of vision. 'You should get yourself checked out, old boy.'

'Quit fussin', Mayor. Do I look like her, bleedin' and buckin'? Don't need no quack, no sir, hic.'

Ismay will not stop flapping. 'Gentlemen, we can't just let her die on that Persian rug, I mean…'

Banastre nods. 'Kid's got a point. It is a Persian rug. Move her over there to the bare floor.'

'I say, you terrible cunt,' grunts Ismay, balling his fists, 'Inhuman, rotten bastard.'

The Commander chuckles, Nancy goes blue and Ginger guides Ismay to the door, breeches and shoes balled up in his quivering arms. 'And let's call it a night there, young chappy-me-lad, eh? We'll take care of all this little exuberance, eh?'

'But…'

'You know what's good for you, son.'

And he's out the door. Gone. The boy's vexed, but he knows what's good for him and his business to complain, if that is what he has a mind to do.

Banastre thinks about lighting up more opium, keen for the buzz not to end here, but Ismay's bleating and Nancy's choking gone done ruined another good night.

'We gots to gets the bastard what's doin' this, Ginger.'

Conté swims through the murk and stops to tread water and get her bearings. The Landing Stage is barely in sight through the pea soup of fog and industrial smoke. Even at this time of night, the river is clogged with vessels queuing for a berth or heading out to sea.

She spots Harriet's legs doing a butterfly kick and swims hard after her.

'Harry! For God's sake, wait for me. Harry! Stubborn Irish sow…'

Conté sees a huge steamship smashing its way through the water on a bearing straight for Harriet.

'No. No!'

Harriet can't hear the warning and she vanishes to the depths as the vessel churns through. Conté races into the wake of the ship, but Harriet is nowhere to be seen. Stricken with exhaustion, panic and fear, she scrambles towards the Landing Stage, tossed around in the tumult like a discarded doll.

Then Conté is swallowed herself by another big wake, disappearing into the black depths of the mighty Mersey swell in a torrent of despair.

#6 HARRIET & CONTÉ

July 4th, 1850

Ten years old. Old enough to think you know who you are, young enough to become a frightened child again in a heartbeat of terror.

Thunk. Rough splinters of wood spray everywhere as the bullets strafe through the thin, canvas skin of the prairie schooner. She can smell the lush swamp land out there and hear the crickets chirp, oblivious to the murderous intent of the raiders now upon them. Then she looks across and sees him, her Daddy, her whole world, pinned to the floor of the cabin by his own weight. There's a small hole in his throat, then blood starts to seep out and he chokes crimson bubbles, unable to breathe, before coughing up viscous eddies of thick, dark, red liquid. It isn't good.

Harriet is on her knees, barely aware of her own screaming, her own helplessness as his eyes roll to the back of his head. No time for words, no time for nothing. She spots the Sharps rifle still clutched in his hand as the rest of him fits and then goes limp. She unfurls each white knuckle as more bullets fizz past her ear, one ricochet bouncing off the metal frame of the caravan and grazing her hip. That should hurt, but she feels nothing right now but the urge to let the bastard who has just killed her dear Daddy have it between the eyes.

She is on her feet when crawling would be safer, but she has no fear. Something else has taken over. It feels like the wagon has stopped and this is confirmed as she climbs out of the back to witness the massacre of this small and very harmless charabanc for the first time; migrant folk heading south to start a new life but hopelessly exposed on this Mississippi trail through dense woodland trails that run serpentine to the swamps and plantation lands all through the Mississippi Delta.

Mainly French folk, with a smattering of Italians, Germans, Jewish, Dutch and Russians and two Irish, all united in being forcibly displaced from home and travelling together, safety in numbers. Except there was no safety, it only made them a bigger, easier target for predators who are far more dangerous than any snake or alligator. Now they lie dead, wounded or scrambled into the trees, gator chump in the shallows. Women with babies, men arrived here to buy land and move their families in. Cut to pieces by flying lead by unseen assailants in this pretty glade of dappled light and thick evergreens. Daddy told her about the natives, warned her to watch out for them, and Harriet looks out alright, but none have shown their faces. One thing she knows is that they don't intend upon leaving any witnesses, as the shooting is relentless and from all angles.

Miraculously though, still nothing hits her. God saves her. Then the gunfire peters out and stops, leaving cordite smoke to wisp across the killing floor. She watches the trees and the undergrowth, priming her rifle, slightly aware of this being her last stand, but only feeling what she has just seen. Harriet Farrell strides out into the clearing, bold as brass, heart full of righteous fury – almost too much for such a young one to bear – brimming over her senses like searing lava. Tears want to come, but the anger wins and her voice is more powerful than she could have ever imagined.

'I'm not afraid of you. My Daddy taught me to shoot. Show yourselves.'

The early evening symphony of the big river swell, insects as big as the palm of a hand, and rustling cypress trees catches her senses as she waits, gun primed. That smell of spent cordite rides uninvited up her nostrils. Will they have painted faces? Will they have designs upon eating her? Well, not before they eat some of her lead.

'Daddy!' she hears herself cry, wounded and lost, a voice outside herself.

So many guns, from all directions. Wouldn't they have risked shooting each other? Doesn't seem to make sense, but right now Harriet isn't able to make sense of anything. She grips her rifle harder and raises it, defying the grief and a new wave of fear that threatens to upend her into her own grave.

'But I'm only ten.'

Rustling in the undergrowth. A young girl steps out and watches Harriet, who makes to point the gun at her. She looks African, Creole was the word Daddy taught her. Her hazel eyes are big but mighty, wild and wily.

No matter. She's one of them and she's getting it. Harriet aims at her head.

'I would not do that if I were you,' she says, or rather pronounces, with all the refinement of an English duchess. Out here, in all the blood and guts and mud. 'Parlez vous Anglais? Deutsch? Russky? Nederlander?'

Harriet is fazed by the voice but continues to train her aim on the girl. She can see that she carries no weapons, but whoever she is, she isn't one of her fellow travellers, which makes her one of them.

'Your friends killed my Daddy.'

The girl smiles and walks towards Harriet. Slowly. 'No. Not friends of mine.'

Harriet's face screws up. The fury makes a swift return and she stomps over towards the strange creature in her dungarees and straw hat, feet bare and at one with this place. The gun is inches from her chest. If she unloads, there won't be much left to tattle.

'Prove it.'

'My name is Conté Marie-Louise Louverture. Grand-daughter of the revolutionary hero Toussaint Louverture of Haiti. What's yours?'

Harriet jabs Conté in the chest, hard enough to make her recoil.

'Murderer. Give me one reason not to kill you right now where you stand.'

Conté stands her ground. 'Because you've clearly never killed anyone before.'

'Perfect time to start.'

But Harriet Farrell is choking back tears again, praying for the nightmare to end, praying for Daddy to wake her up in her little bed in her little bedroom in their little house in Clontarf. They had to leave Ireland because The Hunger was killing everyone. Now, she stands here in this strange place with the lush, moist ground swallowing her up. Her tough talk feels pathetic and

Harriet is reduced to not knowing who or what she is, now that Daddy's gone to heaven.

'What's your name?'

'Harriet Farrell.'

Dammit! No! She's the enemy! Don't tell her anything!

Conté reaches out her hand. Harriet can see she is the same height, probably the same age.

'Harriet Farrell, you need to come with me. Before the bushwhackers return in greater numbers for their spoils. I promise you will be safe.'

'Bush-what?'

'Bushwhackers. Nasty types. They did this.'

Something about her belies her young countenance, like she's a long-lost elder sister preserved in aspic in order to come to Harriet's aid in this hideous moment. Conté takes her hand and she lowers the gun. She goes to look back, but her new companion guides her into the thick, long grass, feet squelching beneath them. Harriet can only trust her when she can't even trust herself.

'But everything I have is back there. Daddy…'

Conté pulls her arm, a little more forcefully this time.

'Don't look back, Harriet. Take it from me, I did and I still regret it.'

Harriet's shoes have long gone, unable to cope with the mud, rocks and bracken. How long have they walked? Up, up and up into hills, the lush tropical grasses give way to tall pines, needles and jagged stones. The girl … Harriet struggles to remember her name … uses the Sharps to push aside vegetation on what is barely recognisable as a trail. She holds a hand out for Harriet as they reach a stream.

Rustling in the trees. Behind them? In front of them? Where? Harriet's senses are bamboozled by it all. Against all her fear and loathing, she takes the girl's hand and they climb down a ravine, near as dammit to a vertical drop. The sound of a rapid stream is quickly upon them, like beating toms. If Harriet were alone, she'd have missed this drop entirely and fallen into eternity.

What kind of dark magic exists in this place? Just who is this girl?

Contay? No, Conté. She spelled it out as they walked earlier, right down to the accent on the 'é'. She's literate then, and mighty cute of mind by the looks of her. It has taken this long for the panic to recede enough to allow Harriet to recall her name. She doesn't look like any native that Harriet could imagine, but it dawns upon her that she hasn't seen a real live one yet in all her time here. Then again, the way Daddy put the heebeegeebees up her about them, she was kind of glad about that.

They scramble down to the stream, which is shallow enough to wade through. Harriet senses someone again, and she spots them from the corner of her eye. They vanish when she tries to spy them.

'You're safe with me, Harriet. Come on, nearly there.'

Safe? Really?

Through and between a dense clump of pines, it seems that the forest could go on forever, up and up and up. Harriet considers running again. Is she a captive? What kind of further mean and cruel horrors await her? She sees bright daylight and a wide clearing, then the last thing she expects; a neat settlement of wooden huts along a short drag. No tipis, no cannibals dancing around fires, just this tidy mountain haven.

A tall man, again wearing dungarees and barefoot, passes them and nods. His skin is deep and brown-red, his eyes bright and friendly, if mighty shrewd, just like Conté's. Others of his ilk walk past, none of them have Conté's appearance but so similar in gait and demeanour.

'Are they going to eat me?'

Conté frowns and chuckles. 'No. Silly.'

'They killed my Daddy.'

'No, they didn't. We saved you from the bushwhackers. The men who took your father's life. I told you. White men, white devils.'

Harriet glances back from whence they came, considering a run for it now; she has an idea of the way back.

'Why should I believe you?'

'Because they saved me. A few years ago now when I was very little, but I remember.'

'So what? Oi, that's mine.'

Conté gives Harriet's gun to a passing woman, the same complexion as the others. 'You must be tired and hungry?'

'You … they killed my Daddy.'

'No.'

'Yes.'

'Look, outside the cities and towns, this whole state is crawling with greedy white men. All kinds of nasties come here from far and wide to prospect and plunder. Criminals who think they can take whatever they want from whoever, especially us. We heard they were making to attack your caravan and fended them off, the evil weasels. Tough shoot, though, if you ask me. Hostile little bunch.'

'*Little*?'

'This here is the Choctaw people, or at least those who have remained on the ancient land. Most of us, them, got forced upriver and then West. Many died. Many, many, many.'

Harriet struggles to keep up with her chatter, which lurches across several accents in one sentence. What a strange kid. Exotic, even.

'They don't look like natives. In the faces maybe, but not in the clothes. Don't look like you, either.'

'What does a native look like, then? Tell me, Harriet Farrell.' Conté gently tugs Harriet, and they start to walk into the village. 'We've learned to fit in with the laws and customs, give the white gangs fewer excuses to steal and pillage. Though that doesn't stop most.'

Harriet is aware that they are moving, but still feels trapped in a whirlwind.

'So are we going after them now? You and your men?'

There it is, that smile again. 'Not *my* men, and no. I'm sorry, Harriet Farrell. They cut into our territory and we sent them a message and that is all. They'll be back to take whatever they can plunder from the wagons, and then they'll scram somewhere else with richer pickings, I guess. I hope.'

Harriet stops dead and tries to breathe, to summon back the protective fury she had earlier. Conté strokes her back. 'This is all wrong.'

'But – for the grace of God – I spotted you from my position, up in the tree, falling out the back of that wagon. That's my role, you see. I'm a spotter and a tracker.'

Harriet studies her again. 'But you're not like them … Oh, I give up.'

'We're foundlings, Harriet Farrell. You too now.' Conté views her with kind eyes, 'Sorry. You Irish with that name?'

'Yes.'

Conté looks happy with herself. 'Ha. I knew that accent. Dublin?' Harriet nods. 'How is it over there?'

Harriet flinches at the odd question. 'How do you think? It is the way it is, which is why I am here.' She stops again. 'Wait, wait. Where are you taking me?'

'Food. Drink. Rest. Come on.'

Conté strides off, leaving Harriet in the dusty road. 'We may not look the same, but we are one spirit. That is the way out here by the great river and in the forest. Get used to it. You coming or not? Your choice, Harriet Farrell.'

Harriet Farrell throws her head back and gazes up into the cloudless, deep blue sky.

'What choice?'

Twelve-year-old versions of the girls in Choctaw smocks, braids and face paint howl with sheer glee as they race each other on horseback through the undergrowth. Harriet Farrell is a different kid, moving with easy stealth, at one with her home on the banks of the great river, sharing the forest river spirit.

Conté speeds up as she spots a low, fallen tree and jumps the obstacle with ease. Harriet is slightly in her wake and tries to copy her friend, but her ride's back leg clips the trunk and she reels off, her fall broken by the lush vegetation.

'Harriet. Harry?' Conté pulls up and dismounts. She approaches Harriet who lies prone, eyes shut. 'Quit teasing me,

Harry. If you were dead, you wouldn't be wearing that gibbon face.'

She kicks Harriet in the ribs and she opens her eyes, chuckling. 'I'll beat you next time.'

'Yeah, yeah. Always a race for you, isn't it?'

Harriet's stricken horse whinnies and they get up and approach her. The problem is immediately clear; a broken hind leg.

'Heck, Harry. I wish you'd be more careful. Such recklessness. Poor thing.'

'Yes. I'm sorry.'

Conté pulls her pistol, convinced that her friend is not sorry. Harriet Farrell is never sorry and she knows a lie when she hears one. Ever since she saved her from that raid, her friend has shown a hard edge, impossible to penetrate. She doesn't do tears because she ran clean out of them that day, Conté figures.

'Not half as sorry as you'll be when the elders find out. All cause of your goofing.'

She hands Harriet the gun, who looks down at her horse in distress.

Bang. The noise came from the river. Conté goes to investigate, pulling aside some bushes.

'Harry. Come and have a look at this.'

Out on the river, a group of gunboats have shanghaied a larger vessel. Another warning shot is fired across its bows.

'Coming.'

Another gunshot, this time from Harriet's trusty Sharps. The whinnying stops. Harriet crosses herself and joins Conté.

'Varmint river pirates again. Worse than bushwhackers.'

Harriet shrugs. 'One and the same.'

Aboard a Mississippi steamer, passengers cower as roughnecks prowl the deck of the vessel, their petrified victims lined up on one side, the crew on the other. Banastre, sporting a mop of greasy hair, scraggly beard, filthy denim coveralls and clutching his Smith and Wesson, climbs aboard from below, and his fellow pirates part like the Red Sea for their leader.

He approaches an ageing crewman as his lackeys collect valuables from the cowed throng.

'You know the drill as well as I know these waters, old Pappy. This is why I came to you first. You don't look like no old fool.'

'You'll dangle for this, swine.'

Banastre presses the barrel of his gun between the crewman's eyes. 'Guess there's no fool like an old fool. You go fetch the captain. Tell him that Banastre Dunwoody is taking his ship. Make it easy for me, and I'll make it easy for him.'

'Banastre Dunwoody?' There's a lump in the old timer's throat, as if the name itself means something terrible. He looks into Banastre's smiling eyes, both crazy and serious. 'Fetch the captain!'

'That's m'boy. Fetch the cappy, Pappy.'

Banastre is fêted by his mates. A steamer like this is worth far more than the passengers or contents, and this represents an audacious catch for ransom or resale. Today is a good day, but this here Banastre has grander ideas and visions. This is only the beginning.

A bullet fizzes past his head and lodges in the paddle casing. Banastre spins in the direction of the shooter and pulls his scope. Two Choctaw kids fire potshots at them from the riverbank, too far out of their range to cause any real aggravation. One of them nearly got lucky, though.

Banastre tilts his chin and chuckles. 'Just some little savages playin' soldier is all. Lookee. Cute.'

#7 COURTSHIP IN THE COTTON FIELDS

August 9th, 1862

Papa says, 'And may I introduce, ma petite Chou-teau. Harriet.'

Harriet appears at the top of the winding stairwell dressed to the nines in the finest overpriced French colonial couture available about town, the picture of a Southern Belle in peach and lace, topped off with the most demure of bonnets. Such a *vision* that Commander Banastre Xavier Dunwoody lays eyes upon for the first time.

They walk and walk. Down the pony track, then through the reeds and honeysuckle azaleas to the cotton fields beyond the fence, following the lilting rhythm of singing harmonies. Men, women and children till the field, getting their work done before night falls. Banastre and Harriet talk about all the pleasant things; fashion, dance, theatre, art. She can see that the man is cultured enough to be able to call himself a gentleman and worldly enough to be able to catch her out, so she remains alert to his sensibilities and to the details of his actions. They stop and admire the tangerine sunset, due west across the plain. Whitewashed huts, where the chattels live, spread across a verdant carpet dotted with fluffy white specks, the precious yarn that will never make them rich. Soon the yardarm will be reached and the whistlers and singers will head back for supper and rest. God help them for what is coming.

'Conté will prepare a room for you. Will you stay?'

Banastre shakes his head. 'I'll speak with your daddy, then I'll have to get away.'

'So late at night? You'll never catch a boat.'

'The river isn't safe for a man like me, Miss. Yankees got their gunboats patrolling, itching for skirmishes. It kills me to say it, but we're past the point of trying to fight them, though I'll never shirk a scrap if presented with one. I'd be a fool to die in a petty firefight with the plans I got.'

She knows some of what plans they are, information that was so hard to come by. Harriet eyes him, seeking the right balance of coquettishness. The time to ply him for information will come, but it isn't now. 'Of course. I'd have taken you to be a fellow who is ready for a skirmish, sir. For God and the South, of course.'

'Huh,' Banastre chuckles. 'My services are required elsewhere, Miss Harriet. Which is part of my issue here. With you.'

'Tell me? I am intrigued and a little in awe.' Yes, positively moist with anticipation.

'I cannot, Miss. But, to speak plainly, if we marry, you will have to leave this estate. You will have to leave Louisiana, leave Dixie. So there it is. You know the deal straight and true.'

Harriet was waiting for this moment, and he delivered. Of course it is a pre-condition; everything hinges not only upon her answer, but how she answers. Even a bull-headed, murderous bastard like Banastre would feel the need to ask first before pressing ahead with a marriage, such is the power of that social convention. Further, it will help his cover and level of respectability if he travels with a willing and loyal wife of good stock. She knows that he knows.

'If you woo me, I may follow,' she responds, with a long-practised quiver in her voice. To men like Banastre, the chase is better than the catch, but she remains wary of his every move.

'I'll take that with me, then. Dilly dally all the way.'

'Sir, if I might be plain too, then?'

'Surely.'

'Speak with Daddy. I do want you to.'

She's glad that Conté isn't here to witness them and especially her. Every fawning, fucking word is wrung out of her, driven by the noble cause. He smiles like a shark, his fine chin strong and square.

This is a man who lined up poor farmers on the edge of a pit and watched on as his firing squads blew their brains out. This is a man who personally instigated a torture camp on Fort Sumter island that was so cruel that even the mandarins at Richmond debated upon whether or not to court martial him. Instead, they gave him a new commission, one that suited him down to the ground and the very reason he stands before Harriet right now. She notices his holstered gun and immediately curses the betrayal of her own eyes.

Banastre nods, impressed.

'A Smith & Wesson, ma'am. A revolution cast in iron.'

'I ain't seen one of them before. We use rifles here, but only for leisure shooting and culling.'

He pulls the gun and deftly spins it in his hand, offering it to her.

Even without firing it, the sleek power is evident. One quick move, a slug to his head, and it can be explained as a shooting accident. But then they'll find another Banastre to send to Liverpool and all that long and deep reconnaissance work will be dashed. A mad moment.

Banastre picks some rocks of varying sizes and sets them upon the fence. 'Here we are. Tin can alley.'

'You mean to test me, sir? What a lark.'

'Call it an initiation. Any woman that I marry must be able to shoot. One day it may come to it, if the Yankees push us.' Harriet pulls her best aghast expression. 'Only joking, sweetness. They'll never make it that far.'

She backs away and Banastre joins her, sidling behind. He places both hands on her shoulders as she takes sight, then slips his hand to her waist, adjusting her pivot and weighting. She can't help but feel a quiver, a tingle at his touch and she curses herself again. If it has to be a part of the act, then so be it, but don't enjoy it. Never enjoy it. His warm breath is in her ear.

'Now squeeze that trigger. It's primed to be sensitive, on a hair, so be careful.'

Harriet obeys, taking out the biggest stone.

'Excellent, Miss. Bravo.'

This isn't her first time with a Smith & Wesson, or indeed any other good brand and calibre of pistol, but she knows how to play it. Good but not too good.

Banastre compels. 'Encore.'

She takes out the second and third. Smaller and smaller. Three left.

'Wow,' she mews. 'I want one.'

'Ha. Very good indeedy deedy, mademoiselle. Encore.'

And the fourth. She adds some jitter and misses number five, then misses again for number six. Then she adds a spoonful of girlish petulance and a dash of disappointment as she stamps a foot. This is what Banastre expects, so give it to him. He places a hand on the small of her back, squeezing her ass in the same movement. Is he prone to taking advantage of her, out in the field? What will she do if he tries? Is she really ready for this? Can she ever be?

'I missed,' she grunts, keeping it cute by adding another stamp and passing the gun back to him. She folds her arms as he reloads six slugs. The more girlish petulance she gives out, the more his guard seems to slip.

'You did, but you did good. Not many can handle a small arm so well first time, Miss.'

'I'm gratified.'

'So you should be.'

Banastre unloads two at number five and another two at number six. Both stones are hit twice. The man is some slinger, she'll hand him that.

Harriet claps. This butters his ego nicely.

'I thank you, Miss.'

'Bravo, Commander.'

He bows and reaches down to his ankle, pulling up his trouser leg to reveal a Colt .45 holstered to his calf. For a second, her blood curdles.

'Why sir,' says Harriet, 'Did you come here expecting trouble?'

'I go everywhere expecting trouble, Mademoiselle.' Yes, and if he doesn't find it, he causes it. Banastre pulls the gun and offers it to Harriet, still on bended knee.

'For me?'

He nods. 'Mais oui. Bien sur, mam'selle.'

'Merci beaucoup.' Harriet takes the gun. Better than a ring, for sure.

Banastre dusts off his knees as he rises up again. He notices the singers working the fields behind her.

'Look at 'em. Happy as Larry. Can't say I care much for that.'

'I wouldn't say that.'

'Why do you treat them so nice? I can't say that I understand.'

Harriet has this rehearsed, but it still rankles in her belly. 'You see how they work when they're not maltreated.'

'But it is a scientific fact that they don't live as long as us. Many more die as infants if you let them breed too much. Thrash them hard and restock when necessary; plenty more where they came from. Your family should know this, the generations you've been here. It's your business, your livelihood.'

Harriet wants to get off the subject. 'I dunno these things, sir. Ask my Daddy. I just stay friendly with them. They like me.'

'I'm sure they do, but you can't be a soft touch. That leads to the wrong kind of thinking, dearie. It is a delicate, intricate system perfected over a long, long time and our way of life depends upon it. Worlds depend upon it. May I speak plainly?'

Harriet nods. 'It is the only way to speak, sir.'

'I know what folks around here say about the Chouteaus, Miss Harriet. Things I heard ain't too generous or wholesome, but there's truth in it. Almost put me off coming, it did.'

Almost, but for a fat vat of cash. Harriet nods, against every instinct in her being. 'Yessir.'

'But I'm not here to lecture you. Relax, belle. All in good time.'

'Okay.'

He massages the shooter in his palm, cocks the barrel and closes an eye, aiming at one of the figures in the field.

'Two slugs left. What do you reckon? Must be 100 paces. One headshot? Two headshots?'

Harriet frowns. She can see his game.

'Commander Dunwoody. You are a rake, sir.'

He drops his shooting hand for a moment.

'What? Why would you stop me? If I wanted anything, why would you stop me?'

He raises the pistol again and Harriet can hear her own heartbeat in her ears. This is a test, a damned, dirty test.

'I implore you to lower that gun, sir. Now, sir.'

He rubs his finger against the trigger, getting the maximum sport out of the situation. Perhaps this is why he hasn't found a wholesome bride to date, although she knows that Banastre has been through more women than cigars.

55

'Why, sweetness? Do tell me.'

She must think quickly, dammit.

'Because?'

'Yes?'

'Because they're all our best workers right there. You hit any of them and the yield will be affected before we can replace 'em. Morale will drop and they may even revolt. That's our delicate balance. And yes, heaven forgive you because I happen to like 'em. Is that such a crime, sir?'

Banastre bites his lip and then lowers the shooter. 'Fair, I suppose. On the first point rather than the second. But if I'm a-gonna marry you, you gotta learn. Sweetness. Remember that all of this will be mine, you included. What then?'

Lumps in her throat; hard, jagged rocks in her belly. She can only nod.

'Then is then and now is now.' How the thick-as-two-short-planks act works a treat.

'Surely.' Banastre holsters his gun and offers her an arm to link. 'Let me parlay with your Daddy, then. Get the formalities out of the way.'

She accepts and they begin to make their way back to the homestead. Harriet can sense Conté, stashed and camouflaged high up a Cypress tree, her trusty Sharps from all those years ago clenched in hand. So, she was here to witness it. Of course she was. God knows what Conté thought was going to happen, but it firms up Harriet's resolve. That was a victory, but it could have just gone so wrong. This is the life she has just committed to, and then some.

Conté tracks Banastre with the long barrel, almost wishing upon a bird or feral cat to make her misfire, but the deal is ready to be sealed and no one is dead. It has to be a good day.

Right? Right.

Banastre finds Papa Jean-Pierre most agreeable and he will leave Les Cyprès with a date for the nuptials and a solid arrangement for a dowry, transferable to the checking account of Commander Banastre X. Dunwoody upon witnessing. A quick toast with

Monsieur Papa's best brandy, a Rebel salute, then he kisses Harriet's hand and is away on his fast horse. Business done and dusted.

Ah, the romance of the South. They wave him away as he thunders up the pony track and into the gloopy Louisiana night.

'Bravo, Jean-Pierre,' says Pélagie, the actress playing the mother.

That reliable old ham Vaughn relaxes his shoulders and lights up a cigar, relieved that he has arrived at his curtain call. He relaxes his gait, shaking off the stiff-backed Louisiana cotton farmer act.

'You didn't think it was a little too much? Maybe I fluffed a line or two. My accent was more Parisian than New France.'

'Who cares? It did the trick,' says Conté.

Vaughn smooths the wax on his moustache. 'Humour my curiosity, but what will become of my character now?'

Conté pats his shoulder. 'Tragically, before the wedding, he will die of a sudden bout of yellow fever and your doting wife Pélagie will also perish, herself of a broken heart. This will sweeten the deal for Dunwoody further still, and the estate will be sold before it can disappear behind enemy lines and hasten the departure to Liverpool. I did not agree to that part, as it will see everything and everyone be sold on, which is a heinous betrayal. Dunwoody gets control of everything. Harriet's money is his money, the estate is his property, Harriet is his property. As am I.'

Vaughn glances at Harriet and looks genuinely crestfallen, giving the glimpse of a real father. He's seen enough of Banastre to know most of what this means. 'I'm sorry for you. Both of you. I should not have showboated there. Forgive me.'

Harriet nods. 'It's the plan, the only plan. Don't be sorry. Take the plaudits for a fine performance. We are performers ourselves, after a fashion.'

The actor puffs his cheeks out.

Conté rolls her eyes in the dime-a-drama of it all. 'Playing out an epic, Southern tragedy in five acts. Ain't that so, Major General?'

A sweating, rotund man in full, true, blue, Union livery walks out from behind them, flanked by a pair of sturdy adjutants.

They've been waiting behind the false walls in the lobby of this secret fortress for several hours now, monitoring the visit of their mark, recording everything in notebooks, ready for plan B if Banastre became less than agreeable to marrying Harriet; to capture and interrogate him. Pity.

Nice that Butler deemed this all worthy of his personal attention. His tone is gruff, blunt and heavily Bostonian. 'Good work, Vaughn. I almost believed you myself.'

'Thanks.'

'Get yourself back to Broadway, sir. You'll be paid in the usual way via your agent. Off with you now. Chop chop.'

Vaughn clips his heels, bows and makes his way back inside to grab his valise.

Butler rolls his narrow eyes, which seem far too small for such a huge head. He doesn't do delays or niceties.

'May we discuss?' Harriet is keen to keep it civil in spite of Conté's misgivings about him.

He dabs his bald pate with a handkerchief. 'Damn this heat. Never lets up.'

Harriet says, 'Get used to it, sir. If you really are going to occupy New Orleans, you'll have to take a home and office in Louisiana.'

'That, my faithful agent, is on a need-to-know basis. Let's walk and talk, if talking's what you want from me.'

Butler glances at his pocket watch, permanently in a hurry. He strides out, feet thudding against the decking and down the steps to the path that leads to the stables. Swathes of New France are now under his unofficial governorship and his style is the polar opposite of what washes down here. He carries a permanently abrasive demeanour, remiss of airs and graces. He is squat, obese, oily and unkempt, leagues below what is expected of a gentleman or an officer, the antithesis of the dashing Southerner. While his public persona has him reviled as *The Blob* in these parts, with merchants in the territories controlled by the Union openly selling chamber pots with his likeness at the bottom, both Conté and Harriet know that this is the tip of the iceberg. He is the grand architect of the new espionage in the Union ranks and the closest thing they've known to having a real father, although the latter description might be pushing it a bit.

'Ask away then. I can see that you're about to burst.'

'Sir, the support mechanisms that you have put in place over there seem a little flimsy, given the gravity of the operation.'

'A little flimsy?' grunts Conté, as if she's stepped on a stone in her bare feet.

'We encoded and relayed to your office a list of supplies and a revised logistical structure. Did you receive it?'

'I did, Ms Farrell.'

'Did you manage to digest it, sir?'

It wouldn't take much for him to digest anything. 'Affirmative.'

'So you'll see to our requirements then?'

'No.'

'No?'

'You will take what you are given and like it, Ms Farrell. That is the end of the discussion.'

'Sir, if you please. We have laid the bait and the trap is sprung. I entreat you.'

Butler oozes ennui, as if this is all just part of his humdrum. That is probably one of the things the *good folk* detest about him. 'An acceptable day's work, if a touch hammy for my tastes. No need to continue with the melodrama, huh,' he grunts, eyeing her up and down, 'Entreat. Really.'

The two agents trail in his wake. Conté takes up the slack. 'So is that it?'

'Oh, not you again, Miss Louverture. You're like a bleating sheep. Verily, verily, baa, baa.'

'Conté, leave it. Quit while we're ahead?'

'Ahead of what? You know just what he's sending us into, Harry? You ever been to Europe? Britain?'

Butler interjects. 'Yes. Many times. Have you?'

'I was asking her, not you. *Sir.*'

Butler sniffs and carries on galumphing, not interested enough in the conversation or them to pursue the line. Behind them, Pélagie helps Vaughn load his valise aboard a pony and trap, and waits ready for the wandering thespian. Both of them are already forgotten by Butler. How long before he forgets about Conté and Harriet?

'We mean to say that you could give us more logistical support, sir.'

Conté grunts, 'Don't speak for me, Harry. *I* mean to say that this operation is the biggest, steaming pile of bullshit I ever saw. Sir. You want to send us an ocean away? We want more guarantees. Demand them, I say.'

'Demand?' he retorts, spikily.

Harriet finds herself as the buffer between them, as she always does when they are in his company. 'What we want to do is…'

'You'll handle yourselves well. A slick unit. I have every confidence in both of you. And don't think that we won't be watching.'

'Major General, you know what you're asking Harriet to do and by virtue, both of us. We need real support over there. An office in our consulate. A company of trained men. A unit that can be worthily called such. That's the bare minimum. You read our list.'

'Money buys men and loyalty. You'll have money. We have excellent connections in the city. You will be well provided for.'

Conté won't let this go, as much as she will never let anything go, but Harriet is all too aware that Butler couldn't care less. 'But who will have control, sir? You've seen Dunwoody. He's a hyena. Everything is about The War to him. One slip and we're dead.'

'Then think of ways to curry his loyalty, blind him with love or some such asinine notion. It is what I recruited you for.'

'You probably should have caged him back there and saved Harriet and me from this game. This is foolhardy, I tell you.'

Butler waves his hand as they approach the stables. 'Are you having collywobbles, Ms Louverture? I can replace you, if not her.'

Harriet protests. 'I cannot do this without her. You know this.'

Conté fumes. 'Yes, and still he threatens us with it. He knows our history and uses it against us.'

'That is what espionage is all about, dear,' mews Butler, satisfied with himself.

'We come as a unit,' interjects Harriet, anxious to get something – anything – from him before he rides off.

'And such a singular, peculiar unit that is,' grunts Butler, but he remains just about convinced. 'Choctaw-raised, Irish and Haitian-Creole. How novel, how cosmopolitan.' Butler pauses, more to give room for his own amusement than to humour them. 'There we have it.'

Harriet says, 'We do need official support, sir. A few local gangs are hardly…'

And he's walking again, pounding the ground with every step. 'Enough from the pair of you. Seeing as you come "as a unit", do you accept this commission or not? Well?'

Butler pretends that they have a choice in the matter. Harriet knows that they've come too far to step back. 'Of course we do.'

Conté says, 'Yes, but there's…'

'Then you accept my command. Or shall I have to start again and put the pair of you under a gagging order? Ship you out to Mexico or somewhere equally godforsaken. It would be a mutual inconvenience, but more for you than I.'

Conté shakes a finger at Butler, and he smiles, never losing his waddling momentum. 'Don't you dare threaten us. We've already done so many terrible things on your behalf.'

'Then you can do some more terrible things, dear. I really don't know why we are having this conversation right now, but it is ending this moment.'

'Conté…'

'No, Harry. We've been on the sharp end of this and soon we're going off the edge of the world. He needs us more than we need him for all his acting. And he needs to be told.'

Butler stops at the door of the stables, and his saddled nag bristles in waiting for him. 'I will consider myself told, then. Now get on with it.'

'Sir, with respect, we do need more assurances. More logistical support. More protection,' says Harriet, flogging the dead horse with all her might.

Conté prefers a tack of open hostility. 'What makes you think that he'll listen to you over me? That he's white and male? He barely counts as human.' Harriet guides Conté out of Butler's path, knowing that she won't get any further with him this evening or any other evening. She might even get both of them canned and shipped out to Chihuahua, the way she is going. 'I shall write you from hell, then.'

'It will be your duty to do so, Miss Louverture. Care of Martin's Bank, as per your briefing. Remember to use the correct cypher.'

He mounts and pushes his horse through the two of them. His boys follow at a steady gallop.

'A pompe à chiasse. Branleur, sous-merde! Pah!'

'I understand, Conté. I really do.' Harriet places a hand on Conté's shoulder, whose face is like a tropical storm. 'But what choice have we? Think about it.'

'Pah.' She shrugs it off and heads in the direction of the servant's quarters to the rear of the homestead. Her swinging shoulders warn Harriet not to follow.

'Divide and conquer,' mutters Harriet, before heading back in the direction of a fake home that she will soon depart forever. She suspects that won't be the last time Butler employs such tactics.

#8 PRINCESS GRACE

June 5th, 1863

She waits. Quiet tonight. Not quiet enough, as was the plan communicated by the lady. That 'big noise' this client told her to expect; just where is it, then?

She is Princess Grace Monolulu and she knows horses. She is 15 years old, Edo West African. A business leader, wise beyond her years, owner of stables and horses in the name of her pops, King Monolulu. Business doesn't interest King Pops, only horses do, so it is Grace that brings in the trade and manages that side. It is a neat arrangement that has been in place since long before they disembarked here themselves, praying that this would be their final destination after so many years of displacement and threat. His name is all over the horse's livery, but she is the brains and trade is better than brisk. It is a good enough reason to settle in this city, greater for now than the many reasons not to.

So, a diminutive African girl of 15 always has thoughts ready, in idle moments, to transform from grief, trauma and anguish to those of food, so goes that hazard of her regular brief to wait and wait. Waiting here, waiting there and everywhere. Waiting tonight about Salthouse dock, a special service for a special client who pays very, very well. Spicy beef stew and dumplings will be waiting for her on the stove back at the stables, bubbling and ready, King Pops' special recipe. Keep that in mind, then. Everything is worth the wait tonight for this particular, peculiar client.

The dense forest of huge masts denotes vessels lined up, waiting for cargo in the overcrowded berths. It is a wonder how they ever manage to disentangle and embark for the river. But here is a curious sight, climbing up an iron ladder, dripping wet and anxious across the brow. A woman, clad head to toe in a woollen one piece that is dragging her down in its saturated weight, combined with a clear fatigue that threatens to haul her back into the dirty drink. Grace stops for a second, eying the odd black lagoon creature and looking about her for any company. No, she is alone. The woman presses a finger to her lips and approaches. Then she notices the bump protruding from the lady's belly. This is all not quite what she anticipated.

'Ma'am? You are indeed alone?' she asks. 'Where is Miss Conté?'

'Thank God it's you, Princess. I can always rely. Please, bring over my horse. No time for niceties.' The mistress uses please and thank you as befitting her status, yet rare to hear. Grace likes this and likes her, which is all the more reason why it seems so odd that she is married to a man like her husband. They've not been in Liverpool for long, but they have already established quite distinct reputations.

'Yes, ma'am. As you ordered. Where is...'

'You are such a reliable business. Now I'm mighty pooped, if you don't mind my imposition. May I mount?'

Grace prepares the seat and Mrs Dunwoody places a dirty, bare foot in a stirrup, pulling herself astride her gelding.

'That's better. I'll tie up round the back of 101 Canning. You can collect her from there tomorrow as you see fit. I'll see to it that there's an extra thrippence in it for you, for your trouble in waiting so long this evening.'

Grace continues to scan the dock and river. 'No trouble, but thank you kindly, ma'am.' The lady nods. 'Where is...'

Mrs Dunwoody rides away at a fast gallop. Grace stuffs her hands in her pockets and gets to walking South, following the same direction towards Canning Street. Peculiar that Mrs Dunwoody's friend was not with her. Mrs Dunwoody's friend is *always* with her. Maybe it is quite sad. Who knows? It isn't her business to know.

Now that her main order of business is complete, Grace has another important issue to address before she can go home to her King Pops' wonderful, tasty stew.

After a day of footslogging, pony care and stabling across the city, this is probably the last thing Grace wanted to have to do, but she makes it a priority to know the faces and movements of every important person in the docks and surrounding areas, from Peelers to scallywags to gangsters. She knows that a certain watchman is due to go on duty at this hour, and if she is quick, she will catch him at the start of his shift.

She scampers across the cobbles, past a huge warehouse on Goree Piazza and onto the old Strand that straddles the water's edge. The magnificent Customs House bears down on her, the jewel of Liverpool's skyline with its Ionic limestone columns and huge, ornate dome. Always but several paces away from either utter misery and penury or ostentation and wealth in this city. Fortunately, Grace knows her niche, and it is thus:

What keeps this city moving? Gas, coal and horses.

What keeps this city growing? Navvies and horses.

What keeps this city prospering? Ships and horses? No. Not quite. Ships, chattel slaves and horses. And they're here, onetime and existing, for all that faux noble, honky tonk legislation about abolition that was passed in Westminster nearly thirty years ago.

Horses and slaves. It preoccupies her thoughts every night, every day and right now as she adopts a brisk, confident stride. Behind her, the path to the Landing Stage will be teeming with life in a few hours, with new victims for this city or those en route to New York, Canada, The Tropics, India, pouring in by the boatload in a daily avalanche of incoming people. The wealthier of these itinerant souls make up the majority of her clients; those who need good horses but aren't staying in the city for long. She knows what it is like to pass through port after port, but for very different reasons to them.

With her King Pops, she was forced on endless treks across savannah and through jungle, further away and further away again from home until home vanished forever in the mind if never the heart. It should have ended in death, slow or quick, or rape or murder or the lash. That she is here at all is testament to their little miracle.

Espying tall, spiked iron railings designed to deter thieves from the warehouses, she recalls for the thousandth time how her Daddy cut a hole in a fence and took her in the dead of night without rousing any of the captors or fellow captives. How they then slipped away on a stolen horse, only to be recaptured and sent to the pound on the Gorée Islands, the godforsaken place that invades her dreams. Their fate looked sealed as a drum. Goree Piazza, so-named after that terrible place as if that is an honourable tribute, is behind her now. Grace doesn't need to look back.

'Wait sir, I speak your tongue. Wait I implore you!' she yelled, at the top of her lungs again tenfold in English, Portuguese, Spanish and Dutch. 'My father is a genius with horses, he can show you. Please let him show you, he will make you some money. Please, sir. Do not whip him, he is of tremendous value to you. As am I. Can you not see that I speak your tongue and many others? I beseech you.'

Appeal to their greed. It worked then and it worked that evening.

Their voices. 'Take her in the back and shut her up.' Even at a tender age, Grace knew what 'shut her up' meant, but she had to remain strong for both of them. Keep pushing.

'He is the famous horseman King Monolulu, just a second of your time, behold and you won't regret it,' she yelled, like a sideshow ringmaster trying to drum up custom from passers-by. One laughed at her weird behaviour and this rippled through the throng of gaoler rapists, enough to put them off their violence for a moment, evoking some of their own civilisation in this terrible bastion, a sandstone edifice jutting out into the Atlantic with coffin ships moored below, ready to feed the industry of pain. 'Behold the King!'

Guffaws. 'The king, is he? Famous is he? What about you? Are you a princess, then?'

Only greed and comedy would break their savagery. She gave them both.

So, curiosity tweaked, they put it all to the test about her Daddy and discovered that he had very useful, saleable skills indeed. Who knew? Slaves were moved across the sea, but so were horses, and good horsemen were always in demand. As she could decipher and negotiate in any language for her father – who was perceived as mute and dumb save for his horse skills – Grace came with the package. Their value together increased a hundredfold in an instant. It saved them from the middle passage and set them on their way here to Liverpool, after a hundred ports, several indentures and four shipwrecks. The sights, sounds and smells of their incredible journey to this place remain fresh on this late Summer evening. They will never diminish in her long decades ahead.

Down the side of the Customs House, she can see the cobbles and townhouses climbing up Duke Street and away from the city. One last errand this evening to get her ride home.

'You stole my horse.'

'Requisitioned it. It's Queen's property now.'

'No, you stole my horse.'

'Move on, bloody scamp. Do you know what time it is?'

'Listen, Constable Starkey – yes I have your name – my father and I have connexions about this town, in case you did not know. You would be foolish to ignore me.' Starkey is removing his civilian wear and pulling on his blue jacket. 'Been out gallivanting tonight, have you? Call yourself a watchman.'

'You calling me a fool?'

'Yes. That is the best I can call you.'

'Why don't you just piss off back to wherever you came from? Or a cotton pitch, whichever you like. Just get out of my sight.'

'That line does not work with me. I have met much worse than you.'

'Want to test me on that? How's about I drag you down to Castle Street by your short and curlies and auction your skinny little arse off in one of the coffee houses, um?'

'Ignorant fool. That business stopped decades ago.'

'That business will never stop in Liverpool, so away with you.' Unfortunately, he seems to be correct on that single point, if nothing else.

'You arrived here not long ago yourself. How can you be so mean?'

'Beat it, I say, before I beat you. Hanging around like a bad smell.'

Starkey turns his back on Grace, making to shut the iron door to the bridewell in her face. She espies the keys to the stables jangling on his waist.

'Wait. I will pay you.'

Starkey stops and turns. Grace emits a huge grin and nods.

'How much?'

'The going rate.'

He licks his lips. Greed opens so many doors, or in this case keeps them open. Grace dips in her pouch and fumbles with some imaginary coins.

'Well? What's the going rate?'

She kicks Starkey hard in the balls. He collapses like a stack of marbles.

In a young life that has packed in more experience than fifty times its span, Grace has learned many things. Two of them are at play here; firstly, to always appeal to a white man's greed if his common decency is absent, and secondly, to wear strong, heavily-toecapped boots when at work, for they have a substantial variety of handy uses.

She picks the keys up as he groans on the floor like the pig he is.

'Mr Ake! Mr Ake help! Assistance!'

'Idiot.'

'Lock her up, Mr Ake! Jesus, Mary and Joseph, me knackers.'

Grace steps back into the yard and unlocks the gate, where the constabulary keep a stable in almost as immaculate order as her own. That is all down to Mr Ake, of course. He would never sanction the theft of a horse for quick profit or sale, but he was a good reason for her to think twice about coming here this evening, which was something Mr Starkey was probably relying upon when he thought he could rustle her prime mare from a client on Wapping and stash her on constabulary grounds.

More whining from Starkey. 'Mr Ake! Come quickly, I say, sir!'

And there is Rosalinda, the white, Arabian mare – in good, bristling fettle she is glad to see. It is such a relief, as that ingrate scaffold-dodger rustled her very best horse and Lord knows what he might have done to her. Grace guides her out of the paddock and mounts her, spotting a giant figure from the corner of her eye as she canters out of the yard.

'Mr Ake! She's stealing one of our horses, sir! Can you not see it? Daylight robbery! Mr Ake!'

A fellow African, towering over Starkey, head to toe in a blue uniform; emperor, lord and master of this bridewell, chomping on an apple, black cat circling around his ankles. Grace knows him well, as does every manjack and woman with half an ounce of wits about them in the docklands who also know to avoid his path. He picks the lad up by his collar and clips him around the ear.

The irritant of a thief constable, who isn't a small man himself but looks like a doll next to the giant, clutches his loins and perseveres to moan and groan before Mr Ake picks him up with one hand, like he's a mischievous toddler, manoeuvring his entire frame back inside the dark lobby. The large man ignores Grace and she canters out, still uneasy in his presence but grateful in the knowledge that the accepted order around here has prevailed. A private levy is paid in monthly instalments to ensure protection from the constabulary, as it is worth their salt to every gang in the city. Young Starkey is too stupid and cocky to realise that he has overstepped his mark.

'Thank you, Payton.'

Without acknowledgement, Mr Ake slams the slammer shut and she trots into the narrow alley that leads out towards Duke Street and back down to the Customs House. She pulls out a pocket watch and glances at it. Her work was long and hard today, but she thanks her spirits and their God for it as she does every morning and every night. Home time at last.

On the East bank of the river, by Otterspool Promenade, another figure gasps and scrambles ashore, looking like some half-dead sea monster in the moonlight, a shapeshifter slowly turning back to human form as it crawls and struggles to its feet. Conté coughs up salty, filthy Mersey water, heaving it back up, getting as much out of her guts as possible. Dry retching, she then pulls seaweed out of her hair and turns back to the river, scouring it for any sign of Harriet. How in hell did her friend make her agree to this operation in such a vulnerable condition? She should have said anything, done anything to keep Harriet at home but, to take stock of reality, that was never on the cards. They share wilful traits. Now, all looks lost.

The likely sum of it all churns up her guts yet further. Either the vicious swell or the propeller of that steamer will have done for Harriet, strong swimmer or not.

No sign of any life in that inky drink, let alone human. Several times did Conté herself almost succumb to the current, tossing her around the swell before she managed some sort of stroke in the direction of the rendezvous with Grace at Canning Dock. Then she was swept over again and forced to take a longer route, possibly three times the distance, before finally finding a favourable ebb. What can she do now? Contact Major General Butler at HQ via coded letter? Hope and pray that they send help? Why should any of that matter, even The War, when she has surely just lost the dearest person in the world to her?

Sure, if they'd just died together, she wouldn't be having this problem.

Remember the struggle is what Harry would say. Get home before Banastre, clean yourself up and play dumb. A fiendish charade to have to contemplate, but the only choice. Hellish when the emotions are bubbling and boiling up from her belly, but she must away, post-haste. It should have been her to perish, not Harriet.

Conté breaks into a run, her bare feet smacking against the cinder track and then onto cobbles as she finds the least exposed route up the hill and over in the direction of the residence. A couple of Irish women whistle after her as they ply their trade on Duke Street, reminding her not to attract attention. She ducks down an alley before any more curiosity is aroused, hurdling fences through several garden allotments and back through into the servant's quarters to the rear of the mansion house at 101 Canning Street, sweating and gasping and carrying an anvil of grief across her tired shoulders. How could Harry have survived? Maybe she should go back and look for her, dead or alive. The onset of grief chokes her.

Barrelling through the stable doors, into the back yard and down the steps into the servants' quarters. Then straight through into the kitchen. A hot kettle sits on the stove, and Harriet has her feet on the table, inspecting them for dirt and grit, woman and bump perfectly dandy after a late-night dip.

'Shall we get a bath or have hot tea first?' asks Harriet.

Conté tilts her chin as the anvil drops. 'Tea. You serve. I'm off duty.'

#9 ALL OVER TO THE ISMAYS'

June 6th 1863

They tried, they failed. The culprits will dangle, Ginger assures him. Ho hum.

How Banastre would have dearly loved to stand at the quayside in Birkenhead and let his pregnant lady Harriet launch the ship in front of a host of dignitaries and the gentlemen of the press, but that might be a tad too vulgar and rich for the palates of the British Government. Instead, the vessel will be launched into the Mersey at noon sharp today with minimal fuss and to keep the powder dry, whereupon it will head out of Liverpool Bay and into the shipping lanes South West on a bearing for the Indies in order to join the Confederate fleet. Ready to begin punching some big old fuckin' holes in that blue blockade. What he would give to see the faces of those Union bastards, so cocksure of their Naval prowess, when they espy this colossus heading for a broadside, rammin' speed. What a fine, fine thing that will be. Mouths and asses will drop like lead anchors.

The magnificent craft looks like it could shunt its way right across to New Orleans, through anything or anyone. Naturally, as a symbol of the cooperation between the merchants and traders of the city and Banastre's paymasters in Richmond, Virginia, some sort of discreet ceremony is deemed necessary and young Ismay came up with the perfect proposal, once he'd come to his senses the morning after the night before. It involves a delightful jaunt by carriage to the North of the city.

This is where the elite of Liverpool's shipping tycoons have chosen to build their residences, in a row of grand terraced mansions, the rival of anything in Regent's Park, St Petersburg or Bath. Built to a height that rises above grazing cattle and ewes, the golden sandhills and beach with a prime view of the mouth of the river, Banastre can see why a rich young engineer such as Ismay would choose this place to settle his family pile. Horatio Nelson himself once said that this view rivals the Bay of Naples, and Banastre will not impugn him. British seapower in trade and in maritime engineering can be seen in plain sight, with hundreds of vessels of all shapes and sizes moving and ducking between

71

lanes at the mouth of the river and into the open sea, ordered by buoys and the rigorous detail of the Liverpool Pilot. Such a wonderful spectacle of chaos; giant timber and iron geese and goslings, jostling for lanes about the crowded water. One day, he will bring all this mercantile majesty and magnificent mayhem to the Mississippi, when The War is won and he sails home to Dixie.

'My vessels are informed of when I am in residence,' announces Ismay, as Banastre, Ginger and the other dignitaries sip his champers and view the river through a row of brass telescopes installed for the occasion. 'When a White Star ship passes, it will sound its horn and I will know that it is safely on its way.'

Harriet nods and smiles, doing her best not to give away the opinion stashed in her head that Mr Ismay is just another pompous little prick. He'll fit in splendidly well with his new brethren at the club; the greedy pricks, the nasty pricks, the rich pricks and the stupid pricks.

Ginger says, 'Now that's what I call the personal touch.'

Touché, prick.

Banastre, on the other hand, is mightily impressed. Perhaps he was rather too quick to mock young Ismay on their first meeting. Cotton, tobacco and sugar might rule the roost in this city, but this young fellow and his opulent mansion terrace are visual proof that there is a future in ferrying civilian passengers across the Atlantic. To the South, of course.

Harriet sits by, massaging her belly, bored and fatigued by all the awful male bluster. As the drink flows, the tone will descend and the bluster repeat ad nauseam. Ever the same pattern, but today she has to be party to it.

'Darling?' she mutters, trying to be discreet in her interlocution to her husband.

Banastre glances back at her as she perches behind the men – with the other women in the gallery – upon the grand veranda terrace, purpose-built to impress with a full view of Liverpool Bay, the distant Welsh Mountains dancing in the heat haze of another stifling day. He offers her a telescope rather than an acknowledgement.

'Sweetness. Come look. Come.'

Ginger says, 'Yes, do. Have a look for the baby, too.'

Harriet says, 'Ha. Very good Admiral Harrison. Now, darling, if I might have your attention for a moment…'

'Call me Ginger, m'girl. She's a sturdy lass, isn't she, Banastre? What ho. Fine, fine figure of a woman.'

Banastre says, 'Steady, Ginger. We're in polite company. Keep it clean.'

Ginger emits florid, filthy vibrations, bankrupt of virtue. Yes, Admiral of the Oafs. She knows his kind well.

Harriet rubs her husband's arm. 'Banastre, please, I don't feel very well. Is there somewhere I can go and lie down? Could you ask Mr Ismay for me?'

That look across Banastre's immaculate face, his chiselled jaw twitching and containing sudden, explosive ire. She knows it, feels it, hates it. 'Of course, sweetness. Just wait a few more moments so that we can all see the passing of my ship. Take a look.'

His ship.

Harriet glances through the telescope. Love, honour and obey. *His* ship, the *CSS Banshee* juts through the surf, bullying the water and all other vessels out of its path as it clears the mouth of the river and finds the open sea. Banastre's Banshee, truly a vessel in his image, willing and able to destroy anything or anyone in its path. Yes, his damned lucky ship. When Harriet says that she feels ill, she means it. Her husband may not know it, but this whole agonising show is rubbing defeat right in her face like coarse rock salt into a deep gash. What makes it worse is that Conté can't be here to share her gut-wrenching chagrin, but perhaps that is a blessing for her friend.

'White Star Line can explore routes to the South soon enough, once your debacle is resolved,' says Ismay, twitching himself but with excitement at the vast potential explained to him by Banastre and Ginger over brandy and cigars the other night, before the unfortunate and unsightly event occurred that does not need to be mentioned again.

Invest and evangelise the great project in the Southern States of America. He can see the billboard. Banastre gives him his best shark grin.

'Let's keep talkin'. What a fellow you have found me, Ginger. Just look at this place. I am astounded.'

Ismay's house ain't nothing special in comparison to the opulence that Banastre has seen in Tennessee, the Carolinas, Louisiana and the other Rebel states, but it pays to be fluent in hyperbole in this city, and Ismay soaks up the flattery. Maybe he'll forget the slight after that cooze expired, maybe he won't. Maybe he'll forget the face on him moments earlier, when he was doing him on the chaise longue for a bit of variety. Maybe he won't.

Ginger bounces his portly frame around the decking as he watches the *Banshee* pass muster, wiggling his grotesque, pachyderm ass in boozy glee. Harriet settles back in her seat for a long day and an even longer night.

Banastre eyes the telescope himself. 'Ten tons of Welsh dynamite couldn't sink her. Here she is a-comin'.'

Harriet twitches. Ten tons? Where did he get that from? More hyperbole.

The Confederate Saltire is hoisted on the mainsail. Horns sound from the vessel and the surrounding fleet of gunboats also headed South. All other river traffic gives the flotilla a wide berth, which is no mean feat in this bustling shipping lane. The *Banshee*'s cannons fire a ceremonial volley, away from any wrong attention now. This is a great day for Dixie.

Cheers and applause from the small throng. Directors of The White Star Line, gentlemen of The Athenaeum and their lady wives fête Banastre with more champagne and pats on the back; forked tongues and greased palms.

Harriet takes up his side, gritting her teeth through it like any other of the daily ordeals inflicted upon her by her husband.

'So proud of you, dear,' she whispers in his ear, back to being the perfect impostor.

'Never badger me in front of my investors again. I will not tolerate it,' mutters Banastre and for a second, she wants to run the blade secreted in her petticoat through his cold Reb heart, for all her own calculated, careful logic and years of planning. What would Conté say? Would she persuade her to do it? Shove the blade in herself, even? Harriet hasn't been away from her friend for more than a few hours, but she sorely misses her.

Ginger dances around like an excited, red testicle. 'Man of the moment! Men of the moment! To The Athenaeum! I say let's get bloody blotto!'

More drinks, more huzzahs and hurrahs, but Harriet is already considering her other, more pressing problem, given her status with child and the failed plot. What next, Major General Butler?

#10 THE CROWN

June 7ᵗʰ 1863

His skin is coming out in black hives, and he knows that isn't dirt. Gruel for the last three days and nights and a whole lot of time to think about how he came to be here and the consequences for Sarah and the children.

Pat gets a space to himself away from all the others awaiting trial upstairs, which should be a blessing, but he'd much prefer the threat and stench of a crowded cell to this solitude. Some might be given penal servitude, others shipped out to Australia, others might swing, but they are common criminals. He has elevated status in here, he is political, or so they said at the arraignment.

They don't hang around for justice here in Liverpool, but that isn't what is bothering Pat right now. He listens for the corridor, for heavy boots to make their way down to him and for some grock of a Peeler or sinister type to come through the door and make him revisit a world of pain, one he discovered back in Ireland when he fell foul of the British and their traitorous Irish lackeys. Royston has pissed off some very powerful men in the course of supporting them two girls, however noble he thought he was being. Who bears the consequences? In his long history of feeling like a mug about his boss' business ventures and misadventures, this just about tops everything.

Pat debates with himself as he picks maggots out of his supper; has Royston forgotten about him? Sarah and the children, even? Maybe that would be better all round. For Chubb, for Sarah, for him.

Because there's no sense in denying it. He's fucked.

Keys jangle and the heavy cell door swings open. Two burly men leer back at him. They're probably from Quinn's gang, the Goochies, The High Rip or some other such hoodlum-for-rent outfit, and they've been hired to come here and fill him in, probably by whoever Chubb's pissed off this time with all that malarkey at Cammell Laird. Pat knows the look of men who are about to give him a hard beating. One of them holds up a set of thumb screws and grins back at him.

'More fine work while you're wining and dining yourself, Royston,' he mutters to no one in particular, especially not these two grocks.

'Eh?' grunts one of them, stepping Pat's way. He puts down his delicious dinner and stands up to address his guests.

'Alright boys. Get on with it, then.'

No place for children or women here.

The Crown pub sits on the permanently busy thoroughfare that is Lime Street, a drag of gin palaces without rival in this or any city, and as fine a place for a good old slosh as any. In spite of its name, never was there an establishment more dedicated to the cause of Irish freedom and independence. It is wall-to-wall Fenian. Will Britain ever allow its nearest and oldest colony to cede? Not without a fight, but as they enter through the cloying tobacco and heavy stench of piss and hops, it is clear that the drinkers here are ever ready for that day, by the song that they are singing:

'*High upon the gallows tree swung the noble-hearted three. By the vengeful tyrant stricken in their bloom; but they met him face to face, with the courage of their race, And they went with souls undaunted to their doom. "God save Ireland!" said the heroes; "God save Ireland" said they all. Whether on the scaffold high or the battlefield we die, oh, what matter when for Erin dear we fall!*'

The singing stops dead, as does the drinking and everything else. All eyes are upon them.

Sarah McCartney pushes her way into the pub and the patrons let her know immediately that it is no place for a woman, and certainly no place for a woman with a baby in arms and five young kiddies at her side – closely joined to mother duck – and ever-so-slightly terrified at the sight of grown fools acting the maggot.

'Aw. Ye puttin' me off me ale y'are.'

'Aw, what's with the sour puss and her sour kids? Ah sure that's not right. Ye should be home, knitting and darning and wiping arses and such. Not right I tell ye. Out with yers.'

'Isn't that Paddy Mc's wife?'

'Nah.'

'No, I'm fuckin' telling ye. That's Paddy Mc's wife. Oh what's she doing here? That's desperate bad so 'tis. Bad luck.'

'Fuckin' yes desperate bad luck so 'tis.'

'Oi, Mrs. Are ye Paddy Mc's wife? What are ye doing here, love? This is no place for a woman.'

'Defo not a place for ankle biters either.'

'Agreed so.'

Sarah fixes her hands upon her hips. The Crown is pathetic. Every man in here is pathetic, and yet her husband would rather be here every night than at home with her and their children. He tells her that this is where he does his business. What business is that? Getting put on trial on account of that toe rag Chubb? She feels sick about it, but not half as sick as the prospect of him dangling on the end of a rope soon.

'Sir, can you direct me to Royston Chubb?'

The men look at each other and decide to stage a ridiculous, poorly-rehearsed charade. 'Who? No one of that name here. Never heard of him, Missus. Best you be going home.'

'No one of that name, no. Never heard of him. Royston's not here. Not seen him tonight or any other time.'

'For fuck's sake, Diarmuid.'

'What?'

'It's a good job no Peelers have come in here looking for him, then,' she mutters.

'Wha'?'

'Gentlemen,' announces Sarah so everyone can hear, pulling the children in closer, 'I know he's here, as well as I know my husband is rotting in the cells beneath St Georges' Hall right now. So someone, please, lead me to Royston Chubb. We haven't got much time.'

Through the back into what is loosely described as a lounge, but can be anything from a bare-knuckle boxing ring to a distillery. Huge and dirty stained-glass windows betray what once was perhaps a more gentrified and genteel establishment. Sarah and the children jostle through to a long table and the patrons pull it back to reveal a solid oak trap door. Diarmuid, him with the loose tongue and equine, wonky face, stamps his foot on the door three times and then pulls it open. Some fancy code they've got here.

Sarah glances over the edge to see Royston Chubb camped out in the cellar hugging a jug of Poitín, curled up on a hemp sack, snoring.

'Mr Chubb?'

Nothing.

'Mr Chubb, I really need to see you. It is regarding my husband.'

He stirs and scratches his arse, turning over.

'Mr Chubb!' she yells at the top of her voice. Chubb jumps awake.

'Wha'...'

'It's me. Sarah.'

'Who?'

'Sarah? You know.'

'Oh. Aye. Sarah. Sarah. What do you want?'

'I want to talk to you about Padraig.'

Chubb gurns in derision. 'Aye. Real shame that, dear. Never mind, eh?'

'Oi!'

'What?'

'Have you no loyalty? No heart for these poor children?'

Chubb becomes aware that everyone up top is watching this play out. This isn't what he would call keeping a low profile. 'Ah I have, I have. Me and Pat there, we had an agreement so.'

'What kind of agreement?'

'Well, erm. Do we have to talk about it now? Can ye not come back tomorrow?'

'Unless you want six starving children and their fuming fucking mother to come down there and join you for supper, I suggest we talk about it now.'

'Now there's no need for that. I assured Pat that you will be well looked after.'

'I don't believe you, Mr Chubb. You are a slippery customer.'

'No, I'm not a slippery customer. I'm just a businessman. A slightly unfortunate one.'

'You slipped out of Cammell Laird's, leaving my Pat to get arrested. I'd call that the very definition of slippery, so. How did you manage that?'

'A man has connections.'

'Ah, good. Then I want you to use them connections again to free my Pat.'

'There are limits, dearie.'

'Don't you call me dearie, you shithouse. What are you going to do, then? Huh? I'm going nowhere until you tell me. I'm listening, your boozy friends are listening.'

'Yes, so we are,' grunts Diarmuid.

Chubb leers back at him in annoyance. 'I'm sorry, but can ye not see that I'm in a wee bit of a pickle myself so?'

'My Pat has put his life on the line for you countless times. The least you can do is help him.'

'Well, it's the truth so. What do you want? Cash? I can sort ye out.'

'And even if I did believe you, which I don't, I'd rather have a living, breathing husband than a dead one, granted that he's a fucking numbskull who keeps the wrong company.'

'Well, I...'

'So what are you going to do about it, Mr Chubb? Last chance, before I go tell all and sundry about where you are hiding and what you did. We're waiting.'

Diarmuid and his entourage are enjoying this evening's entertainment. 'Yeh, we all waiting, Roy, Bundle of Joy. Why don't you tell us what ye going to dee?'

'Will ye keep your big, red conk out of it, Diarmuid Carroll. Fuckin' hell.'

'Well?' says Sarah. She holds up the baby for Chubb to see. He scratches his pate.

'Ah right. Right so.'

He's out, again. Harriet is exactly where she is expected to be this evening for a lady with child, which given her recent misadventures shouldn't be a bad thing, but word has been sent to Butler and both of them are crawling the walls waiting for new instructions. Even via the fastest transit, it might be weeks before she hears anything. Rumour has it that the Rebs are assembling for an incursion into Virginia, buoyed by recent advances and by a surge of successes at sea. The blockade is starting to buckle, as is their campaign all these leagues away from the main Theatre of War. Soon there will be no home to return to.

She sits in her parlour and reads her French novel. Conté would be welcome to join her, but chooses to have supper in the servants' quarters this evening in spite of the reality that Banastre will not return home until after midnight, if at all. Harriet could not feel more isolated and bruised, less so due to the absentee husband, more so about the absentee friend. She remains unforgiven for that swim and rather suspects that said friend will spin this out until they get their next orders from Butler's office.

'Bah. Ugh.'

Harriet primes her pipe and lights it. What else is there to do then but ruminate and fret?

Without invitation, the parlour door opens and in strides Conté with a sense of renewed purpose. 'We had better make this quick, Harry.'

Harriet raises an eyebrow, surprised at the incursion and at her tone. Almost upbeat. 'Make what quick?'

'Come with me.'

Down into the bowels of 101 Canning Street and up through into the yard. There wait Mr Chubb and Mrs McCartney, replete with six offspring and a headful of problems.

'So then,' says Chubb. 'We've got a wee favour to ask.'

Harriet glances at Conté, whose eyes sparkle. She's not looked this cheerful in weeks. 'Elaborate, please, Mr Chubb.'

#11 LEATHER LANE

June 7th, 1863

This is starting to become a regular part of an evening's entertainment.

The latest ruffian that made to waylay him lies a-twitchin' and a-groanin' with a slug to the belly, and Banastre debates with himself whether it is more humane to finish him off or more prudent to let the doctors try to help, prior to his performing an interrogation when, or if, the scoundrel is deemed fit to talk.

After several pints of hard, plain Irish stout chased down by three or more gills of thick, molasses rum, it is tempting to discharge and leave the mess for the Peelers, but no. This is the third attempt on his life in a few days, the second shot from a second rat, with a third still at large and who knows how many out there waiting to take their turn. Something whiffy is afoot, so he cajoles his addled senses enough to preserve this fellow for investigation. Lying there in agony at the slug he just took, the boy doesn't know how lucky he is.

Banastre pulls a whistle from his watch pocket and emits three short blasts that echo out into the pea soup of the main thoroughfare leading to the Town Hall and Cotton Exchange, where Dale Street becomes Water Street, the very cradle of this city. Peelers will attend presently, at least the ones in Ginger's ass pocket.

Good work has been done in this short time, so dammit if some common cur is going to try to assassinate him and then not spill the beans on the whos and the whys. Laws, this time; the attacker will not die or vanish like some cheap Vaudeville act. He will give answers.

And where in hell did Ginger get to? Fat pussy.

Banastre spits and curses, his jet black eyebrows twitchin', his wardrobe chin grindin'.

'Damn it, rapscallion. Some fool you are, boy. Who ordered this? I killed the last man who made like you, you know. Shot him in the face. He tried to get me after a drink too, thinking me slow and easy, hic, so unless you want to end up like him, you'll spill your beans good, son.'

'Ugh,' grunts the distressed wrong' un, writhing about the york stone slabs in a pool of his own crimson goo. Two sturdy Peelers, head to toe in black and spotting natty new frock coats and stove pipe hats funded by his own donations to The Liverpool Constabulary, appear at the end of the alley, truncheons at the ready.

'Constables.'

They squint and recognise him on cue. That accent, that egg-laying stance, that musky cologne. All of them know about the American. A big unit of a Peeler speaks up first.

'Commander, sir. It was difficult to see if it was you. Foggy night, sir.'

'What's your name?'

'O'Driscoll.'

Another Irish. Bah. 'O'Driscoll. Recognise this maggot, then?'

'Yessir.'

'Well?'

'It's Terry Lennon, sir. Erstwhile thief operating in the docks and bonded warehouses.'

More groans. A small gang of Peelers has now arrived. Another one of them boots him in the same spot that took the slug. O'Driscoll glares at him.

'O'Driscoll, get this heap of horseshit to a physician. I want him saved, cleaned up and delivered to me.'

'That's very charitable of you, sir. I'd let him die on the pavement.'

'No, you miss the point. Just send a fast runner to the Royal Infirmary and tell them that the Mayor will stand the bill with no expense spared. See if they can save his bacon. If so, I have questions for him.'

Hats are doffed. Now they get it, slow on the uptake.

Banastre primes his pipe with some aromatic Virginia bush and lights up. They manhandle the inept assassin up by his knees and armpits, and he screams in agony.

'Quiet, manjack. I'm trying to think.'

'Thank you, sir,' says O'Driscoll as they brush past and onto Dale Street.

'And if he bleeds on them new uniforms, be sure to send them directly to my staff for laundry. 101 Canning Street. You know my lodgings.'

'Yes, sir. We do. Thank you kindly, sir.'

'This is getting irksome. I am irked, hic. Huh.'

Lennon, the ruffian rat, has passed out. Best thing for him, aside from a bullet in the head, but not before time. The Peelers flag down a hansom cab and requisition it for their mission.

Midnight. Nah, must get home to Harriet. She frets so when he is on evening business and even more so when he is drunk, especially after the other recent episodes. 'Damn Frenchie. Ain't no good wife to me. Always bellyaching.'

Banastre about faces and strolls back into the pub, somewhere he knows that he is always welcome. All this bothersome palaver has given him a second wind. Screw her.

Harriet waves a palm back and forth over the gas lamp as she sits propped up in bed, enjoying the heat that threatens to scorch her hand, waiting for the husband's return, baby kicking, bitter acid bile rising up in her pipes. Who is he with tonight? Nancy? Oh no, Nancy's dead. Annie then? A boy? He's partial, as is his friend, the Mayor.

She has a first edition of the latest Victor Hugo next to her for company, inciting her to revolt from beneath her warm and comfortable quilt.

She permits herself a deep breath and looks out to the purple skies and ethereal fog beyond the open sash windows, an opaque veil draping over the ornate rooftop silhouettes of a city always up to mischief. Regardless of the weather, she insists on fresh air in the chamber. Cawing seagulls echo incessantly, day and night, and she pines for pelicans and flamingos, majestic wading birds. All there seems to be in Liverpool are these greedy, common gannets.

Harriet returns to Hugo, who can offer another world, neither here nor there, which is just about right tonight.

Creaking on the stairs and then on the landing. Familiar, shuffling, pompous, drunk footsteps of a poltroon. She can hear his voice grunting at her from outside the door.

'Guess what, sweetnessh? You shall never guess what, hic. More killers! I tell ya! Well, they don't fuckin' kill Commander Banesh, Baneshtre Shavier Dunwoody. No, they do not. Hic.'

Conté's voice, brave to confront him in this state, although Harriet so wishes that she hadn't. 'Sir, you will wake up the entire street; I entreat you.'

Low, drunken belching like a toad. That morose chuckle. Harriet debates with herself on whether or not to climb out of bed and head him off at the pass, in case he fancies taking a slice off Conté in one form or another. Mercifully, she can hear him shuffling towards the door, clearly too spent for any more shenanigans. She places Hugo on her bedside table and dims her lamp, settling into the pillow as if fast asleep as Banastre barrels through into the chamber, pulling off his braces and farting like a Gatling gun, a dashing Duke just full of Southern charm.

'There she is. There's my Frenchie Duchess. Is it too late for a kiss, Ma Petite Chou-teau? You'll never guesh. Shomeone tried to murder your beloved again tonight, and I am shorely in need of the tender lovin' and mercies of a good wife.'

Deep breaths, Harriet.

#12 THE CLINK

June 8th, 1863

A crackling coal fire provides light and heat every night that Payton Ake is on duty here. He likes to be comfortable when writing, reading and keeping his ledgers. He perches behind his oak desk, his central domain and haven rolled into one. Behind him is a dank, narrow passageway leading to a row of cells. The warmth of the fire doesn't extend down there.

There is an assault of malodours on this place coming in from the docks and alleys nightly, and his ritual battle against them is sanitation. The trusty mop and bucket stands by, with a solution of sandalwood and ether used to rid the pest smells of effluence, booze, tobacco and masturbation. He prides himself on a clean shop, to the extent that he has considered taking a patent out on his sanitary concoction. Perhaps Captain Frank would support him in that venture? He would know investors. Another pipe dream.

Mr Ake scribbles into a thick ledger with a fountain pen. *Monday June 8th 1863. Prisoner #00622781 Terrance John Lennon of no fixed abode, attempted murder of an American gentleman. Held over in cell G at Campbell Square Bridewell by order of Constable P.D. Ake and Chief Officer of the Liverpool Constabulary Captain John Frank.*

Happy with his work, Ake closes the ledger and places it in a cabinet, locking the door.

He returns to his half-eaten apple and his reading. The book is Dickens' *Hard Times*. He shakes his head.

'Doesn't happen like that.'

He pulls out a notebook and scribbles in it with a pencil. Another attempt at *The African Leviathan* has been crossed out and replaced by: *The Great Journey, from Africa via The Americas to Liverpool by P.C. Ake.*

He pauses and scrubs out 'Ake', replacing it with 'Smith'.

'Smith. Maybe. Jones?'

Ake nods and returns to Dickens.

A clacking of hooves on the cobbles outside interrupts him again. Ake chomps the last of his apple and puts his book down. The boy's back at last.

Keys rattling in the mortise lock of the oak door. It opens and Starkey bounces in, drenched like a wet hound. Ake watches him.

'Well?'

'Awful pissy out there, so it is.'

'Well?'

Starkey shoves his hand in his pockets, straightening up like he owns the place. 'Well. The Captain was a wee bit fazed by your note. He made me attend while he summoned his staff to pass messages across town. They didn't even offer me a glass of milk or a biscuit or nothing while I sat on the back step in the rain. Miserable, so it was.'

Ake snaps his fingers and Starkey fishes in his satchel, pulling out a sealed letter. Ake takes it but doesn't open it.

'Small wonder that you're curious about the nature of this note, Mister Starkey? Especially after your salubrious adventures over the water. Fame and fortune has smiled upon you since you stepped off that Irish barco, eh?'

Starkey doesn't know where Mr Ake is going with this. He shuffles on his feet. 'I am of equal rank to you, so yes.'

Fresh off a boat, into the Constabulary, and he has the same status as a man who has been serving the city hard these last two decades. Such is life for an African Leviathan that he has to listen to such needless reminders from imbeciles like Starkey.

'Attend your pony.'

'But it's tipping it down out there. Can't I warm myself on the fire first?'

'If I see any dung in the yard by the time of the dawn watch, you'll be for it. Out.'

Starkey sulks, re-buttons his coat and slips out of the front door. Ake gets up, deadbolts the door and cracks the wax seal on the letter.

Make it look like he went in his sleep. Burn after reading. JF.

Ake traces a finger around the handwriting, nods and tosses the letter into the fire, making sure that it is completely engulfed and destroyed. Then he takes his bunch of keys and heads down the passage towards the cells.

Behind the cell door, Lennon is lying in a ball on the floor. Empty bottles of surgical spirit surround him. O'Driscoll brought him directly here, even though the American gave the order to take him to the Infirmary. O'Driscoll takes orders expressly from Captain Frank, not the Mayor or some American with a vested interest. He is one of the dwindling number of good officers in these bad times.

Ake leans down to Lennon. The prisoner moans in delirium. He places his massive hand over Lennon's mouth and nose. In seconds, the prisoner starts to convulse, froth seeping out from beneath Ake's iron grip.

Hardly fair, is it? After all, Ake knows who paid Lennon to do the job, but that knowledge could get him replaced, turfed-out of his home or killed. Much as Captain Frank is fond of him, he has a ruthless streak that is beyond prediction or calculation, so discretion is the better part of valour. Follow orders, keep one's mouth shut, mind one's own business, be reliable. Keep it simple.

More convulsing from Lennon. Then it stops. He stops.

Ake returns his body to the same foetal position that he discovered him in. He makes the sign of the cross and mutters his standard. 'May perpetual light shine upon him.'

He walks out of the cell, shuts and locks the door and then returns to his desk. He takes the ledger and blots out the entry on Lennon. Then he picks up a mop and bucket and whistles an old ditty as he cleans the floor with a sandalwood solution, proud of how spotless he keeps this tidy shop. Writing can wait tonight.

A lemon and orange sunrise comes up behind him as he strolls along the squalid, dank row of court houses; black-bricked hovels, dens of disease that he yearns to take his children away from. Even the sky always seems bruised and sad over this end of town, just past the central docks towards the south of the city. Abject poverty is everywhere. An old woman, or perhaps a young woman who looks old, squats in the gutter, adding to the human slurry. He might be off-duty now, but he could take issue with that on the grounds of public indecency.

He ignores her and pulls out the key to the heavy, fortified door, which is the only barrier keeping his family safe while he's out at work. There's just no decency around here, especially when it applies to the young, old or vulnerable. Some locals may know not to tangle with the giant Peeler who lives at the end of the street, but there are too many who would never have got that message.

Five children sleep in the same bed as Mr Ake enters and pulls off his coat. He locks and deadbolts the door behind him. Dry rot permeates every wall, even though he douses the place from top to bottom every spare moment with his solution. He must remember to move the bed away from it.

Payton Ake knows that the gifts that keep a roof over his children's heads and a meagre existence in this cruel town aren't about his reading and writing, rather something altogether not for these sweet cherub dreams. His babies have seen enough, with their Irish mother in heaven after the consumption got her. He wishes that Captain Frank would raise his wage high enough for them to escape Starling Street and the court houses. He wishes for so much more again from that man.

Mr Ake strokes the red hair of the eldest one, his daughter. He knows about the Irish in this city. Better than most of the Irish themselves.

'Good morning, darling. Thank you for looking after them.'

#13 ST GEORGE'S HALL

June 10th, 1863

The reverberating tones of a piano recital can be heard through the walls at the trial of Patrick Eamonn McCartney of Scotland Road, on the charges of Conspiracy to Commit Mass Murder and Aiding and Abetting an Act of Seditious Criminal Damage.

Some are saying that it was a botched Fenian conspiracy to strike a blow for Ireland, others that it has something to do with the protection rackets run by Chubb's mob over that side of the water. The truth of it may or may not be revealed to the court, but altogether these charges can and should equal his person doing the hempen jig sometime soon. McCartney must know, along with the watching gallery, one that includes the board members of Cammell Laird, that the real business of this trial will take place in the bowels of this great hall, where entertainment, dance and musical performance sit directly next to correction and justice as if they are the best of siblings.

Judge Morris, a crusty, semi-decrepit, bewigged practitioner shipped in from Manchester – who couldn't be a better pick for the prosecution in terms of his impressively merciless record of black caps and death warrants – shuffles and scribbles on his papers before waggling a finger in the direction of the dock. He's not one to mince words.

'Take him down while I consider.'

The Attendant barks. 'All rise!'

Banastre studies his diminutive mark. Christ, he's no bigger than a whippet.

Padraig (not Patrick) McCartney leers up at the gallery to see The American chuffing away at his pipe, infamous by reputation, worse again in the flesh. Sarah, a sweet young mother doing all she can to keep her children quiet in all this officialdom, watches her husband as he is accompanied below, a heavy cross to bear on her stooped back. Banastre enjoys the show and misses nothing. Ginger, still suffering from his exploits over the past few days, snores next to him. Banastre digs him in the ribs with his elbow.

'Wh…'

'How long do I have, Ginger?'

'Wh…'

'Hold my coat. I'm going below.'

'You can't do that, old boy. Leave it in the hands of…'

'Enough is enough. Everyone's dying, no one's talking. If this one's gonna die soon, I want answers first.'

'Well then, but I still don't think…'

Banastre pats Ginger's shoulders. 'Don't you worry, old chap. I've made some arrangements for myself this time. Better that way, I think, don't you?'

'But…'

And he's away. Ginger, flustered, lights his pipe.

Under the duress of a couple of burly Peelers, Pat is rolled down the narrow, precipitous set of steps, towards the cells, and away from the relative opulence of the courtroom to a rat-infested netherworld.

He can just about make out the tones from the concert hall next door, Chopin's Nocturnes. In clement weather, he often comes to St George's Hall of a Saturday evening with Sarah and the children and they stand outside the vent to the Music Chamber, listening to the strings and horns lilting up through the grid, dressed in their Sunday finest. Sarah humours him and helps him to make an occasion of it, baking scones if there's money for flour and sugar. Has all that vanished now? The journey back to the gutter is fast and permanent. For them. All he can see are gallows.

The door to the dock above slams and bolts behind him and they guide him down the tunnel and into his accommodation, which is tiny in length and depth but high in ceiling. Not a cell, rather a dungeon. More slamming and locking.

Two huge men wait in the cell for him, patently not court attendants or Peelers. Pat doesn't recognise them, which means that they've been brought in from out of town. More *special* treatment.

One of them holds up a set of thumb screws.

'Not fuckin' guilty.'

Banastre rolls his sleeves up again. Pat's blood flecks the white cotton of The American's shirt. Truth is, the Commander has missed this type of work. 'You're always guilty, paddywhack.'

'This is an illegal interrogation. I demand my rights.'

Pat hangs by his thumbs. One thing about the Irish that Banastre knows is their ability to take punishment, even a half-pint slither of piss like McCartney here. Since it is his first opportunity to directly question anyone in connection with the attempts on him or the Banshee plot, he aims to make this count. Hopefully, the man won't die before he gets the information he wants.

Banastre speaks into Pat's ear, like he's sharing a hot tip on a horse. 'This ain't the first slammer I've visited. As a prisoner or as a patron. Guess you can gather that.'

More struggling and wincing. 'Me neither.'

'Oh good. Then you'll know this routine like the back of your hand. Where's Royston Chubb?'

'This is illegal. I'm on trial and you are interfering with a witness.' Banastre turns his thick signet rings around, balling his hand into a fist.

'Who fed you that line, you inbred sister fucker? Chubb himself? You're dead meat.'

'Ha.'

Pat spits at Banastre, who piledrives a fist into his ribs. He starts using Pat as a punch bag.

Then, he pulls his Smith & Wesson and holds it to Pat's temple. Click, an empty chamber.

'Must remember to put bullets in this thing. How remiss of me.'

The oak door to the cell swings open. A big Peeler enters. Pat looks up and squints as blood oozes into his vision, just about recognising him as one of the few good ones, O'Driscoll.

'Excuse me, sir.'

Banastre frowns and spins on his heels. 'What?'

'The prisoner is recalled for his verdict.'

O'Driscoll nods to Banastre's shooting hand.

'I ain't finished with him. On orders of the Mayor's office.' O'Driscoll releases Pat and catches him before he collapses to the floor. 'Hey. Don't I know you? Sure I do. You're the ass who disobeyed a direct order the other night. Hey, I want to talk to you, ass.'

'Sorry, Commander. I don't take orders from anyone but my superiors in the constabulary.'

'And I know just who that is, too.'

Banastre's hand tightens over his gun, but he thinks twice. O'Driscoll slings the passed-out McCartney over his shoulder and continues in the direction of the stairwell, up back towards the dock.

'Guess I'll have to do something about that jurisdiction issue, then.'

Banastre holsters his gun and primes his pipe. He got his answers alright, maybe not from the source he first thought, but far more revealing.

'All rise!'

Morris, permanent scowl across his brow, lamb chop sideburns twitching, sits himself down. If the watching gallery were judging which way he is about to go by the expression on his face, pity poor Padraig.

Then the ruddy QC for the prosecution gazes up to Ginger in the stalls, shaking his head.

'Oh no, laws no. Surely not,' grunts Ginger. Banastre rubs his paws with a handkerchief as he takes his place next to him.

In the dock, Pat wobbles on his feet, like a drunk. Morris twitches again and nods as the courtroom settles into a hush. 'I conclude that this is a spurious waste of this court's time and resources, hence a desultory squandering of the faithful British taxpayer's money.'

In the delightful Manchester outlier of Cheetham Hill sits a splendid small mansion with considerable lands, rather too grand for the incumbents Gabriel Arthur Morris and his wife Agatha. A childless couple, all they ever want for in life is far behind them, yet even to an old soak like Morris, the adage that money talks still holds firm.

Morris eats his dinner. The doorbell rings and Agatha gets up to leave the room as he continues to enjoy his lamb.

'The defendant shall be released immediately and without prejudice. That is the order of this court. Dismissed.'

Agatha returns with a leather pouch. Morris puts his knife and fork down and reaches inside it, grasping a fistful of gold coins. Perhaps the money isn't the prime mover, as much as it sweetens the deal. They hate the Confederacy in Manchester almost as much as they love it in Liverpool, and that even extends to the more conservative areas. Morris nods in satisfaction and returns to his food.

Outside, in the immaculate, deserted road, Conté canters away from Morris' leafy idyll, job done. She pulls Rosalinda into a hard gallop; forty miles of riding ahead of her.

Cheers and whoops from the throng. Pat is too tired and beaten to celebrate. He winces as he is carried away on the shoulders of his supporters, a merry band of his boozing buddies from The Crown.

'I should consider myself disappointed, Mayor.'

Ginger shakes his head as his companion breathes through his teeth. 'The Chief Constable is a law unto himself, Banastre. As is the judiciary. I'm not sure, old boy. It's an aberration certainly.'

'Well, not sure ain't good enough. Aber-something my ass ain't good enough.'

Banastre gets to his feet. 'I know sabotage when I see it. I want this rat found and skewered.'

'Chubb? Our best men are looking for him. I can assure you that it won't come to court when we find him.'

'No. Not Chubb. Whoever is paying him. You useless goddamn pigfucker.'

Ginger looks puce. Banastre is publicly berating him. 'Steady, old boy. There's a line, you know. That is not gentlemanly behav-'

'-Do you want this deal or not?'

The Mayor's face has turned to jelly. 'Indubitably, sir.'

'Then I'm taking over this town, and I'm finding that Union Spy. Myself. Too goddamn much is riding on it.'

Banastre spits on the teak furnishings and stomps off, leaving Ginger ashen in the empty courtroom.

Pat is lifted into a waiting carriage by O'Driscoll. It barrels off across the cobbles and away from the spectacular edifice of St George's Hall.

Inside, Conté and Chubb sit opposite him. He passes out again.

'Lord bless us. Poor lad, so,' whispers Chubb.

Harriet studies Pat. 'Does he need to see a physician?'

'Can you see now, Mr Chubb? Just who we are dealing with?' says Conté.

'Yes, yes. I see. No one likes a smart arse, do they? What with youse two and his wife, mithering me so.' He leans over to Pat as he slumps on the seat. 'Ye alright, sunshine, eh? Aw, poor lad.' Chubb grabs Pat's hand, and he screams in agony.

'Aargh, me fucking thumb, you clumsy fat fucking gobshite!'

Pat curls up into a ball, protecting his hands, whimpering.

'Alright, son. Alright. There, there. I'm sorry, like. I am clumsy aren't I, ha.'

Conté remains about business. 'You're going to have to find somewhere better to stash yourself than that cellar, Mr Chubb.'

Chubb leans back, taking even more of the seat up, crushing Pat. 'Aye, so. I suppose.'

'You have a good spot?'

'So good that you don't need to know about it, petal.'

'Don't call me petal.'

Harriet's eyes dart between them. There might still be verbal jousting, but the edge has gone. It should be a comfort to know that she and Conté can trust Mr Chubb and his stricken little friend here, that their confidence was not betrayed in spite of the most testing of examinations, but that was far too close for comfort, and Crispin Starkey is still out there swinging his beat. That kid is holding his water, but for how long? Still no word either from Major General Butler, a man who makes Mr Chubb here look like a dainty Russian ballerina.

'We're deeply sorry too, Padraig,' she says, and he barely registers, swimming in and out of wakefulness. 'The United States Government promises that it will make this up to you and your family.'

'Me arse,' he groans, before passing out cold again.

#14 DINNER FOR THREE

June 14ᵗʰ, 1863

Foie gras with gravadlax on wafers as a starter; grazing rather than eating. They dine together tonight in formal dress in the parlour, enjoying the lemony late-afternoon sun as it streams through the huge bay window overlooking the descent into the city. The vista rolls across the imposing and magnificent Gambier Terrace and the grand necropolis of St James' Cemetery. Down, down, down Duke Street to the dome of the neo-classical Customs House, rising out of the sooty fog that consumes the dock estate like a supine breast, majesty and crime bedfellows everywhere the eye travels.

Just the two of them with an unborn offspring, so it might seem odd that they would dress for dinner, but the neighbours can see them clearly, and it is as much about keeping up appearances to them as it is an exercise in rigid formality. Since they arrived here, the Dunwoodys are all about making good impressions, showing themselves as more English than the English. Banastre tasked Harriet with this as her main detail in running an impeccable house, alongside the gestation of his son and heir, of course.

Dear Husband is exceptionally chipper this evening, which makes a change from the sullen, surly and acidic demeanour that has been his standard for several weeks now. What would the dutiful wife put it down to? Business going well? Social success? Good news from Richmond?

Harriet needs to be able to think on these terms in order to tune her performance just right, although the real woman reads the change in mood as a smugness associated with his campaign, which has yet to receive a setback of any substance. The cumbersome rock of pressure upon Harriet and Conté weighs in heavier daily upon their backs. Banastre is never forthcoming about his plans, and she has to adapt to his movements, which suits none of the versions of her; the loyal wife and mistress of his house or the interloper who is trying to unravel his every action.

'Good fish,' he says, slurping up the smoked salmon. There he is, a hint of the boy from Tennessee roaming the woodlands for some trapping and poaching.

Harriet goes back further with his kind than he should ever discover, God willing. She hides the Choctaw in her rather better than he does his feral, bushwhacker side, although that is out of necessity rather than choice. These two have been at war against each other far longer than the Union and the Confederacy.

'Yes, darling. Beautiful fish.' Harriet cuts her food and eats it with delicate precision, rather more like a surgeon than a diner, as prescribed by the courses in etiquette forced upon her by Butler prior to the commencement of this operation. Painful as the training was for a woman of her history, it is all she ever seems to do in Banastre's presence. Even their bedroom antics were choreographed in advance by Butler's experts, with her movements performed like a naked waltz while Banastre was all drunken cock and collapse. It should make her sick to her stomach, but that is just another path to defeat. Conté will never know what she put herself through to gain his trust, not ever. Let her think that she enjoyed it, unpalatable as that is. Her friend would kill him in his sleep if she knew the details.

He gulps down French wine and slaps the heartburn out of his chest, belching.

'Well, excuse me, my good lady.' Manners, an apology indeed! What has gotten into him this evening?

'That's quite alright, my good sir.'

'My good sir. I like that. You are indeed my good lady. I'll drink to that.'

He'll drink to anything. Harriet sees an opportunity to open up a conversation with him. It is moments like this – when the usually cavernous silence is broken – that must be handled with care.

Conté watches on in stiff deportment, waiting on them this evening. Banastre doesn't even register her. Harriet reaches over for his hand, gazing out wistfully.

'Another beautiful day.'

Banastre looks slightly amused at her sudden show of affection. 'I cannot submit how you describe anything about this city as beautiful. Apart from its money, sweetness.'

'It is growing on me. Really, it is.' Harriet is aware that she isn't lying on this occasion, either. Perhaps it is the iota of hope supplied from the likes of Chubb and Padraig; perhaps she is just numbed to it. 'But how long will we have to remain here, darling?'

Banastre shrugs and sups. 'As long as is necessary, I guess. Until the job is done.'

'So it is not done?'

Banastre spears some more fish and smiles like a shark. 'No, dearest.'

Vague! Come on, give her something. She exchanges a rapid glance with Conté. Be careful.

'I would like to see our son grow up in the South. Virginia or Tennessee.'

'Fine places,' he grunts, through a face-full of fish and duck liver. He chews with his mouth open.

'What would you like, Banastre? You never tell me. That would mean more to me than the world.'

Banastre finishes the bottle and taps on it. Conté nods and goes to fetch an encore.

'Another bottle of that rich French plonk would go just dandy.'

'No, sir. Seriously.'

He retains his good humour. She knows that it takes very little to see him retract, even on the brightest of days. All those poor men on Fort Sumter must have felt his wrath on so many occasions, worked like galley slaves to the edge of death, massacred and dropped into a lime pit. It is fully documented in the records that Butler made them study and learn. But still, she can't quite get into his soul, for all the intelligence. Perhaps that is because he does not possess one of those.

'Seriously? We are far too serious, sweetness. Seriousness is all I ever see. What about some fun?'

Good humour or not, she isn't getting an answer out of him with that line. She decides upon a stronger gambit. They are alone in the room for a moment, so it might work. She takes his hand again, steeling up some tears from deep within. The image to summon is always the same; Daddy Farrell lying on his back in that wagon, bleeding out, pants pissed as he loses his fight.

101

And always the same outside; Banastre is the bushwhacker with the smoking gun, grinning and chuckling as if he's bagged a turkey. Even though he was nowhere near Louisiana back in 1850, the awful image sticks in these moments. Her eyes sting because it is ultimately why she is here.

'I cannot sleep darling. Thinking about these people who are shooting at you, wishing you harm. I cannot countenance a world without you, Banastre sir.'

The melodrama wins him over every time. She feels more comfortable delivering it without Conté in the room.

'Aw, don't you fret your pretty little face. It will bother the child in your belly too. This is meant to be a happy evening.'

'I know. I am sorry.'

'You have nothing to apologise for, Belle. You hurt, so I hurt, petite sweetness. I am the fiend here, going this way and that every night, even if it is in service of our noble cause to be a Sovereign state, and I … I know it makes life difficult for you. Do not think I miss these things.'

Most nights, he is balls-deep in whores or consorting with devils, so he misses these things easily.

'Yes, dearest. But must you keep going away? Where is your next trip? When?'

Banastre rubs her hand and looks into her soul. Rare that he does this, but it unnerves her, as it would unnerve any poor being that he has tortured. She digs deep for the strength to lie, to appeal to his knurled sense of propriety on some level. His hard eyes soften, and she feels a deep shift is happening, like he is about to spill it all. An expression of exhilaration washes over his face like nothing she has ever seen in the man.

'You really will just burst when I tell you this, belle. For God and Country.'

'Tell me what, darling? Do not tease me.'

'Well, tomorrow morning Ginger and I will be going …'

She sees the bullet grazing across his forehead before hearing the shot. It thuds into the portrait of Pélagie behind them, commissioned as part of Butler's meticulous preparations. The fake heirloom is ruined by a hole in the canvas right between her eyes.

Banastre frowns and dabs his head, seeing blood. The bullet shaved his temple. 'Ooh. Down, Harriet. Now.'

They drop to the floor as another volley shatters the glass of the giant bay, sprinkling the table like shards of ice.

'Oh my.' Harriet continues the act seamlessly as she joins him under the table. The first bullet that hit Pélagie's portrait came from a lower trajectory at an angle of around 35°. The second volley came from two other snipers in different positions. It looks like they are going for broke this time, whoever they are, and whether or not she gets caught in the crossfire is immaterial. Perhaps Banastre has worked this out for himself, but the Smith & Wesson in his hand indicates that he plans to shoot his way out of trouble, as he always does.

Harriet feigns panic as another set of volleys arrive from all three positions. They'll aim to shoot through the window until they can hit something; she's seen too many sieges to consider anything else.

The door to the parlour creaks open and Conté peers in.

'You,' grunts Banastre, 'Wait for the next shot and I'll cover you. Then take my lady down to the cellar and lock up behind you. Do you get me?' Conté frowns at Harriet, who nods back. 'Hey, goddamn stupid! You hear me?'

'Yes.'

'Yes what?'

'Yes sir.'

Bang. Bang bang. Tinkle, crash, thunk.

'Go with her, sweetness. I gotcha covered.' Banastre clutches her hand, and for a moment she feels some tenderness, maybe even some humanity, flowing from him. 'I'll be damned if my son is not getting born because some hired lowlife gets his ma. This is crossing a goddamn line, I say. Attacking me in my own home. Threatening my son and heir. Go, now.'

And there it is, stone cold, all he cares about. Harriet crawls towards Conté as Banastre points his pistol out of the shattered window, aiming at some chimney pots to repel fire.

'Come on you frickin' rats, show yourselves,' he grunts as she scampers out. She feels a bullet waft past her backside just before getting through the door, thankful that it missed, as she knows there are few things that can slow you down as much as a slug in the ass. She has scars to prove that.

In the corridor and then out into the foyer. Servants look panicked, not knowing what to do as bullets ping around inside the room. They're not used to coming under fire like this in little old England, but for Harriet and Conté, it's just another skirmish in the bush. They know just what to do.

Through a plain door and downstairs into the servants' quarters, then below again into the cellars, locking the door behind them as per Banastre's instructions. Not as per his instructions, Conté pulls a tarpaulin off a large tea chest brought all the way across from Louisiana and kicks off the lid. They each grab a Sharps rifle and a fistful of ammunition. Harriet takes her small Colt revolver, Banastre's engagement gift, and tucks it into her breeches, warmed by her baby bump. Thank the stars that he never ventures down below.

'Tell me that you've kept these oiled and checked,' grunts Harriet as they load 'em up.

'Always,' says Conté, affronted at any suggestion otherwise.

Conté shoves the lid and tarp back over the chest and they head for another door that leads up into the small stable at the rear of 101 Canning. In the open air, the gunshots get louder, but to Harriet's trained ear they are coming from the same direction, which indicates that the assassins haven't moved. Prone shooters are more vulnerable to counterattacks. That's a mercy. Likelihood is, they are not military-trained.

Harriet goes to move, but Conté grabs her arm. 'What if he sees us?'

'What if they kill him?'

'Is that a bad thing?'

'It is when the Rebs send over another version of him to finish his job and we're cut loose, so yes I'll say.'

Conté spits and sucks her teeth. 'I know that something stinks like manure in all of this deal. My instinct is never wrong too. I've been Choctaw longer than you.'

Harriet cocks her Sharps. 'That's as maybe, but we're sitting ducks here.'

Conté shakes her head. 'Don't be so drastic, Harriet Farrell.' Then she curses to the heavens. 'Damn you, Butler. I know you're behind this sabotage. We're being set up to fail, I swear it. I know it!'

She only calls Harriet by her full, original name when she is either mighty scared or mighty angry. This time it could be both. Harriet can only vote with her feet, knowing that Conté will follow her to the ends of the Earth, no matter how severe her reservations. She moves out into the yard, to the side of the mansion, which is where the gunfire is drawn, careful to remain out of sight but able to see the rooftop positions.

'Un, deux, trois,' Harriet whispers. Conté sees them too. One o'clock, six o'clock, ten o'clock, straight from the manual. If they can see it, so can Banastre, although how far is he going to get with four rounds left in his chamber?

'Miss Conté? Mrs Dunwoody? Just retrieving my mare from you, if you please.'

'Get down!'

Young Grace stands behind them with Rosalinda. She obeys and pulls the horse behind the wall. Rosalinda bristles at being jolted, but another volley of shots doesn't bother her too much. Grace ties her up to an iron railing.

Harriet watches the figures load and report, looking for a way to pincer them. One shot from here would leave them wide open, as it isn't a good position. They need to find a way in behind them.

Bang. That was Banastre's pistol. One of the figures groans and slumps. Harriet feels competitive but resists the urge. They need questions answering, not just corpses. The problem is, so does Banastre.

Grace can see exactly what she has walked into, no stranger to a skirmish herself. 'I am sorry. I always collect and refresh our horses at this time.'

Conté grips her rifle hard, looking for a shot. Grace glances back and forth between them, never having seen the like.

'Good timing as it happens, Grace,' says Harriet.

'How so, ma'am?'

'The only way out there is down the path to the front gate and then via the cobbles on Canning Street. You know how to use one of these?'

Harriet holds the Sharps under Grace's nose. She nods. 'Yes.'

Conté strokes Grace's cheek, hoping she stays lucky. 'Best news all day. Take it.'

Harriet's eyes are glued to that roof. 'My husband is trying to pick them off, but I'll bet he'll run out of ammo before that happens, dead-eye or not. That's the percentage, anyway. So you two will hit them with covering fire and I'll take this wonderful nag and bolt hell for leather.'

Grace's face drops. 'What? No ma'am. I cannot allow that.'

Harriet grips her hand, trust pouring from her eyes into the girl. 'Listen to me. Rosalinda will not be harmed.'

'They'll shoot at anything that moves,' protests Grace.

'I know, but we'll be too fast for them.'

Conté checks her gun and then looks over to Grace, gentle in her way. 'Trust us, Your Highness.'

Grace thinks about it and takes the rifle, trying to figure these two odd women out. 'I know what you two are. I think.'

Harriet folds an eyebrow, as does Conté. 'Do you? Well, we will talk about that later.'

'Sure,' grunts Conté. Harriet unties Rosalinda and gently guides her towards the picket door, still just about out of sight of the gunmen. Bang, another Banastre shot and a miss. Two rounds left and then it's a turkey shoot.

'Cover me on my signal.' She climbs up and mounts Rosalinda. 'Can't believe I'm doing this to save that coyote's ass of a man.'

'Neither can I,' grunts Conté.

'Un … deux … trois … allez!'

Conté boots the door open and Harriet digs her heels into Rosalinda. The bogies notice immediately and try to potshot her, but the fire from Conté and Grace is brisk and accurate, forcing them to hunker down for long enough for Harriet to approach the 7ft stone wall and iron gate at a gallop, dropping her knees and squeezing Rosalinda to jump.

'Good girl.' They clear the wall and make it onto Canning Street, hidden again from the shooters. More gunfire and another shot from Banastre. There's no way of telling whether or not he hit his target from here. Effective or not, though, that leaves him with only one remaining round.

Harriet canters round to the terrace facing the back of the mansion and ties Rosalinda up in a strong knot to a gas lamp, taking a good look at the layout. It might not be a Louisiana Cypress Tree or a drop into a gorge, but climbing is a far more natural part of her skillset than this façade of being a lady mistress, although never with the extra burden of an unborn child. She has a strong enough inkling, though.

Conté is a very capable shooter, but she probably won't take either man out from that position. Grace is an unknown quantity but likely the same at best. Banastre barely has a pot to piss in. She almost wishes that he could see her right now as she shoehorns herself up a drainpipe, baby kicking and bowels complaining, but then the jig would be up.

'Damn your eyes, hick swine.' She loses her footing and almost falls, arms swinging for something, anything to grip.

A young man's face appears above the angle of the roof, red hair and at first angry at the disturbance, transporting rapidly to utter disbelief at the pistol-toting pregnant woman clinging on for dear life. He comes to his senses and points his rifle at her, happy to get at least one kill in his sights.

'Take your best shot,' snaps Harriet. He frowns at the fearlessness and bravado. Harriet swings herself across with an agility that surprises herself, just about catching the lip of a Juliet balcony. The lad shoots and misses just as she hooks her leg over the lip and pushes through the French doors.

She hasn't been inside this building, but most of the houses on this street are similar in basic interior layout to 101, and she finds her way onto the landing with ease. The place is musty and clearly mothballed. Unoccupied. Climbing up onto the top landing, she can see that the hatch to the attic and roof has been jemmied. Local boys with local knowledge would know who is home or away, it occurs to her.

She climbs the ladder, pistol drawn and cocked ready. More gunfire outside; she listens out for the calibre, two from Conté and Grace and two from the shootists up here. The young man who spotted her is clearly distracted, but he'll be aware that she hasn't vanished into thin air.

There's a door from the loft to the roof left ajar. He'll be expecting her to come through it and he'll be ready with a pot-load of lead. Harriet looks about herself in the dark room, shafts of light speckled with dust strafe out of a small, boarded-up window. One kick ought to do it and she's right as it gives way and she clears a hole, climbing through and out …

Only now, she's stuck. Damned baby! She admonishes herself; curse the man, not the infant. Funny how, in a moment like this, she finds the energy to think about General Butler and whether or not Conté was right.

Harriet offers yet another silent apology to her child and strains with all her being, pushing herself as hard as she can, becoming reborn into the open air herself before finding some purchase on the slate tiles and climbing through, sharp wooden splinters piercing her midriff.

'Ouch.'

Again with all the agility she can muster, she reaches the apex of the roof by crawling up sideways like a salamander, hands and feet doing the work. There's the redheaded shooter and, below, she can make out the girls and Banastre. At last, she has a clear sight, but where's the other gunman gone?

Bearded chappy, standing over her to the other side. Grinning at her like a shitting bear and taking aim.

'Oh. Rats.'

Bang bang. Fast succession. The beard drops from Banastre's last bullet; the redheaded lad gets one in the face from Harriet.

Phew.

She ducks back down. Did Banastre see her? The idiot with the beard gave her husband a clear shot when he stood up to finish her off. She climbs back down and, this time, gives herself some momentum, swinging back through the narrow gap from which she appeared moments ago, crawling back into the womb.

Now, questions might well be asked.

#15 THE AFTERMATH

June 14th 1863

Of course, Mr Ake doesn't fail to notice the long series of loud reports coming from less than half a mile away as he proceeds on foot towards 9 Catharine Street. He might know something of why there is a gun battle going on within close earshot, but the man of the house that he is about to visit has insisted that his skills are not required for this detail. As of yet. And as with anything or anybody, Mr Ake can only show the deepest loyalty to his friend and mentor, Captain John Frank. However, the mystery of an impromptu late-night visit and high jinks – the length and breadth of the city – vexes and perplexes him.

Ake approaches the grand vestibule. The large, brass door knocker would reach chest height for most adults, but he has to stoop down to use it. For all his fearsome repute, Ake often feels awkward in his own frame in a world built for much smaller, whiter people, but this isn't the worst of things.

The door swings open and Frank's butler, Morrison, a suitably stiff and immaculate ex-army type, welcomes him inside without a word, being used to the visits of many other constables, day and night. You come to John Frank, not the other way around. The Chief Constable avoids the use of Watch property as much as possible, preferring to conduct matters from a discreet distance in the comfort and security of his home, a grand place that reminds Ake of some exotic folly in an aristocratic pile. He follows Morrison past the gallery of taxidermy – lions, dogs, prairie wolves and an adult bull hippo – through into the dining room, where children can be heard playing.

And there it is, the whole happy clan. Ten offspring last counted, playing hide and seek beneath a huge table atop which are the scraps of a sumptuous meal. Loud, chatty Siamese cats prowl the surface, scavenging the used dinners and meowing like gossips. Toddlers grab their tails, and Mrs Frank sits contented, knitting and chewing tobacco while her husband props himself at the head of the table, smoking a cheroot with a baby on his knee.

'Ah, Payton Ake.' That soft, Scottish lilt of an accent, that gentle face. No one would guess what he did for a living if they didn't know him. No one would guess many things.

'Sir.'

'Children, it's Uncle Ake.'

'Uncle Icky,' mews one of the littlest, gazing up Ake's leg like it's a Giant Redwood.

'Ak-ay, not Icky, Archibald,' chides Captain Frank, 'Learn to enunciate, son.'

Daddy drives his kids to be bright, as well he did with Payton himself many years ago. Ake waves down to the tiny, moon-faced offspring. 'Hello Archibald.'

Frank hands the baby to Morrison and approaches. He wears an over-decorous waistcoat, replete with a neat, goatee beard, perfectly slicked back hair and immaculate finery, the maharaja of Catharine Street. And Payton Ake loves his very bones.

'Elspeth?'

Mrs Frank, as she will always be known to Ake, claps her hands, synchronising the attention of the children immediately. 'Privy, hands and teeth, you lot.' A chorus of 'aws' follows. 'Come on now. Your father has business.'

Ake looks into Captain Frank's eyes and sees John looking back at him. Yes, business.

'Stay tonight. Please.'

'No. No sir. I cannot. Not with her. Or the children. Under the same roof. It isn't right or proper.'

'What is right or proper about what you do to me, Payton? Or I do to you?'

'My eldest daughter is in charge of the little ones. I need to be there for her.'

'Strange so. What do you do when you have a night shift, then?'

'She has an ague. I need to be there for her, sir. These things can progress to worse illnesses.'

Ake feels clammy under the collar, and it isn't the woollen uniform or the warm evening causing the issue. John sits on his knee at the head of the table. What if someone came in?

'High time you saw things for the way they are, Payton. What is your problem with Elspeth?'

'My problem is that she knows, sir.'

'Stop calling me sir under my roof. That is an order.'

'Right.'

'You are a good man and she knows this. In this house, we make our own rules. You can see that just by looking at the place.'

Ake tries to breathe, to allow himself to appreciate all the eccentricities of this man, his house and his clan. From the gold leaf on the ceiling to the menagerie of dead, stuffed animals everywhere, there is so much to consider, but it just gets him in a cold sweat. It was far better before his children, his wife, his house, his money and his status. The days when this man was on the up and Payton went everywhere with him. From spit and sawdust to shebeen to hellhole and hovel. They grew into this city together and then they grew apart.

'Sir. John. She cannot approve.'

He presses a finger to Ake's lips. This tableau alone would render many mortal beings in prison for a long stretch, but somehow John has forgotten about the law, perhaps because in this house he can control it more than anyone on the outside. Mr Ake fears for him on this issue. It has been too long since he ventured out to see what the world really has become, relying upon the world to come to him. One midnight flit full of whisky and worry to his bridewell changes nothing.

'Elspeth approves of us; she does. She's a stout hen, the stoutest.'

'And where would that leave her and the children if you were disgraced?'

John shakes his head and pours them both a scotch. 'That is not my point. Drink.'

They drink and John strokes his arm. 'What a perfectly ridiculous, no, preposterous pair we make, eh? Some picture is this. Mr Turner would paint us, if he were still kicking around. Or Hieronymus Bosch.' He traces a finger around Ake's bicep.

'And you are a magnificent landscape in yourself. Aw Payton, don't be like that.'

Ake uproots Frank awkwardly, rising to his feet and backing away. He needs to resort to business, to the reason he came here, and this business is about as far from being a trivial distraction as it gets. This man and his love is killing him a little more every time they meet now, and John just doesn't seem to care. He has become a monster, albeit a melancholic, pained and crazy one. This is just why Ake must revert to "Mr Ake" and John to "Sir".

'Sir, I came here this evening at your request on constabulary business, did I not?'

Captain Frank rolls his eyes and gulps down his drink. 'Yes. I suppose you did. Mr Ake.'

'Then may I ask the real nature of this business? Not our business, the business that had you showing up at my shop less than a fortnight ago?' Captain Frank pays great attention to a stray piece of fluff on his waistcoat. 'Sir. Please tell me. I've never seen you so distressed, even with a gun pointed at you.'

Captain Frank closes his eyes as Mr Ake talks, as if he wants to shut all of this out. He can't. 'Yes. It is important and I was going to ask you.'

'Then ask. And then I'll leave.'

'That's the problem. I don't want you to leave. Ever again.'

'Ask. Please. Sir.'

Captain Frank retrieves his cheroot from the ashtray and sparks it up again. 'Mr Ake, this evening there has been an action taking place close to this spot.'

'I heard it, sir.'

'You heard it. Well, it has become something of a bother. An understatement.'

'Yessir. Why didn't you send me?'

'You see all this?' Captain Frank waves a casual palm around the room, like he didn't hear the last statement.

'All what, sir?'

'This house. The bairns. Elspeth. The properties in Wales and Provence. All *this*.'

'Yes.'

'You know how *this* didn't come out of thin air. There's a price.'

'Discretion.'

'Yes. Yes indeed. You are still the best. How many fools judge you by your appearance, yet you are the brightest as well as the strongest. If only. Pah.'

'Then I wouldn't be stood here, sir.'

'Quite. So then. Banastre Dunwoody.'

'Yessir.'

'You know all about our little project, don't you? I expected so, even though I left few crumbs to follow.'

'There is very little I do not know when it comes to this city. I should offer you information rather than the other way around.'

'Quite so. What is your take, then?'

This makes Mr Ake feel almost as uneasy as the situation with Elspeth. 'The Confederates are winning. Here and over there.'

'I didn't ask you about them, did I? I asked, what's your take on him?'

Mr Ake exhales. He wishes to be home or in the bridewell with his books and journals. 'I don't know, sir.'

'Yes, you do.'

Yes, he does, and Captain Frank wants an answer. 'Alright then. He's pond life. No better than any of the crooks I'll jail day on day, only a better shot and perhaps more wily. Lucky too, but only lucky because you didn't assign me to do the job. I am perplexed by that.'

'You understate, Payton.'

Let's not get back to *Payton*. 'Sir, if you insist upon my full opinion, he's a menace and he may well destroy our city. The powers enthralled by him … Harrison … think that they can contain and patronise him, but he will not stop until he has his full consulate and a victory stateside. You ask me what I think about him and not this war of his, yet it is not possible to separate the two.'

Captain Frank nods. A knock and Morrison comes through the door with a pasty-faced Peeler in tow, stove pipe hat in hand. The lad acknowledges Mr Ake with a nod and whispers into Captain Frank's ear. The question occurs to Mr Ake of what would have transpired had this constable turned up a few minutes earlier.

'Very well. Thank you, Donnelly.'

The Peeler Donnelly makes himself scarce along with Morrison. Captain Frank chuckles, as if privy to an inside joke.

'Canning Street?' says Mr Ake, hardly a mind-reader.

'Aye.'

'Hit or miss?'

'Miss. Again. You're right. He has the luck of the devil.'

'May I ask you again, then? Why did you not commission me?'

'You can ask. I don't have to answer.'

Mr Ake cracks his knuckles. 'I'll go and finish the job for you right now. Don't know why you didn't ask me in the first place.'

'Hold your horses, Payton. I know that this is what you like doing.'

'I don't like doing it. But I am proficient at it.'

'Yes. Of course. Look, I just want to protect you.'

'Me?'

'Yes, you silly boy. Can't you see it? I've been watching over you for years, since things were simpler, better. You might think that you run the toughest gaol in the city, and you would be right, but that is not the worst of Liverpool. I built it to protect you as much as to incarcerate others.'

'I don't understand.'

'This thing has become a blight. A war that has reached across thousands of miles, sullying the minds of good people and making the bad ones worse. And what for? Money? A cotton drought? Slack docks? We want more and more. So we'll end up with less and less.'

'Then the solution is plain. Do you want me to kill him or not, sir?'

At last, Captain Frank stands, a full eighteen inches shorter than Mr Ake. 'Yes. No. Perhaps. My decision is indecision. It seems that you are my only effective weapon remaining, but I am loathe to risk you too. Out there is what I really have at my disposal. An untrained, poorly-disciplined, corrupt rabble, divided into camps according to which side is paying them, political or criminal. One and the same, you could argue. But for some blue cloth and a tin badge, they are just a common gang like any number of scum around the port. I am losing my grip.

The tide is turning before my eyes, and I am so fucking tired of it all, Payton. Do I turn with it? Do I stick or twist?'

Ake knows that his own family's future depends on the answer, as does every answer he gives to John Frank. It is why they cannot be closer, in spite of their urges. 'I cannot answer that for you, John.'

'Of course you cannot, poor dear Payton.' Captain Frank approaches and looks up at Mr Ake, eyes soft again. Deliberation is all over his face. 'I'll sleep on it. Let us hope the world doesn't end overnight.'

He turns his back on Payton Ake, who knows it is time to leave and that his dear love has already made his mind up, lest Mr Ake would be on his way over to Canning Street already.

'Recognise the fellow?' says Banastre, hovering over the corpse, bent upon making an identification. It's the same drill as the other evening, except this time Banastre is relatively sober. That morose expression is back, and Harriet knows that she isn't looking forward to the rest of the evening in his company.

The attending Peeler studies the corpse close at hand. Grace nods at Harriet, who already knows the identity of the young shooter and his profession, care of her loyal stablewoman.

The chappy, a fellow member of the Liverpool Constabulary to the attending officer, has a wound under his right cheekbone where the slug entered and even though there isn't much left of the back of his head, his face is relatively unsullied. Still, the Peeler shakes his head.

'He isn't immediately recognisable, sir. Perhaps from Manchester? Some of their gangs have been known to operate here.'

Harriet can tell that the attending Peeler is a fairly accomplished liar, as they all seem to be, but Banastre isn't buying it for a second. 'Come on, lad. Do your job. I'll make it worth your while.'

The Peeler looks unsteady on his feet, which she long knows is the effect her husband has upon anyone who gets in his way.

'What's this then?' grunts Ginger Harrison, fresh on the scene. He spots the three corpses lined up on the patio of 101, 'Oh my.'

Banastre acts like he's been there all along, eyes glued to the bodies. 'I smell complicit swine in all of this. Have done from the outset.'

Ginger reddens, as is his wont. Harriet pretends not to look at them. Conté is back in character, vanishing into the stonework of the yard. 'Old boy, we should be careful what we say out in the open. For many reasons. This isn't The Athenaeum.'

'Yeah. You English and your famous goddamn reserve.'

'Steady, old boy.'

'Steady old boy, steady old boy. That's all I ever get from you, you ass.' Banastre jabs a finger in the direction of the corpses and tosses a brass badge at Ginger, bearing the Crown insignia of the Liverpool Constabulary. 'That dead boy is a fully-fledged member of Captain Frank's club. And you.' He jabs the same finger at the living Peeler. 'You are a liar, man. I should have you fuckin' keelhauled.'

Ginger tries to placate Banastre. 'Yes, well, you're not at sea now, old boy. Let's just rein it in a moment, eh? What what?'

Banastre starts frothing. This could mean trouble. A little part of Harriet confesses to herself that she hopes it does. 'You knew all along, you boozy idiot. How could you not say anything? You are my friend. *Our* friend. True colours, Mayor. Spill the beans before I spill you.'

They're up to something. Harriet listens keenly, desperate for any clues as the mercury rises.

Ginger wobbles, public embarrassment being the worst of his fears. 'You want to get into another war, Banastre? Right here in this city? I suggest you retire to calm yourself and let the constable on duty here take care of the situation.'

'So that they might stab me in my bed? So that you might in my back? They done tried guns and poison, blades would likely be next. Tell me what's next, Mayor.'

'There is a delicate balance to be had in Liverpool, and that is all I will say to you on the subject in the here and now. Now, we are in the company of staff and a lady. *Your* lady, sir.'

Banastre prowls, glancing at Harriet with derision. 'So what? Let 'em hear it all.'

'No sir. They shall not hear it all.' Ginger is attempting to play the stiff-backed statesman, but Harriet can see through that. From the corner of her eye, so can Conté. He is impotent, drained of all of his influence by the very succubus who is accusing him of collusion. This is just how Dunwoody wins every battle he fights, whether the opponent knows they are fighting him or not. Conté has seen his like so many times before.

'I told you already. I want this city, Ginger. I want it all.'

Ginger waggles a finger, doing his damnedest not to see this unravel in front of all these witnesses, which is probably all he has left. 'Enough, I say. Remember what you have coming up.'

What is coming up? *Spill it, damn it.* Banastre chews his lip and circles the patio like a caged lion, stopping suddenly at Harriet. He strokes her belly, not even making eye contact with her, fixated on his glorious future. The Union Agent within her is choking to death. Can her poor child feel all of this? Not even Conté can risk looking her in the eye right now, for fear of alerting Banastre's hackles.

'You are quite correct, Ginger. But it is time to stop hedging your bets, *old boy*. Whose side are you on? Mine or theirs?'

Ginger breathes, nods and tremors. He replies in a dry rasp. 'Yours. Of course.'

Harriet can see that he knows exactly what he is in the middle of here, and her husband's ultimatum is final. The Mayor is only upright because of whatever their project is, and weak as he is, Banastre has shown the boozy oaf just who *really* owns this city right now.

'Good show, old boy,' says the Commander, mimicking Ginger. 'Then we're still on.'

`

#16 DOING A DEAL

June 15ᵗʰ, 1863

Banastre has work to do in Liverpool, but at last! The opportunity has arisen – by discreet invitation via Mayor Harrison's office – to meet with Lord Palmerston at 10 Downing Street. Any direct beseeching of the Prime Minister by the Confederate States might be seen as bad form, hence the lack of pomp and ceremony today. Just two visitors to the big house. They could be a pair of junior ministers or civil servants. Palmerston is keeping his cards close to his chest lest the vultures on both sides of the House of Commons and Lords attempt to swoop upon any controversial decision, but if ever a situation demanded a personal touch, it is this one.

So then, a fast London and North Western express train from Lime Street at 7am, taking five hours to arrive in the capital of the Empire, a wonder of engineering in pumping, steam-driven flux; although once The War is won, the network that will be installed across the new CSA will make even this impressive performance look puny.

Ginger likes his booze rather more than even Banastre, a feature of his being that has taken on a new level since their little contretemps yesterday. The florid old tar has been putting it away like water ever since they hunkered down in First Class and he is pitching and yawing like a stricken sloop by the time they reach the concourse to the Gateway of The North, Euston Station. Were it not for Ginger's personal connection with Edward Seymour, 12ᵗʰ Duke of Somerset, First Lord of The Admiralty and most senior member of Palmerston's cabinet, Banastre would be tempted to banish his sot of a friend to a hostelry on the way, or dispense with him entirely into the river with a bullet to the base of his irritating skull. The state Ginger is in, daresay he wouldn't notice. The only saving grace is that there won't be any need for this idiot blunderbuss of a Mayor soon if this all goes to plan.

Once they alight the hansom cab direct outside 10 Downing Street, Ginger spews his guts up on the pavement, leaving an awful smell of semi-digested kippers and brandy on the immaculate drag, embellished by another searingly hot day as the sun cracks the flagstones. Banastre's fear of guilt by association escalates, but he chides himself to keep his wits and temperament levelled. This is further than Jefferson Davis ever got, or any of his esteemed cabinet or Foreign Diplomatic Corps. Expectations are high, but immediate impressions are important. Better to decorate the sidewalk than the lobby, but it isn't the start Banastre wanted.

They are guided into the building by staff who take their coats, and Banastre thanks the stars that Ginger is more upright now. Thems in London are just the same as thems in Richmond or Washington. The place looks like a slightly grander version of The Athenaeum, with a gallery of mouldy old farts rising up a flight of stairs, depicting every PM since old Walpole, all Etonian or Harrovian alumni. Banastre knows every single one of them, committed by rote to memory.

The pair wait in the anteroom to the cabinet office on chairs lined with gold leaf. A grandfather clock ticks. Banastre grips his cane tight while Ginger hiccups like a toad, bile and too much rich living repeating on him.

'For God's sake, man. Doncha know where this is?'

'Of course. Hold on, hold on,' says Ginger. Then he emits a ground-shaking belch, 'Ooh better. Getting up a fair tailwind now, old boy. Never fear an old tar.'

'I swear to God, Ginger.'

The double doors ease open, and that famous long table where the future of the greatest Empire on the planet is debated and decided is revealed, along with the two most powerful men in Britain, who look like a pair of butlers that should have been retired from service decades ago. This isn't what Banastre expected – like a deuce of cadavers re-animated in some Voodoo ritual – but Ginger relishes a reunion with his school chum Seymour. He's quickly upon him, pumping his hand. Seymour looks less than impressed.

'Eddie! Pammy!'

Pammy? Eddie? Chummy English Public School names? They are Lord Palmerston, Prime Minister of Great Britain and Ireland propped up by Edward Seymour, First Lord of the Admiralty. The lack of formality is nonsensical to Banastre as the hierarchy in the room is clear immediately, but he isn't interested in British foibles; he just wants the deal.

"Pammy" is the elder of the elders, more lamb chop sideburns than face. Bent over and scarcely able to hold his own weight, he reminds Banastre of some of the simian life he encountered in the jungles of Bolivia. He collapses rather than sits in his chair.

"Eddie" Seymour is a few years younger as a peer of Ginger's and slightly more agile, as if that could be a competition. He beckons them to the end of the famous table.

Seymour says, 'Pammy is unable to speak aloud at the moment due to a slight ague. I will do the talking for him.'

A slight ague? He's half-dead. Might be fully dead by the end of the next sentence.

Ginger snorts, 'Very good.'

Pammy doesn't look too agreeable with this or anything, but he is perfectly capable of stuffing his pipe and lighting it.

Seymour studies Banastre and then returns his beady gaze to Ginger to fire the first salvo. 'You know our neutrality position, Ginger. Lincoln would rattle his sabre at us if he had an inkling that we were even having this conversation.'

Ginger twitches and smiles. 'Yes, Eddie, but…'

Seymour holds his hand up to silence Ginger, who obeys. 'But we understand that this is indeed an issue that is essential to the nation's future prosperity. Ergo your cotton drought that is stunting the growth of the economy in the North West. Ergo the rest of the country. That is all down to this Union blockade of Confederate-held ports. The situation has altered somewhat since we legislated upon it. We can see that the Confederate escalation is going well with superior artillery and cavalry. We have our intelligence too. Thus, it is plain.'

Pammy grunts and twitches. Has he had some sort of brain spasm? Who's the real leader here?

Ginger is thankfully unable to say much. Banastre is keeping his counsel. This is how he got the role of Consul to Liverpool, by knowing his place in the pecking order. As in Richmond, same for London. This here Seymour loves the sound of his own voice, so let him be.

'The Empire needs the Americas and the bounty it brings. All the Americas, not just the useless, frozen bit at the top that we ended up with. Of course, we have India and swathes of Africa. We have Australia. A few rambunctious spots here and there, I grant you. Do we verily want to get into another scrap after the Crimea? Hmm. We could just let you keep building your boats, and turn a blind eye to that. We could, could we not, Pammy?'

Pammy continues to drool. There's a semblance of a nod in there somewhere.

Ginger responds, 'Yes, yes, yes. Of course.'

Seymour hasn't returned to Banastre once. It is like he isn't even there. 'But consider a place for civilised men, a place that already exists and shares our language, customs and laws, even our history. A place settled by our cousins and brothers. We need to pick the right side in this war and then help you rebuild. I've been saying this all along. Now, happenstance…' Seymour glances at his decrepit overlord and emits a thin, bent smile, 'has dictated that my voice may no longer fall upon deaf ears. Your Chamber of Commerce has sent me the recent figures on trade with the former colonies. It is a sobering review.'

'Aye,' says Ginger, 'It is Eddie. It is.'

Seymour slaps the mahogany. 'There it is then, in black and white, the greatest earner of all in our economy, stricken now because of an infernal sea blockade. Never mind potential, look at the cold, hard economics. But this reluctance to throw our all into the cause of the South is making the markets wobble. We have to commit, lest we lose out. Rest assured, I understand the predicament inside out. One day, America might grow so big and strong that it might colonise us, so we need to have a role now.' Ginger and Seymour laugh at the notion. 'Naturally, I'm being flippant.'

'Naturally,' croaks Ginger.

Banastre stays rock-still, watching and waiting. Come. To. Papa.

Ginger flounders and fawns, 'I beg you, sir. This all is music to our ears.'

Seymour's deep thatch of eyebrows twitch, turning his attention at last over to the American. His teeth are black as coal, probably once belonging to some uncommissioned kid who caught a Russian slug in Sebastopol. 'Why let that lanky pillock Lincoln pull the wool over our eyes, gentlemen? You know where the money comes from in North America and it is purely down to geography. So, yes I, *we*, do have a fair proposal for you today.' He leans in, as if someone is listening who shouldn't be listening, like he's playing truant and scrumping apples at Eton, and he wants to see if these two younger boys want in. 'As an hors d'oeuvre, we will take New York, Boston, Philadelphia, Washington, New England, all lands North of Virginia. Push these jewels all back into Canada, tax the bastards to Kingdom Come. Let them try and have another Tea Party.'

'Bravo.' Ginger sticks to his platitudes and where his bread is buttered, 'Wonderful!'

Seymour has moved all of his attention onto Banastre. 'Now, many of our members beseech us about the slavery issue. Mr Lincoln's emancipation proclamation.'

Ginger nods like a dog. 'Yes. A turgid affair.'

'Turgid. I could not have put it better myself, but we should tread carefully. Legal challenges are inevitable if we are clumsy. But that is all about the wording, sir. Devil in the detail.'

'I'm intrigued, sir,' mutters Banastre, measuring every syllable of his first response. He couldn't be further away from a skirmish on the old river right now, but in an odd way he couldn't be closer either.

'Aye. You have seen the wonders of mechanisation in our Northern cities. With shrewd investment, we will help you take this a stage further and dispense with the need for this type of labour. Send them back to Africa, scatter them like you've done with the natives, whichever, whatever. The nub of it is that the seed just needs watering. Then there is the second problem, how to skin the awkward problem of the lobbies and the courts. How?'

Seymour pauses, like he's waiting for a reply. Ginger attempts to go first, but Banastre kicks his ankle. 'Oof sir! Why...' Not now, the man is getting to it himself.

The First Lord of Admiralty issues a rictus grin. Seymour is several hundred leagues south of sour, but his words are the sweetest thing that Banastre Xavier Dunwoody has ever heard. 'Us British will soon forget about the issue when they see the vast profits coming in. Of course, we cannot give you personal command of our Army and Navy. Or make a declaration of war to Washington. But…' He rattles his fingers on the table, as if he has just come up with the idea, but clearly hasn't, 'were we to give you the considerable heft and might of the Royal Navy to scatter this little Union blockade, in the name of protecting our trade and goods, that might present more of a bind to our opponents in Westminster. In the meantime, Lincoln will declare war himself and full intervention will commence. If he hasn't the balls for that, we'll supply you with enough arms and mercenaries to do the rest yourselves. Hey, presto.'

This is just how the British manage to hold on to such a huge Empire, not just with brute force but with unrivalled cunning. Ginger grins, like the idiot he is, from ear to ear. Banastre remains contained, but his insides are vaulting. Is it as simple as that? Does he even care if he can return to Dixie with this little old gem of a deal in his back pocket? The right levers have been pulled at the right moment. There will never be a better chance than right now.

Pammy frowns and grabs Seymour's collar, beckoning his ear. He whispers, spittle flying into Seymour's lughole and across the table. Seymour isn't vexed. Pammy finishes and Seymour returns to his guests.

'I repeat by way of caveat. It will surely be a hard sell to the House. And we will have to pay off the press to keep them quiet in the short interim.'

Ginger interjects. 'I am sure that any expenses will be covered by our Chamber of Commerce. As for the MPs, the sell is a good sell. You'll get a majority if the wording is correct; push it through on a white paper about trade and commerce? Grease the right palms?'

'Spoken well,' says Seymour, 'You could be in our cabinet, Ginger.'

Ginger grins and slaps the table. 'Aye aye! What what!'

Seymour's face remains sour, in spite of the old school tie connection.

'Transfer the funds directly to my office. My staff will make up an invoice.' Seymour leans in, 'This is delicate. Surgical. Our system takes more than coarse bribes of cash and land to unravel. That is why it endures, why we've never had a revolution. Hence I have no need to remind you about your discretion?'

'We gather, sir,' mutters Banastre. He knows that coarse bribes of cash and land are everything it takes. This man has just solicited one directly, and there is no doubt that he will top slice any money Ginger pays over. Matters not. 'When may we announce?'

'The sooner the better, but it needs to be passed and ratified, so hold your water until then.'

'Understood.'

'I'll have the treaty drawn up and copied to you.'

Banastre reads Seymour well. He knows the prevailing wind.

'I'll contact my superiors, post-haste.'

'Use our courier.'

'With respect, I have my proper channels.'

Seymour doesn't give it a second's thought.

'Good then.'

Ginger pipes up. 'Will you travel to our city for the ratification, old boy? Bring Pammy up with you? The sea air will do him good.'

'There's no sea air that is ever earthly up there, Ginger. It stinks of shit.'

'But you will come, though?' All the man ever thinks about is pumping himself and his cronies up.

'Very well, I think.' Seymour nods and his countenance changes to playful in quite a disturbingly quick transition, even for Banastre. 'Now Ginger, to other business, you absolute goat. Tell me again how you arranged for my pony to go lame at Aintree in The Grand National? Should have shot the bally donkey myself before it started. I love hearing you try to talk your way out of these things.'

A bellowing laugh from Ginger, reverberating around the chamber. Imagine a room full of Ginger Harrisons, all what-whating and blustering. That's what happens in these cabinet meetings and this Seymour is just the chief cock, assuming the role of Head Boy. How many futures have been bought and sold in here by his like? None greater than this, Banastre would wager. Without hardly lifting a finger, he has the world's greatest

Empire in his thrall. As they prattle on, his head spins with it all. This is it. This is really happening, and a river pirate from Gatlinburg is going to bring it home.

They step out of number 10 into the bright sunshine, a cab waiting. Ginger is cock-a-hoop, but on the surface Banastre is altogether more circumspect, mindful of more assassins, even down here. However, a buzz greater than any substance he has ever taken has rushed up his spine and into his brain, try as he might to contain himself.

This.

Is.

It.

'Shall we go and get a drink, old boy?'

That might actually be a good idea as he has nerves to settle before the work starts. 'We'll get one on the train. You're buying, Mayor.'

#17 SHOWDOWN AT LIME STREET
Part One

June 15th, 1863

'Meanwhile, I'm stuck in this hovel with the children and rats while you're arse-farting around with Royston bloody Chubb and his bloody schemes.'

'You don't understand, Sarah.'

'Oh, I understand pretty farting well, Padraig. I saw them take you below, not knowing if our children were ever going to see their father again. I saw the state of your thumbs…'

'Yes. Me poor thumbs…'

'…when you got out of that place barely alive. No, I won't have this again. Get away from him, please. Get an honest job on the docks or shipyards or somewhere.'

'Who'd employ me? Pat the Cat, best lock-picker and burglar in the city? Oh aye, that's a fine recommendation so.'

'That man takes everything for himself and gives you scraps. All we get are cockroaches and rats and I am fed up with it, Padraig. Fed up so.'

'I can easily tell by the mardy face on you.'

'You've a mardy face yourself. Like a dropped pie. Whinge and whine is all I ever hear from you. Why can't you be a man?'

'Then leave. Take the kids back to Ireland. Go on with you.'

'And do what? What is a woman without a husband? Even a fuckin' useless one like you?'

'How dare you call me useless. I'm not useless. Piss off with it.'

'You piss off. Go on. Piss off right out the door. Go and see your great friend Royston Chubb, see what he has got for you next. Maybe a year in the clink, maybe dangling on the end of some hemp. You'll have no thumbs left in a week. We'll be just fine, Padraig. Oh yes, fine.'

'I'm going.'

'Then go then. Eejit.'

'Don't expect me back tonight.'

'Oo we're having rat sandwiches for tea. You won't know what your missing.'

'That's enough.'

'Stop being so gullible. Go and get a proper job for us.'

'I've got a job.'

'Close the door after yourself, Padraig. While we've still got one.'

'Bah. Pah.'

Slam.

Naturally, Banastre didn't report exactly where he was going. Damned inconsiderate of him towards a wife who is plotting to sabotage her husband. Where he clearly only has to ask for information by writing a first-class letter to Richmond, Virginia, Harriet and Conté must keep themselves under wraps and in the dark from everyone, friend or foe. The silence from their side over yonder ocean is deafening and excruciating. Does Butler not even care about the failed plot? Are there no questions or directions? Are they now really alone?

Grace has informed them that Banastre boarded a train for London with the Mayor this morning, on God knows what business. While the cat's away, she gets the insane urge to march up to Captain Frank's house and parley out some sort of agreement, ascertain exactly what resources and logistics are at her disposal, and make some immediate plans to escalate the campaign against the Confederacy in Liverpool. They seem to be holding all the cards despite the presence of an official United States Consul at Paradise Street.

Their cover is deemed so precious to the war effort that Haines Dudley – Lincoln's trusted representative here, and perennial cleaner of faeces morning, noon and night – has no knowledge of them. And as for Frank, is he really a Union ally or just in their pay? What is his angle? Why can't she get more information and go direct? Sometimes, it would be good to get acknowledgement that they exist from someone. *Anyone*. It is so tempting. All it would take is a few words, but that would mean disobeying Butler's orders.

*LAND, A PENSION AND A WAGE! JOIN THE
UNITED STATES ARMY HERE!*

The banner is curled up from the bottom, covered in all
manner of effluent. It might as well represent this whole
campaign.

Naturally, Banastre himself tries to avoid Dudley aside from
the occasional encounter in the clubs, and the feeling is mutual,
so Harriet can only observe the U.S. Federal Consul and
Consulate via this ridiculous routine of promenading with Conté
up and down Paradise Street in a well-practised charade every
Friday morning, watching that inauspicious building adorned
with a resplendent but incongruous golden eagle statue above its
doors, spying on their own side. Why doesn't Dudley get some
protection in place? Is he really that wholesome? Three, four or
even more times a day without fail, the United States Consul is
there personally with his staff, cleaning the frontage down and
repairing any damage before replacing the banner:

*LAND, A PENSION AND A WAGE! JOIN THE
UNITED STATES ARMY HERE!*

Then he returns inside to work on the affidavits in an attempt
to prove the shipyard skullduggery and financing of the
Confederacy via laundered accounts, taking The War into the
British courts. Doing things the legal way, the hard way, the
wrong way. Again and again and again. Bless his stoicism, but
damn it too. His staff sit ready to process the walk-ins for the
Army, hoping to distribute tickets for free passage to Boston and
New York to able-bodied men of fighting age, no experience
necessary. Trade ain't exactly brisk.

Poor Dudley. She watches him clean more muck from the
letterbox, maintaining his good humour with the staff, his
outright integrity. He's a sickly fellow, an Ivy Leaguer of
establishment stock and a personal friend of Honest Abe who
helped propel him to the White House. What harm would a
subtle approach to him do? To talk with an ally on their terms,
not Butler's? To sit and pray with him? To consider that this war
is not lost and that the Emancipation Proclamation really means
something to someone this far away from the heat of battle?
What harm really?

'Why do you put yourself through this?' whispers Conté, forming the lady's single retinue as they stroll back up the thoroughfare for the umpteenth time, her heels clacking against the york stone pavement slabs that Harriet is aching to call a sidewalk.

'Because then I can pretend we are not alone,' mutters Conté's governess, who isn't really a governess of anyone, especially Conté. Dudley continues to scrub the mess off the walls with sugar soap but senses the eyes of the women upon him. He turns and doffs his cap. Ever the gentleman, even towards the wife of such an unscrupulous adversary.

Harriet checks her stride and emits a neat curtsy as a riposte, joined by Conté in the formality. Does he really know of her? He will not know Harriet Farrell, Irish-Choctaw stray, but he surely will be all too aware of the Southern Belle wife of the man who is trying to humiliate him on a daily basis; the chattering classes are too hard to avoid in this town. Possibly, probably, ifs, ands. Dudley is cut from the same cloth as Mr Lincoln and it is a reminder, for sure, that the real gentlemen ain't necessarily Southern in this battle. Few, if any, men are blameless in all of this, but some are more blameless than others.

Conté breaks her train of thought. 'We need to prove that we can do this alone, Harry. Without anyone's help. We need to empower ourselves. Screw Butler, screw all of them.'

'Fine words.'

'Do you not agree?'

'I agree more than ever. And that is the cross I must bear.'

So just where is their commanding officer right now? The one who should be providing the reassurance? The flesh and bones behind the coded messages delivered to their deposit box in Martin's Bank? What has become of the man who recruited them when they were still children playing adult games of deception, costume play, petty theft and sabotage back in that other hotter, stickier, sultry melting pot of New Orleans? Conspicuous by his absence.

Is he in Boston? In Washington? In occupied New Orleans itself? Major General Benjamin Butler, whose corpulent physique and gruff manner lead even his allies to call him The Fat Man, is everywhere and nowhere and that's how he likes to do his business.

A young lad approaches and whispers into Harriet's ear. She slips him a penny and consults a pocket watch, which looks odd against her summer outfit of cream lace and bonnet.

Harriet leans into Conté's ear. 'Padraig's been spotted in an Irish shebeen on Lime Street. He's drunk as a skunk and telling everyone how he is going to meet Banastre off the train.'

'Oh dear. Something must have snapped.'

'Yes. Hardly surprising.'

'After his brush with your beloved husband? Oh Banastre, my dreamboat.' Conté flutters her eyelids rather too convincingly.

'Give it a rest, Conté.'

Harriet nods and smiles at Dudley as he gets back to the work of being a gentleman and not winning the war. Banastre and the Mayor will be arriving on the express from London at 8pm sharp, hungover or drunk. The nature of their business is unknown, but it cannot be good news for their campaign.

'We had better get up there, then.'

It has just gone half past seven in the evening, and the trains are ever reliable between the two richest cities in the Empire. Princess Grace waits at the junction of Hanover Street with a pair of sturdy nags for them. They will need to get in and out before Banastre arrives, for Pat won't last five seconds if the husband claps eyes on him. Consequently neither will they.

'*High upon the gallows tree swung the noble-hearted three. By the vengeful tyrant stricken in their bloom; but they met him face to face, with the courage of their race, And they went with souls undaunted to their doom. "God save Ireland!" said the heroes; "God save Ireland" said they all. Whether on the scaffold high or the battlefield we die, oh, what matter when for Erin dear we fall!*'

It evokes an ancient memory for Harriet, of Clontarf, of Westmoreland Street, of Temple Bar, of Dublin. All her Daddy's favourite pubs, true rebel songs, but now she couldn't look more like an outsider. The ruddy-faced child that accompanied Augustus C. Farrell to all those alehouses is still Irish at her very core and always will be, but comforting this place is not. There is an edge in the air that comes with being set in enemy territory, the jewel port of the British yoke, the air of something about to snap.

Aside from behind the bar of The Crown, most of the clientele are men, so two ladies dressed for promenading rather stand out. Rolling, fishy, glazed eyeballs greet them as they cut through the throng, looking for that man who is hidden in plain sight. It seems Harriet isn't the only one with agitation on her mind.

Padraig McCartney holds court at the back of the pub, guzzling from a pottery jug of poitín, a favourite gut rot of the thousands who have come to this city since the British created a terrible famine from nothing over the water back in the 1840s. Liverpool is what it is now because of that event, and don't they know about it.

'I guess they have a point, Conté. But they ain't helping themselves in here.'

Conté nods, registering every leer as if it is about to manifest into a physical threat.

Pat swigs the liquid down like water; his singing as bad as everyone else's, only louder.

'God save Ireland! Said the heroes; God save Ireland said they all. Whether on the scaffold high or the battlefield we die, oh, what matter when for Erin dear we fall!' He spots Harriet. 'Mrs Dunwoody, Lord Bless us and save us. And who is it with her but the sweet Creole coleen who's always a-smilin' and jokin' with us. Little ray o' sunshine so am I to you. My steadfast friends come and say hello to your wee little leprechaun pet who's always up to some paddywhackery of some kind or other so he is, hic.'

He belches like a toad.

'Not edifying, Padraig,' says Conté, many eyes upon her.

'Couldn't give a shite, Miss.'

Harriet looks about herself. 'Where's Mr Chubb, Pat?'

Pat looks around himself. 'Lying low still, I reckon. Shite on that, I say. Get these good women a drink. Will you have a little drink with me? Before I go and put a hole in your husband's nasty fucking skull? Um?'

He pulls a revolver and waves it around. His drinking partners laugh, but still remember to duck as he swings the heavy piece around the room. It's bigger than him.

Conté interjects. 'Pat, he'll kill you. And us. Don't die of bravado; you're smarter than that. You don't mean to do this.'

His earnest little face wobbles, tears brimming. 'And you. See, that's the bit you're worried about. Isn't it just? Our little secret. Don't suppose you'd mind if I told all me buddies in here about it, though? Hey! Guess what 'tis about these two fine ladies! Lay anyone in this room thrippence to a guinea they'll never get it.'

Harriet's knuckles whiten, and her hand grips the snub Derringer hidden in her petticoat. May the Lord forgive her for what she is considering. But who's to say that he hasn't blabbed already? Even a rumour could grind everything to a halt and result in a hasty retreat on the first steamer out of here, at best. Dead in a ditch at worst. Then Banastre really will have the whole place to himself.

'Will ye put some money down on it?'

A short chorus of ayes and whoo-hars about the throng, even though the drinkers clearly have no idea what he's talking about.

Pat lurches to his feet. The flotilla of empty pots and jugs on the table indicate that he's been out all day. This isn't like him, but that gut rot is hard enough to change anyone's character. 'How about you two fine girls? You happy for me to spill the beans for the sake of our wager?'

They shake their heads in unison. A scrap breaks out behind them at the bar. Two navvies going at each other with fists and clubs. Pat isn't the only one who's been out on the lash all day. What a desperate den.

Harriet tries to seize Pat's flickering attention. 'Go home to Sarah. Go home to your children. Please.'

Conté pushes one of the brawlers away. 'If you Irish are ever to get independence, you'll have to learn to stop fighting between yourselves.'

Pat grins and waves a hand, swatting away the slight. 'Yes, I agree. Go and tell them to stop, then.'

Guffaws. Men dance around them, getting in their faces as another rebel song turns quickly into a stomp. The brawl continues and they barrel into the two women. Yes, this is just as Harriet remembers it.

They turn back to Pat, but he's vanished.

Conté says, 'Where did he go? Dammit. He's a sharp one for a little boozehound.'

Harriet cranes her neck beneath the table. 'Look.'

The table is right above the open trap door to the cellar, ever handy for a fast getaway. Harriet and Conté push past and through the drunks.

'Ah, come on now.'

'Will yer not stay for one?'

'I'll give them one so.'

'Don't be filthy, Cormac.'

'Ah, stay for one will youse.'

'Ye pretties. Plump and preggers and an African Queen so.'

'Fine ladies! Phwoar, so.'

They squeeze down the dirty hole and into the cellar, ripping their clothes in the hurry to catch Pat. The evening sun streams through an open door leading to a flight of steps out of the cellar and more steps up to the yard. They are right across the road from the station concourse on Skelhorne Street, a particularly rambunctious little drag packed with drifters and grifters and ne'erdowells, all vying to survive in the slalom of competition, survival and vice. It is dripping with menace and inebriation. They dodge beggars, trollops and chancers, pushing through the flesh market and towards the hansom cab ranks, catching sight of Pat, who is running now, albeit in a drunken lope.

They chase him, slaloming workers and gentry to the platform as the steam locomotive driving Banastre's train is easing to a stop. Harriet has been on enough train journeys to know that first-class passengers alight at the front on arrival, and she expects to see Banastre jumping off the car any moment now. Close enough to get a shot in, she raises her Derringer, but Pat does a volte-face, standing and watching, tears streaming down his face, smacking the gun against his hip. She just can't shoot him.

Harriet grits her teeth as she finally gets it about him. She saw it in the face of her daddy when he told her that they had to go to America; she sees it in the destitute of this city. It is the complete absence of faith and hope and now she sees it in Pat. He's no more capable of shooting her husband than old Dudley back there. 'Is that really what this is about, Padraig?'

Pat staggers on his feet and then darts away to the side, just as porters start opening the doors for disembarking passengers.

Harriet and Conté remain rooted to the spot. Banastre carries a ten-parts-drunk Ginger around his shoulders. They've clearly been at it themselves, although the Mayor is in a far worse state. She tucks away her gun and Conté follows suit. Banastre frowns, perplexed by the welcome party. Ginger staggers and mutters as his friend navigates for him. Banastre's eyebrow is raised.

'Sweetness? What are you doing here? And why the cap gun?'

Harriet thinks on her feet.

'My little joke, darling. So you don't go running away again without telling me first. Remember that I'm handy, am I not?'

'You should not be away from the house in your condition. It is not seemly.'

Snot and drool pour out of Ginger. Seemly, eh?

Harriet doesn't need reminding that Banastre hasn't got any sense of humour that was earthly, but even she would have to admit that it was a lame cover. Banastre struggles under the weight of the grinning idiot Ginger, thankfully distracted.

'This is the last time I'm doing this.'

'Got us a pair of trollops, Banastre? Good idea, old boy. I'll have the fat one.'

Banastre rolls his eyes and Ginger spews up port and cheese over his shoes. It dribbles out of his nose as he retches.

Banastre recoils. 'Bah. You, maid, Corty.'

Harriet, for the ten-thousandth time, mutters a correction. 'It's Conté.'

'Run along fast and get the Mayor a couple of porters and a hansom cab. Quickly, girl! Vite, damn!' Conté emits a curtsy and jogs away in the direction of the station master's office. Harriet tucks the pistol back into her petticoat, wary of Pat reappearing at any moment. 'Don't look at me like that, woman.'

Harriet tries and fails to recover her demure face. 'Like what?'

'I'm not in the mood, Harriet. I'm busy saving our cause and you're out playing cowboys with your slattern. The Good Lord only knows what you two get up to while I'm out at work. Well, it has to stop, I say. Think of our public image.'

'Would you have me stay at home? It is summertime. The fresh air is good for the baby and I'm growing our reputation about town.'

'My ass. Don't rile me. It ain't right and proper. Behave like a lady.'

'Darling Banny, please now. I get so bored and restless. I want to go home. Real home.' That's a far better line, but where is Pat?

Conté approaches with a porter and a cab driver. Both are fully aware of who awaits them and move at a keen pace. Where *in hell* is Padraig?

Banastre is thankfully distracted from his own annoyance by the state of Ginger. 'Just quit embarrassing me. Be dutiful. Ain't too much to ask, is it?'

Harriet says. 'I guess not. No sir.'

Banastre nods. 'No sir. Come on then, lollygaggers. I've further business this evening and he needs to get sobered up.'

The porter and driver collect Ginger and take up the slack. Banastre shakes the vomitus off his boots and strides off in the direction of the cab rank, ladies following. Harriet espies – in a glance – Pat watching them from behind a kiosk. A hot well of fear bubbles in her guts and Conté squeezes her hand. He wouldn't dare.

Would he? With drink, anything is possible. Conté shakes her head at Pat, pleading with her eyes for him to remain static. Even Banastre catching sight of him will be enough to spiral everything.

'Where's that damned maid?' grunts said beloved husband from twenty yards up ahead. Harriet drags Conté back into step.

'We've got to find out what he was doing in London,' whispers Conté, careful of the earshot.

'And just how do you propose we do that?' says Harriet, eyes front.

As Pat loses his marbles in the shadows, Conté distils an idea that has been fermenting since before this evening's antics. It's time to raise their game before Dixie gets out of sight. Will Harriet like it? Too bad if she doesn't.

'Leave that with me.'

Banastre leaves the group and heads across town in his own cab. It would be awkward for Conté to tail him directly, but Ginger is in no state to notice the Commander's maid as she slips away back down Skelhorne Street, assured of making her way on foot in better time than his ride. She knows where he is likely to be headed, given his bellyaching about having more business today.

'Dammit. Hurry up, man.'

Banastre pulls the cord hard and the bell to number four Water Street chimes again. Thudding steps emanate from within and several locks are unbolted in the heavy door.

It swings open.

'Good evening, Commander,' says Mr Rollo, not in the slightest flustered by the late intervention of his valued customer.

Banastre waves a docket under Rollo's nose. It bears the seal of the First Lord of The Admiralty, his prize from a long trip to London and back.

'Urgent communiqué. It can't wait. You got ink?'

'Yes sir.'

Mr Rollo nods and opens the door for him. Banastre shoves past him.

Across the way, between the colonnades of India Buildings, Conté watches the bank.

Ten minutes is all it took. Banastre is out the door without so much as a by-your-leave to Mr Rollo. She waits for him to flag down a cab before jaywalking across the thoroughfare.

After such a cavernous silence from Butler's office, it has been a fortnight since Conté has had cause to visit this place. Time was, upon their first arrival in the city, there were daily communiqués. Further proof that something is off.

Mr Rollo is, of course, accommodating at short notice, as usual, in his evening jacket and carpet slippers. Only the most exclusive customers get an out-of-hours service from the ever-present manager who resides in the upstairs rooms. He asks no questions.

He hands over Commander Dunwoody's docket. She opens it to find that the copy ink is still moist on his signature.

'Do you have a pencil, sir?'

It is unusual that Conté stays here for any longer than an instant, for fear of being spotted, but she is now safer here than any other part of the city. Rollo attends passively as she gets to work, scribbling down the decoded message officially sent by Banastre to Virginia no more than ten minutes ago, now intercepted and in the process of being deciphered. As the code starts to make sense, her stomach starts to churn.

'Are you quite alright, ma'am?' asks Rollo, whose job it is to be never any the wiser.

'I think I need to sit down, sir.'

The crowded pub is unusually subdued as Pat returns through the main doors. He looks broken, unable to fathom himself, never mind anything or anyone else.

'Give me a jug.'

A fresh refill from the still, a jug emerges in front of him. He pulls the stopper.

'That Sarah. She's a good woman, fine woman,' says Diarmuid, only half as drunk as he normally is.

'Mmm.' Pat goes to take a swig but stops, staring at the woodwork in the bar. He can feel eyes on him. Friendly but intense nonetheless. He could do without the sympathy. 'Too good for me.'

He takes a deep swig, intending to drink himself all the way to oblivion. Chubb climbs up the steps from the cellar and the drinkers part ways for him.

'Now then. I heard ye was causing trouble, little bollocks.'

'So you bothered your arse to come across town for me, did you? Careful of that, someone might stick a knife in you.'

Chubb throws some money at the barman for Pat's drink and moves in next to him. He leers at the other patrons to give them space. Diarmuid sniffs the air and frowns. He makes his way to the back room to collect pots and jugs.

'I had fuck all when I came to this city,' Chubb says, glancing around the pub. 'Not like all this is much, mind. But I'd stopped appreciating it, son. Wanted more when God had already decided I had enough.'

'Oh, there he is. Giving me lessons now, isn't he?'

'Let it go, Padraig. If I followed up every grudge, I'd be under the sod a long time. He who seeks revenge digs two graves.'

A flicker in Pat. He puts his jug down, face stiff. Then he melts into tears. Chubb hugs him like his own.

'Me fuckin' thumbs, Royston.' Pat's moans are muffled against the bigger man's embrace. 'They're me livelihood. That American shithouse. That Limerick bastard. Them British fuckers.'

Chubb rubs his head. 'Aye, I know. But let it go. Them's the power; we've got to remember that.' Pat nods, edging towards acceptance, bitter as that is. Chubb pulls him away and grips his shoulders. He holds up a shiny coin for Pat. 'Now, are ye going home to that fair and temperate wife of yours for a shellacking? Yer putting the drinkers off their jugs so. Not good for trade.'

'Yes. Suppose.'

'Aye, suppose.'

Pat takes the coin then sniffs the air. Smoke.

Diarmuid pushes his way back into the bar area, panting. 'Fire! Fuckin' fire, like!'

Chubb's moment with Pat dissolves and they glance to the back of the pub where flames dance across the opaque, stained glass. Bang! The window shatters with the explosion.

'Manure bomb,' grunts Pat.

'Aye,' says Chubb, 'That little shit Starkey no doubt.'

'I warned you about him so.'

'You did so, and you don't have to keep reminding me so.'

Bang! Another explosion takes the rear door off its hinges.

'Really?' grunts Pat.

#18 ANOTHER NIGHT IN THE BRIDEWELL

June 19th, 1863

There has been an almighty ruckus over at Goree Piazza after a French crew got into a scrape with some of the local traders, probably something to do with contraband, unpaid fees or vanishing cargo. Will they ever learn about this city?

Either way, some of the blighters thought that they could go in heavy-handed and took cudgels, blades and small arms to the party. A couple of them ended up dead, one in the Mersey soup and a gaggle in the Infirmary, besides a motley band distributed among the bridewells of the Central Docks. A mob of angry imbeciles for the better part, with a few harder cases among them.

Those ones, the toughest of the tars, were despatched to Campbell Square and were suitably cowed upon the sight of Mr Ake, but he does feel the need to rattle his truncheon across their bars should they continue to indulge in further Gallic chatter and bellyaching. They will be hauled up in front of a judge tomorrow who will rule against them and slap their masters with a fine, who will, in turn, drop the ringleaders into the brig of their ship and then the matter will end. All such events have the same conclusion of sore heads and sorry lips. Naturally, no questions will be asked around the traders of Goree, as fees have been paid well in advance to assure their complete impunity and anonymity in this matter – and just about any other matter – making the market a sovereign state enclaved within that other sovereign state that is the City of Liverpool.

11.45pm, near the witching hour, and things have finally quietened sufficiently enough for Mr Ake to pick up some reading, but he is promptly and impertinently interrupted by a stiff rap on the door. Malachy, the black tomcat who has made this garret his home, hisses, resenting the interruption to his paw-licking and mousing.

'Confound it.'

Mr Ake evicts the cat from the counter and hauls his huge frame up, striding over to the door and unbolting it. Every Peeler will know that Ake's is a full house this evening, so the interruption is almost sure to be unwarranted. He cracks his jaw and opens up. This had better be good.

Captain Frank's eyes smile at Mr Ake from the step. Twice in a few short weeks? This is unprecedented indeed.

'Will you invite me in, then?'

'This is your bridewell, sir. As they all are.'

'Are you alone?'

'Except for Malachy, yes. And some French grunts in the cells.'

'Then pish to the formality.'

He opens his arms and hugs Mr Ake. From a distance, it might look like a small child embracing his parent or favourite Uncle. Mr Ake is prone to hugging him back, in spite of what logic dictates.

'John?'

'Payton.'

'John!'

Captain Frank rises to his tiptoes and Mr Ake lowers himself down for a brief but lingering kiss. It feels good, but they both need to remember where they are and who they are. The yard is quiet as the grave tonight, but Mr Ake knows from long experience that this doesn't necessarily mean that no one is watching. John Frank steps through and admires the tight ship.

'I would have expected you to summon me to your house again.'

Captain Frank waves his comments away. 'Our business. I slept upon it. I cannot afford to send notes any more. The service is in chaos and no man can be trusted, save a few. Save you.'

Mr Ake nods. Prepared for any assignment. 'Yes.'

'I will meet with them. Tomorrow evening at 7pm, my house. I want you to be there. Seen but not heard. Only ask for and take his weapon, that is all.'

Mr Ake can't help but betray a little frustration across his brow. The other night, John was complaining about the state of affairs with this war and the corruption and greed. Now, here he is, pulled back into it. He would clip this American off the face of the Earth without a moment's thought and any other that followed in his wake. The Liverpool Constabulary do not follow the whims of a rogue state. What do you want, John? For pity's sake, say it. But none of his mindset will be revealed to the Captain.

'Very well.'

'Hmm. I can see your disappointment in me. I am disappointed in me. Permanently thus.'

'I am vexed. Beset with worry, but not disappointed. Never so.'

'How can I break your ice without breaking your heart, Payton Ake?'

But Captain John Frank did that a long time ago. Mr Ake averts his gaze as his visitor looks up at him. Captain Frank notices Malachy and gives him a stroke. Malachy doesn't usually take so well to strangers, but the Captain is very much a cat man.

'Dunwoody. I want you to watch him. Special detail. Him and his wife. Especially his wife.'

'Why his wife?'

Captain Frank flinches, as if he wants to say more. 'Watch them and report directly to me.'

'Yes sir. How can I watch two people at once?'

Again, Ake's question vanishes into thin air, as if he never asked it. 'I've heard news from London. Big news. We have to be on the right side of this, or we are all doomed in this city. My children and your children.'

Mr Ake takes a moment to digest this. He looks into Captain Frank's eyes and can tell that his ship is sinking. He is doing everything not to let himself be pulled down with it. Protecting an animal like Banastre Dunwoody goes against everything in the Captain's soul. 'Payton, it doesn't need to be said, but I will say it regardless: use the utmost discretion. See but do not be seen. You know the drill.'

Mr Ake smiles and cracks his hammerhead knuckles.

'I was rather hoping you'd give me something. I can't stay holed up in here much longer. You say that you're protecting *me*, but this place is a slow death.'

'There he is again. At last.' Frank smiles and strokes Mr Ake's arm. The hairs rise on the back of his massive hand and Mr Ake edges away to a safe distance. 'I know. Sorry. Abandoned you at your post, did I not? But a good post it is. Efficient, tidy, clean. Pity that the business has become so dirty.'

The Captain glances around the reception. Mr Ake has made it as inviting as a bridewell could possibly be, with a warm fire, scrubbed floors and neat, if austere, furnishings.

'A little adventure wouldn't go amiss, even babysitting.'

John Frank nods and smiles. 'Well, let's hope that this isn't too much of an adventure, eh?'

Mr Ake nods in unison. 'Captain Frank? John?'

'Payton?'

'If we can get through to the other side of this...'

Frank reaches up and touches him on the nose. Mr Ake is not sure whether or not he likes it.

'That is what I hope and pray for. Not just for you and I.'

Mr Ake nods. 'What's really afoot, John? There is more, is there not? You can tell me.'

Frank smiles and slips his riding gloves back on. 'You said, I recall, that you offer me information rather than the other way around. Let's keep it that way. It works. It has always worked.'

'Righto, sir.'

'It's way past my bedtime, Payton. Elspeth will be waiting up for me.'

'Aye sir. I imagine she will be.'

'Good. Nice to see you, Payton.'

'Nice to see you. Sir.'

John Frank doesn't look the slightest bit awkward, yet he has a way of inspiring unease in Mr Ake when there isn't another human or animal on the planet who could achieve such a reaction. He glides to the door and Mr Ake holds it open, ever unsure of whether to be Mr Ake or Payton in the presence of this man, feeling the weight of both identities, as distinct as oil and water.

'Goodnight then.'

'Goodnight, sir.'

And there it is, the answer from Captain Frank himself. He mounts his horse and canters out of the yard. Mr Ake watches on, already mindful of his cover for the assignment and for the interim management of the bridewell while he is absent. At least he might get out the door more often.

#19 TRUE ALLIES

June 20th, 1863

A sultry afternoon on Canning Street, or as sultry as this city gets. The humid heat almost reminds Harriet of the South, although really that is like comparing a warm flannel to a Turkish Bath. Her husband promenades up and down the hallway with Ginger, who arrived via cab half an hour ago. They have said nothing of substance, but their game is now apparent.

The Mayor bid greeting to Harriet (with no recollection of his slurred, inebriated insinuation last time they met, or even anything about last time they met) and scoffed down two large measures of Banastre's best brandy before reluctantly agreeing to walk the short distance to their engagement. How that man has a nose for every liquor cabinet in town. He paces with Banastre, as if they are inspecting the carpet for mites.

The two uptight gentlemen exit the house, mercifully.

Harriet sits on the stairs and lights up her pipe. Conté joins her and, unusually for her, borrows a puff of the fine tobacco.

'It's habit-forming. Be careful,' says Harriet.

Conté shrugs. A sealed envelope pops through the front door. Harriet climbs to her feet, picks it up and opens it. The handwriting is poor, but legible.

Newsham Park bandstand. Noon. Yor frends.

'Can we stop again? I am wrecked.'

'We're nearly there, are we not, Mayor? Do you not know your own city?'

It is an easy, level-enough stroll, but Ginger is never steady on his feet. It is as if the old tar is still on board one of his frigates upon a choppy surf, rolling about the deck. A few times, Banastre considers having to save him from falling into the gutter, only for Ginger to magically right himself to an even keel at the last moment. It dawns upon him that this man is not used to walking anywhere. Perhaps dry land is still anathema to him after years at sea, and only regular libations will correct the imbalance.

Ginger rose to Mayor in quick succession after his retirement from the Royal Navy, but that was more about rank and privilege than aptitude or intellect. Seymour was right, he could have chosen the Whitehall cabinet, but the richest city on Earth proved to be a greater lure. The simple answer is that there are probably more pubs and brothels per square mile here than anywhere in the country, even London.

'The simple deduction is that this Frank fella is an utter oaf who can barely wipe his own ass and relies upon the privilege bestowed to him at birth?'

'Yes,' pants Ginger, 'No. Maybe.'

'You tell me. You know him.'

The Mayor is too out of breath to form a reply. He gasps to a stop. 'Here it is, then.'

Number 9 Catharine Street. As grand a terrace of mansions as there is to be found in this city. High promontory, with splendid views down over the port via giant bay windows that would not look out of place in a cathedral. A place where Captain John Frank can survey every part of his jurisdiction at a glance. Banastre knows that, for all the pomp that pretty much supersedes even his own place on Canning Street, this is just a case of meeting the town Sheriff and laying down some common ground rules in a lawless place. High-time Frank agreed to this, too, and Banastre figures that his own influence has become too much to ignore. Time at last to parlay.

As much as Ginger bleats about his sway in the local chambers, clubs and Cotton Exchange, owning a town requires the cooperation of muscle on both sides of the law, not just a few lackeys in Ginger's pay and cronies in the clubs.

A rap on the brass knocker. The door swings open and Banastre expects a butler but is faced with a huge African man in the uniform of a peeler.

'Damn.'

The Peeler holds out a palm. 'Your gun, sir?'

This sticks in the craw, feeling like a surrender. But it is the price of this meeting; a little trust, a little faith where there is none. He hands over his Smith & Wesson. 'I want it back later. In the same state I gave it you. Don't go playing with it, boy.'

'Surely. Sir.'

'And just so you know. Any double crossing this day will be met with all the hellfire that the Confederacy can throw at you people. Your boss would be foolish to break a truce, mightily so. As for you, you'll end up on a fucking boat or a rope. Just making myself nice and clear from the outset.'

'Surely. Sir.'

'Surely indeed.'

They enter without a further word. Ginger drags himself over the step and shuffles past Frank's bodyguard, nervous as hell.

'Hold your water, Ginger. Remember, I do all the talking.'

They are served tea by a modest glasshouse at the back of Frank's lawn, away from prying eyes and ears except for that menacing totem of a man standing by and to attention. Banastre insisted upon checking the fences and the gullies to the rear of the terraces to alleviate the worries of another attempt on his life. Frank eyes him like he is some sort of post-colonial court jester and Banastre doesn't care too much for the dour Captain's complete lack of deference or grace in his company. Hardly love at first sight.

'Shall I be mother?' says Frank, pouring tea for his companions. The Sheriff is head to toe in tweed, his blazer draped over the back of his chair, waistcoat unbuttoned, with his sleeves rolled up, ever debonaire like a nouveau riche Highland Laird. Yes, just a Sheriff, though. He consults a pocket watch, as if these two interlopers are to be given a time limit on their audience.

'Frank isn't a very Liverpool name?' says Banastre, watching his every move.

'What is a Liverpool name? I'm from Glasgow. Via many other places.'

'I'm also from many other places.'

'Enchanté,' says Frank, as if he's chatting with his neighbour over the garden fence. The Captain drops two sugar lumps into his cup and stirs his tea, tapping out the spoon on the gold rim of the china.

Ginger can only blink at the exchange, as if he is a dog being shown a card trick. Frank hands over a china cup and saucer. Darjeeling. Banastre sniffs it and puts the cup and saucer down on the table. Ain't drinking that, it could be poison. Smells like poison, or a rat's ass. Same difference.

'So, yes. To the matter. Your attempts to shift my person from this mortal coil.' Banastre nods towards the big man standing by the rear of the house, out of earshot but close enough to be seen. 'Surprised you didn't set *that* on me.'

Frank sips. 'He would make short work of you.'

Banastre readily accepts the bait. 'Like your other imbeciles did? Don't think so, Cappy.'

Ginger pipes up, fearing a confrontation. 'Now, now, gentlemen. We came here in good faith looking to find a workable resolution …'

'Shush, Ginger,' mutters Banastre, carrying enough threat in his voice to make it count. 'I won't say it again.'

Frank purses half a smile in amusement. 'Do you always let some American swamp rat use that tone with you, Mayor Harrison? The city really has gone to the dogs when an interloper can command such deference. I confess to being disappointed.'

Ginger shuffles in his seat, wary of how this might develop. Banastre eyes the giant again, but leans in closer to Frank. 'The rank of Captain is not from the Constabulary. I know a Navy man when I see one.'

'How very perceptive of you, Commander.'

'Then I cannot see your logic, your regimen. Why kill me? You British, there is much to admire, but you have gone too far off the edge into folly, and you will lose your Empire in time. Your kindness to your subjects is your weakness. Here and in your colonies.'

Frank couldn't care less. 'That's another debate.'

'It is. But can you tell me … why?'

Frank kicks his legs out beneath the table and folds his arms, throwing his head back like a sullen youth. 'Commander

Dunwoody, would you like me to give you the keys to my house?'

'I don't follow, sir.'

'Or the keys to the city? You have this stout fellow enthralled, although I've long since learned not to trust him or his cronies from The Athenaeum. On the grounds of stupidity rather than any Machiavellian flair, you'll understand.'

Ginger pipes up. 'Oi!'

'Mayor Harrison here would give you the whole caboodle in order to line his pockets. But for me, well...' He shakes his head, making eye contact with the giant. 'Well, it isn't about money. I have money. I am more corrupt than any other man in this city, and that's some going, I promise you. There is nothing left that you can give me that I don't already have, right here in this prison that I have made for myself.'

Now he looks full of melancholy. Is this another test? Banastre can't feel the reassuring weight of his Smith & Wesson against his hip. Was this a mistake? Could he take that obsidian mountain on, hand-to-hand? Frank's talk don't make all this sound so promising. Rather he looks like he is losing his grip.

'So there is nothing left that I can give you? Money? Kudos?' Frank shakes his head. 'And that is why you are trying to stop me? Is this a turf war, Cappy? Is this all about pissing on your territory? With due respect to Ginger, I couldn't care less about that. The tide is turning and this place will become the single most important spot in the British Empire before long, thanks to the trade that I will personally indemnify. London will be the second city to Liverpool; your gracious Queen will build her palaces up here. We will build another New York but bigger and better, right here. We are winning this war.'

Frank sips tea and nods, as if the most obvious thing in the world has just been presented to him. 'Yes, I know you are.'

'You know, you know.' *How* does he know? 'Then just why are you trying to put me in the ground?'

Frank smokes and considers. 'Because I don't like you, Commander. You are an awful cunt and I've met some awful cunts in my time. But you are extra special, sir.'

Banastre considers this for a moment, then throws his arms up and his head back, laughing at the sheer absurdity of it all.

'Sweet baby Jesus. We got a right one here, Ginger. Here was I, racking my brains and it's just plain old beef.'

Frank looks almost offended. 'It is a very reasonable gripe, Commander. You disrupted a balance that took me years to establish, within and without the Liverpool Constabulary. You requisitioned mayhem by paying gangs to do your bidding. Vandalising the legitimate United States Consulate, for instance.'

'Really? That? It's just a bit of shit on his doorstep. A jape.'

'Who made you legitimate, Commander Dunwoody? Who voted for you? You are a criminal who works for criminals.'

'And what are you, then?'

'If you have to ask, you will never know.'

Frank smokes. Ginger wrings his hands. The Peeler pulls on some leather gloves, as if that is meant to intimidate them further.

'What's laughing boy doin'?' asks Banastre. 'He's making me twitch some. You don't want to see what will happen if I twitch too much.'

Frank chuffs away, letting the question stew in the air for a moment. 'Payton. Stand down.'

The Peeler's hard face drops. He wants to protest. Banastre knows insubordination in ferment when he sees it, but the giant step back. Thadda fella.

'He should cheer up. His world might end soon,' grunts Banastre.

The joke is lost on Frank. 'You came to see me. That's a start, I suppose. No one from the other side of your little spat has bothered so much lately.'

'But you haven't been trying to kill Mr Dudley, have you?'

'Because he minds his own business. Keeps it clean, literally. Like you should have.'

'Where does that ever get you? Meaningless injunctions, bureaucracy. The only sum of that is defeat.'

'More so that yours is an unrecognised, illegal state.'

Banastre takes this in. This fella is more crazy again than he thought, but he can work with that. At last, there is something. 'Very well. I acknowledge that. But you shall see that we will have a legitimate relationship soon with a full consulate. Sanctioned by your Government. But then, I guess it will be too late for you, Captain.' Captain Frank stirs his tea again, even though it doesn't need stirring. Banastre sees the play, right in front of his nose. 'And you know this, don't you?'

'Yes.'

Delicious, delightful. This week gets better and better. 'Promise me a truce until then, at least. It will cost you nothing. What else is free in this city that will have such an incalculable value, unimaginable wealth, in just a few short days? I'm not here to run your city; I'm here to cut the deal of the century *with* your city. You don't have to shoot me to be a part of it. We got bigger things going, both you and I.'

'I wouldn't quite go that far, Commander.'

Frank looks back to the house. Banastre eyeballs the giant again. They stare at each other. What the hell is going on there? Lord knows.

'Listen to me, this ain't so bad! It will be glorious. We will usher in a new era of...'

Frank holds up a hand, possibly the only man on the planet that could silence Banastre Dunwoody with such a gesture, but he knows that power is fleeting. 'Spare me the pitch. I gather the drift of it. Now, please, fuck off, both of you.'

'Ha. Good enough.' Banastre sniffs and thrusts out a hand. 'So, no more attacks? No more cockblocking?'

'What a perfectly vulgar expression. You odious man.'

'You know the meaning.' Captain Frank offers back a limp handshake and Banastre grips it. Then he leans back and winks at the giant. Frank stands up and walks away towards the house, nothing more to be said. Whoever put the bug up his ass, it isn't Banastre's concern to remove it. 'Whoo-whee. That was tense.'

The giant emerges onto the lawn and approaches them. He hands the pistol back to Banastre and then walks away himself.

'Let yourselves out,' he says without looking back.

They feel a spot of rain, for the first time in weeks. 'Come on. Now we've settled that matter, we can take care of the other.'

'What other?' mutters Ginger, like a big, lost puppy.

Banastre cracks his jaw and an enormous grin, a man finally where he should be, on top of his world. 'There's a new sheriff in town, and he don't take no bullshit.'

Mr Ake swings the lid of the case back to reveal a mix of currency and gold sovereigns. It was dropped here by a Martin's Bank courier while they were talking, a cheap bribe as per the form of the aforesaid odious man, even though it was made clear that this is not about money. Frank sips his tea, singularly unimpressed.

'I should give this to you, Payton. Should I not?'

'Why did you ask for it?'

'I didn't. But such men only understand guns and money. They want to feel like they're buying something. It puts them in control.'

Mr Ake nods. A fraction of the loot would solve every problem, forever. It bores an immediate hole in his resolve. 'You could give it to me. Or some of it.'

Frank caresses his arm.

'Make your own way out, Payton. Elspeth and the children will be home soon. I will take care of that.'

Mr Ake, as ever, does what Captain Frank asks of him without further question.

#20 AN ILLEGAL GATHERING AT NEWSHAM PARK

June 20ᵗʰ 1863

On horseback, Conté, Harriet and Grace arrive at a bandstand set in the splendid rolling greens of Newsham Park, to the east of the city. This is where the new money lives, but promenading gentry and picnickers are rarer today, thankfully. Perhaps word got out about who was attending the grounds.

Chubb and Pat lean up against the structure. Chubb chews on a liquorice stick while Pat looks wired, if mercifully sober.

Conté goes straight to the smaller man. 'How are you feeling? How is Sarah? The children?'

This could be construed as code for "are you still going to screw us?" but Harriet sees that Conté's intent is less cynical. Kinship emerges in unexpected places sometimes.

'A bit frazzled, suppose,' mutters Pat.

Chubb is more about business, as usual. 'You're quite sure you weren't followed, girls?'

'We grew up in a Choctaw village,' says Harriet.

Chubb exchanges glances with Pat. 'And what the fucking hell's that got to do with the price of fish?'

'They gave money to Ireland during the Hunger,' says Pat, nodding at Conté. She smiles back at him with her eyes, like he's a prodigal brother.

The women dismount. Conté unhooks the saddlebag of her horse. Chubb lifts the flap and glances inside.

'You can disappear now, Mr Chubb. As you wished.'

Chubb's eyes light up and he offers a conspiratorial nod to Pat. 'Aye, that's vanishing money alright so. We could go to New York, Padraig. Take your wife and ankle biters. Buy land. Buy a pub.'

'Or Tahiti. Somewhere warm where I don't have to shiver me bones.'

'Aye. Tahiti. Captain Cook, like.' Chubb dances a little hula.

Conté looks disappointed. 'So that's that then. Our bargain is complete.'

'In exchange for our silence,' grunts Chubb.

'Yes.'

Chubb buckles the saddle bag up and Pat reaches down, kicking the lid off a sturdy chest. It contains the other saddle bag of gold from days ago. Incredulous, the women watch Pat haul and hook the bag up to the other side of Conté's saddle, straining under the load.

'Friggin' weighs a ton, like.'

Conté frowns at the action. 'What are you doing? You need the money. To vanish.'

'Pat kept a little back. One coin, for expenses. And we're going fuckin' nowhere.'

Conté checks the bag. 'But most of it remains. Gentlemen, why are you doing this?'

Harriet shakes her head, smiling from ear to ear. This is some turnaround.

Chubb chews as he talks. 'Let's face it. You three didn't come here to send us on our way, did you?'

'You might be right. We can't do this alone. But you do have a choice, Mr Chubb. From here on, you always have a choice,' says Harriet. The men take their hands out of their pockets and stand firm.

'That's more than any English would give us. They dismiss us as thick, lazy, inferior, inbred. We build their cities and their railways. We fight their wars. They starve us out of our own country. But you know what? Pat came here and survived, didn't you, Pat? Built the legend that is Pat the Cat.'

'I did so, Royston. Weren't all plain sailing like, as you know.'

'All our pals. Our families. All we have is here. We didn't come to Britain, Britain came to us and wiped us out. Liverpool is all that's left, so Liverpool is Ireland now. Suffer as we must with that, so.' Harriet, Conté and Grace all look at each other, then back at Chubb. 'And it's where we stay, ladies. So you need an army? You got one. I'm not hiding any more. Neither is Pat, or any of us.'

Pat places two fingers in his mouth and whistles. Hundreds of figures emerge from over the rise. Conté espies the legions of rough-looking but seriously out-of-shape Irishmen before them, clutching shillelaghs, clubs and sticks. 'Wow.'

Chubb stands tall and proud, as if he is a Roman General. 'I'm done with all this titting about, so I am.'

Every single one of them is a drunk or a physical wreck, an utter mess, but this is the single best sight Conté and Harriet have had since they arrived on these shores. At last, they have their unit. Grace, watching all along, joins their side.

'And I'll help, Mrs Dunwoody. In every way I can.'

Harriet beholds the fervent mass and Conté nods like she is listening to a beat. Here's the city that they never knew and it is mighty. Just maybe, it is the real Liverpool gathered here today.

No one in the crowd of several hundred people notices the horse tied to a tree trunk on the periphery of the park.

Starkey sits up high with a telescope, eyeing the huge throng that has assembled. He picks an apple from a branch and sinks his teeth into it, before spitting it out. 'Pah. Fuckin' worms. Eeeuw.'

He jams the glass up to his eye like he's watching a peepshow.

The large recruitment banner still hangs over the entrance:
LAND, A PENSION AND A WAGE! JOIN THE UNITED STATES ARMY HERE!

Dudley scrubs shit off his front doors again, whistling as he works. He becomes aware of three horses towering over him.

Harriet points at the banner. 'Had many takers, Mr Dudley?'

Dudley shakes his head without even glancing at her. 'Are you here to mock me again, my lady? If not, there's a spare bucket.'

Two huge American flags frame the print of Abraham Lincoln on the wall behind Dudley's oak desk. The place is immaculate, indicative of how much time Dudley spends cleaning it personally. It would be unkind to consider that this and scrubbing shit is all he ever does towards the war effort, but they've both noted it.

Dudley peruses Harriet's stack of diaries and Conté's notes with a magnifying glass, moving on to the code sent by Commander Dunwoody to his High Command containing some deeply concerning news about Whitehall. He keeps peering up at the three women opposite him, screwing his eyes up. 'Why have I heard nothing of this? Who keeps me in the dark?'

Harriet and Conté occupy the Chesterfield chairs on the other side of the sumptuous bureau. Harriet feels the baby kick and jumps but continues with her line. 'You know Major General Butler well?'

Dudley frowns and emits a tiny hiss. Conté can see it written all over his face. It makes more sense now, why they were ordered to steer clear of the official channel, but a house divided cannot stand. 'Butler keeps secrets from even us, so it is no surprise that you were blindsided, sir. We relayed urgent news to him, and still there is nothing back.'

The Consul leans back and massages the bridge of his nose. 'How do I know this isn't one of your husband's tricks? Do you know how much poo I've had to wipe off my windows? Dogs, horses, humans, a filthy detail. You should see how much detergent we get through.'

Harriet leans in. 'The point is, sir, you always wipe it off. No matter how much of it you get. Without fail, without complaint. Without prejudice.'

The cogs in Dudley's brain can almost be seen moving. 'Well, quite so.'

Conté continues the tag team. 'You've challenged the illegal shipbuilding in the courts. And you've hit a wall, sir. We prefer more direct action.'

Dudley nods like a dog and then it is written all over his face. 'Hang on, that business at Cammell Laird with all the Welsh explosives. That… was you?'

Conté smiles, at last proud of their efforts. Maybe they can mean something after all. 'Mr Dudley, you are a decent man and you have played this with an honourable, straight bat.'

Harriet continues from Conté seamlessly. 'But next Monday, the whole world is going to change.' She glances up to Lincoln, who almost nods back down at her. 'Hell awaits and it's no place for decent men. Or women.'

Dudley studies the three of them and looks at Grace, who has put herself in the corner. 'And what's your tale, Missy?'

Grace smiles. 'We haven't got long enough, Mr Dudley.'

The Consul considers the trio of strange women and their even stranger mission.

'Follow me to the cellars. I have something to show you.'

Even the basement is in pristine condition, with not a cobweb in sight. Column by column of paper files in alphabetical order are further testament to Dudley's tight ship. At the far end of a cavernous room, he opens the first of a long row of trunks and pulls out a blue Union Cavalry Private's uniform, holding it up.

'We had to put them in airtight vessels to keep the moths off them.'

The women nod. Conté is first in with the important question. 'How many have you got?'

'How many do you need?'

#21 SHOWDOWN AT LIME STREET
Part Two

June 21ˢᵗ, 1863

Pissing rain outside. The Crown is as packed as ever, boards covering the blown-out windows, scorch marks on the walls and furniture. Raucous, rambunctious, rebel songs rattle around the walls, damning Oliver Cromwell and just about every other greedy English interloper into Eire.

The double doors swing open and Chubb enters with Pat, both men wearing boozy grins.

Pat fishes the gold coin from his pocket and slaps it down hard on the countertop. Chubb pulls out a thick club, his shillelagh, rapping it on the bar. 'My fuckin' round. Get 'em in! Everyone's on the piss, tonight!'

Cheers abound. Pat is in his ear. 'Our fuckin' round, Royston. Our fuckin' round.'

'Aye, son.'

Chubb and Pat pour themselves out of The Crown, followed by a huge entourage, joining countless others who have turned up on the street. The whole city is out celebrating with them this night, it seems.

'Everyone back to my house?' grunts Chubb.
Pat, still at his side, starts peeling away. 'I'd better get home. I'm on a curfew, like.'

Chubb looks like he's going to protest at the early exit of his favourite crony, but too much has gone on between them lately. He kisses Pat on the head and ruffles his hair. 'Away with you then, ye little bollocks. Don't be causing trouble.'

It's a moment, but then Pat's eyes widen and a surge of horror rises up from his guts. Banastre steps out in front of them, striding down the cobbles with a deadly purpose. A hoard of Peelers packing long sticks and clubs back him up, the corrupt ones Pat knows to a man. This is worse than a couple of Starkey's shit bombs.

Chubb sees them too, now. 'Ah, fuck.'

Banastre raises his Smith & Wesson and shoots Chubb between the eyes, killing him instantly. Screams as Peelers on horseback wade into the small crowd, batons swinging.

The American devil makes a beeline for Pat, who is gasping for air. 'You demon. Satan be gone,' says Pat.

'We have unfinished business, Mr McCartney.'

Pat spits, aware that Peelers are closing in, surrounding him and the others. 'Away. Away with you. Evil diabhal.'

'I own this city now, so you better play nice and tell me who is paying you. I may let you live. I may let your wife and children live. I may not, but you gonna inform me presently either way, boy.'

Pat glares back, helpless, staring down the barrel as the man who is the closest thing he's ever had to a father lies twitching, dead at his feet. 'No. Not Sarah. Please no. I'll tell you anything. I'll tell you, Devil.'

Behind him, a manhole cover has been lifted. Strong hands and bodies absorb Pat, and he drops down to the sewer beneath. Banastre shoots into the crowd, taking a couple more down. Pandemonium ensues and the Peelers are ready for it. They steam into the throng on horseback and on foot, hooves trampling, truncheons swinging.

Dressed in his civvies but known to the Peelers, Crispin Starkey stands at the side chewing a cud of fine tobacco, altogether proud of his work. He takes in the symphony of violence, particularly the corpse of Chubb, does a little jig on the spot and saunters off, hands in pockets. So many opportunities in this Liverpool, everywhere the eye wanders. He had to leave Limerick in a hurry, but he's so glad he chose to come here.

Then Starkey spots him; the golden goose. In the thick of the action, the man who paid him solidly for this information stands proud, at last content in the eye of the chaos, a place he was born to be. The glow from the street lamps bounces off his pale green eyes. It is His Satanic Majesty and, truth be told, he can see that the American doesn't mind his new badge too much. It's kinda sexy.

'I said, I own this town.' Banastre Xavier Dunwoody yells, firing his gun in the air before stomping off away from the trouble he has created. Starkey swoons a little, before slipping away down a narrow entry with the stealth of a rodent.

Ginger waits by a carriage as Banastre approaches. 'Curiosity satisfied?'

'Not really.'

'Oh?'

'I took care of that potato-faced ape, at least.'

'What-ho. Good show. I think.'

Banastre shakes his head. 'No. Ain't good enough.'

'Not long, and it will be right as rain, sir. I'll vouch. Don't let a few common paddywhacks get under your skin. They're nothing. It's in their breeding to be workshy and drunk.'

'Shut your saggy ass, Ginger. I've heard enough from you.'

Banastre mounts his horse and races away from the devastation he's caused like he's on a cavalry charge.

Mr Ake stands by and watches as Banastre gallops along, breezing past like an apocalypse. The American recognises him, offering a brisk salute laced with sarcasm. On cue, there is a huge peal of thunder and a flash as the roof of the Crown takes a bolt, the steeple collapsing, as if commanded by Banastre himself. Shrieks of terror ripple down the street at the biblical timing. Mr Ake holds fast and still, watching on as a troop of the worst officers from the Liverpool Constabulary do the American's dirty work, paid handsomely to a man, now completely unrestricted by the edicts of their Chief Constable. Is this really the end of the world?

He debates with himself whether or not to return up the hill and entreat John, telling him about what he has just seen. But what is the point of that? What will he get back apart from doe eyes and frailty where there once was passion and strength? Instead, he leaves his "colleagues" to their work and heads away in the direction Commander Dunwoody went. Heaven help this city. The rain starts to pour in, riding a sudden squall; hard and

163

pelting, rods of water slicing through the humid air as a stream of blood flows into the drains.

Heaven help Captain John Frank, for even Mr Ake knows that this is on him.

#22 THE MORNING AFTER

June 22nd, 1863

Sunrise in Newsham Park. The mood is sombre among the men of the *cavalry*, but those who survived last night intact are all present, if not entirely correct. Deathly silent, bruised and beaten but remaining in their droves, several hundred Fenians in ill-fitting blue Union Army uniforms line up for inspection as Dudley and Grace check out a new delivery on the back of a wagon.

'What an earth have you got for us now, dear?'

'We borrowed it from the museum on William Brown Street. Well, I say borrowed…'

'Oh?'

She pulls the tarpaulin: a Napoleonic era cannon, replete with rusted iron shot balls. Dudley shakes his head and strokes his bald pate.

'Oh. Very good, Grace. Very good.' He claps his hands together. 'Right, then.'

Crispin Starkey lopes up to the front entrance of the Dunwoody mansion in full peeler uniform, boots polished, hair slicked, like he's calling on a young lady for a date.

He rings the doorbell.

Conté answers. Starkey stands exaggeratedly wide, pushing his pelvis out, cap in hand.

'Yes?'

Starkey smiles and raises himself up onto his tiptoes. 'Aren't you going to invite me in, then?'

'No.'

'The Big Boss Man not home, then?'

'None of your business.' Conté goes to shut the door.

'Suppose I'll find him across town. The Athenaeum. Or The Coffee House on Castle Street with all them nice ladies upstairs. Or Leather Lane. Or the Town Hall. Suppose it won't take me long altogether to find The Big Boss Man, I don't think so. You see, I know him and he knows me.'

Conté stops. Harriet emerges behind her. Starkey bows. 'Ah, your ladyship come to greet me. Charmed so. Good morning to you.'

Harriet cranes her neck. 'What do you want?'

'Ooh. Some of that lovely gold your eejit man and his culchie friend refused. Can you believe how stupid that is? Did I say some of it? I meant fuckin' all of it. You going to let me in, or am I to keep blabbing about this and that on your doorstep, then?' Harriet nods and gently guides the door open, but Starkey stays rooted, enjoying this little game of his own creation. 'Ooh, The Big Boss Man, did he stay out all night again? What kind of Daddy to your Babbee does that, eh? Shocking, so, 'tis I reckon.'

Conté grits her teeth, quickly scanning the exterior for anyone watching. 'Get inside.'

Starkey grins, salutes and steps in, eyes all over her. 'Aye, aye, chicken pie.'

A horn. The deep bellow of The SS Leinster, an Irish Sea steamer, moored at the Landing Stage. Droves disembark, but far fewer souls embark for the journey back. The sign reads: *Dublin Ferry, North Wall, steerage only.*

Pat accompanies his children and Sarah towards the gate. Each of the kids holds a hemp sack with the exception of the baby in Sarah's arms. The sum total of everything they have is not much more than the clothes on their backs. He gazes over his shoulder in the direction of Goree Piazza and stops, mesmerised. Is this the last he'll ever see of this place?

'Shite,' Pat mutters, just as a sudden, rapid horde of incoming steerage passengers wash into them. Then he turns back to Sarah, but she's not there.

Where are they? Where in hell?

'Sarah? Sarah!' Pat's guts tremble and – in an instant – he is alone in a vast crowd. The human traffic is raucous and incessant. Peddlers, hustlers and grifters are upon the stage, appearing in a flash, ready to make promises they'll never keep to the hungry and desperate or to skim the pockets of those who have anything to their name. Pat shoves his way against the tide and climbs a lamppost like a salamander, proving his hoodlum name of The Cat in the most desperate of moments. Where? Where? Where? For an agonising few seconds, he can't make out his family in the hubbub. He recalls the shot to Royston's head and all the screaming and panic on Lime Street, just before they pushed him down, down, down through that hole and closed the grate. Nothing could be heard down there but the swish of piss and shit and the scurrying of rats.

'Sarah! For God's sake!'

'Padraig! Over here, you numbskull. What's the matter with you?'

He glances down and behind him. They're at the foot of the post. They were there all along, at his side, where they should be. He jumps down and embraces her. The incoming traffic funnels around them, and his desperation washes over into relief.

'I'm sorry, Sarah. I'm so sorry.'

'Why, love? Why are you sorry?'

'Because I made this happen. This is all on me.'

Sarah caresses him, the sweetest of women. 'There's nothing to regret and nothing to stay for, Pat. We've family over the water. It's our true home. That's all. We made a go of it here, but it wasn't to be.'

'Yes. I know. I just…'

'What good to me or them are you dead?'

'I'm sorry for being a terrible husband, so.'

Sarah nods, adjusts the baby and passes him over to Pat. She picks up a hemp bag with her meagre belongings and slings it over her shoulder. 'You're a fine husband and an even better father. Just give yourself the chance.'

'Say that to me the next time I land home drunk.'

'Come on, husband, pappy. Boarding time.'

They file through the gate towards the boat and away from this city forever.

Over at the Seraglio, Banastre wakes up on the same chaise longue that he used to share with Nancy. He misses her. There's no one quite as good. Another anonymous cooze lies next to him. He peels the crusty satin sheet off his bare body and then hauls himself up to his feet.

His pocket watch lies in a bundle of clothes on the floor. It was relieved from a steamboat passenger on a raid once, back in another lifetime. Quite the heirloom. He consults it and considers Harriet and the baby.

'I stink of bad cooze. Need a hot bath.'

As Commander Dunwoody lumbers out onto Castle Street and hails a hansom cab, Mr Ake watches him from an alley. He might be the biggest, toughest fellow in Liverpool, but he knows how to stay hidden when needs be, even in broad daylight, even in the bright morning sun. He'll always find the shallows and the shadows – in a savannah, the hold of a ship or the streets of a city.

He mounts his strong, black steed and trots out, tailing at a distance. Makes a nice change from the bridewell.

Conté slides a slice of mutton pie in front of Starkey and he promptly shovels it down. He looks far too at home here. Thank God most of the staff are off sick with typhus.

Next to him on the table are gold coins, heaved in here by Conté and stacked. Small wonder the little prick looks happy as Larry. 'So where was you hiding them?'

Conté and Harriet sit opposite him at the kitchen table. Conté speaks back. 'In the horse trough.'

'Clever so. I didn't think to look there.' Starkey taps his temple. 'Smart girls, you two. Pretty too, like. I might take a fancy.'

Harriet eyes Conté, Conté eyes Harriet. What now? 'Will that be all, Mr Starkey?'

'Mistress, you may call us Crispin. Or Chrissie. Or Chris. Any of them.'

'Yes, Mr Starkey,' replies Harriet, her face as straight as when he entered the household.

Starkey stuffs the last of the pie into his mouth and dusts the crumbs from his hands. 'I gots to move the bits next, you know. I need help so.'

Conté shrugs. 'Not our problem.'

'Now, here I was thinking we was all starting to get along. Then you start with that arsey tone again.'

Harriet tries to compensate. Let's not lose this over ruffled feathers. 'Conté will get you a horse. Won't you, Conté?'

'I want a sturdy one. I like that grey pony owned by that funny little witch friend of yours. Roolapindi.'

Conté squirms in her seat. 'Rosalinda. Yes.'

'Good nag that. I'll keep her into the bargain, so I will. She here? The horse whisperer imp? I owe her something I do.'

Harriet nods. 'Grace can be here.' Conté seethes. 'I'm sure she'll be happy to help.'

Conté is rooted to her chair.

'Go fetch then,' he orders, face full of pie. 'The master will be back soon, I'll bet. Even he has to come home at some point, so you had better shake a leg. You don't want him seeing me here, do youse?'

Conté pulls a short, sharp blade from her lapel and whips it in the direction of Starkey. It embeds in his shoulder. He looks back in shock, climbing to his feet.

'Harriet, leave him to me.'

Harriet jumps up and circles Starkey, who pulls out the blade. 'Ow!' He reaches into the small of his back and pulls out a Browning pistol. 'Silly of youse. That smarts, so it does. I'll have to slot youse both now, so I will. Explanations later and a big reward from the big man.' He points the gun at Conté. 'Pity as I quite fancied you, so.'

Harriet darts towards the oak door to the staircase leading to the stables. A cast iron frying pan hangs above the stove. She grabs it and runs at Starkey, swinging. He gets off a shot which pings off the pan. It impacts him on the temple, caving the side of his head in. He twitches and slumps, pie falling out of his open mouth.

Harriet grips the pan. Conté studies the fresh corpse. 'What did I tell you about always packing your gun?'

'I'm at home, Conté.'

'Especially at home.'

She places the pan on the kitchen table. The front door slams upstairs. A dull but raucous and pissed-off grunt can be heard, horribly familiar. 'Where's that goddamn Creole? Run me a bath! Harriet!'

'When are the servants back?' Harriet asks Conté.

'Wallace and the others have typhus, but Penny's at market. So any time.'

'Shit, shit, shit.'

The baby kicks. Damn this indigestion. Harriet wipes her hands down and barrels upstairs, leaving Conté to deal with Starkey.

Conté drags the corpse up the stone steps, his half-destroyed head thumping against the stone and leaving a crimson trail. Mr Ake watches her from the bushes, incredulous.

'I want it nice 'n' hot.' Banastre pulls his long johns off and gets naked as Harriet runs the bath.

'No problem, dear.'

'This ain't becoming of the lady of the house. Running baths, common chores. No, won't have it.' He sits and watches her, lighting his pipe, scratching and sniffing. 'Where's that stoopid-assed maid or yours? Sour puss, sour pussy.'

Conté drags Starkey's dead weight inside the empty stable and hauls him up, with considerable strain, into the trough, dipping him in the water. He bobs up like a ducking apple, an expression of surprise still upon the half of his face that isn't caved in. She searches around and finds yard irons and saddles, anything she can get her hands on to weigh him down.

'What is it? Baby kicking again?' Harriet prepares salts and oils. Banastre frowns, getting to his feet. 'You flat shouldn't be doing that in your condition, sweetness. I'm going to whup that goddamn maid good and proper when I see her.'

'No, darling. I want to do this for you.'

Banastre grunts and heads for the door. He picks his belt up from the chair and flexes it. Harriet knows what's coming next. 'It's plain wrong. High time I did this. You done protected her long enough, that pet of yours.' Harriet, sweating and panting, blocks his path. Conté appears, gasping for breath for different reasons.

'You were gone all night again. I was beside myself, Banastre. What am I to do? Now, why don't you relax now? You've had a long night.'

Her husband grips the swatch, as if still mindful of using it. 'You don't care too much. I ain't blind.' Banastre leans into her, smelling fear. Will he thrash both of them?

Harriet matches his glare, showing steel back at him. Fuck him, fuck him to hell. 'Votre bains est prêt, mon chéri.'

Conté does her best to get into his line of vision. 'Your bath is ready, sir.'

#23 THE COTTON EXCHANGE

June 23rd, 1863

Conté endeavours to avoid serving Banastre at any time, relying upon her status as Mistress Harriet's maid over any tasks that would bring her into the radius of the husband. As the one and only member of the household staff brought here from across the Atlantic, it seems that the Master of the House actively selected her to deliver his breakfast and papers this morning, specific to the subject matter they contain.

In the last week, Banastre has decided that he can't bear sleeping with Harriet due to the fevers and bodily functions of her pregnancy, and he has removed himself to a guest bed, which is a small mercy. Less than a mercy is that Conté is having to spend longer than a second alone in his company, as the outbreak of typhus in the area still curtails the household staff. It is too early in the day even for Banastre to be drunk and then to misbehave in his time-honoured fashion, but she feels a cold sweat on the nape of her neck regardless, as he stuffs kippers into his mouth and scans the paper. He hasn't dismissed her yet, which adds to the weight of this worry. Some lines remain to be crossed, and they are getting mighty close.

She attends to him, hands crossed and back to the wall. He washes down the fish with percolated coffee and sneers at the article in a week-old *New York Times*.

'Yankee filth. Have you read this utter ass wipe?' he waves the paper in Conté's direction, spitting kipper bones. 'No? They're probably just squiggly lines on a page to you. Well, let me indulge you.'

Banastre clears his throat. Conté read the paper cover to cover when it arrived at 4am this morning, as she does every morning with all the Liverpool, London and Manchester broadsheets and periodicals. The news made her sick and angry in equal measures.

'A trade delegation of Federal diplomats, bi-partisan officials, businessmen and representatives from several major cities under Union control have departed New York headed for the port of Liverpool, due to arrive this morning. Spokesman for the delegation and erstwhile Governor in Occupation of the city of New Orleans, Major General Benjamin F. Butler, commented… blah blah blah.' Banastre leans back, rummaging beneath the sheets. He quietly growls, 'So, the Fat Man cometh. Useless pricks in Richmond could have warned me, couldn't they? No doubt the greaseball thinks he can lord it over Liverpool like he does over New Orleans. Fat bastard.'

He balls the paper up and launches it across the room in Conté's direction. She gathers it up from the floor.

'Well, I for one can't wait to see his goddamn jowly walrus ass of a face when he enters Exchange Square. He'll get laughed all the way back to Boston fricking harbour.' Banastre shuffles in bed and eyes Conté up and down and down and up. 'Never liked me much, have you, girl?' Conté chooses not to respond, although she has an arsenal of ripostes for him stored in the silos of a febrile mind. 'Oh, I forgot. You're not a slave over here. You're an indentured servant. Woo-hoo. Well, now, if that ain't the future as some see it. Still, your tight, round little ass belongs to Harriet and Harriet's big, sweet china white ass belongs to me, so you can figure the rest, honey child. I gets whatever I wants on a plate, when I wants it.' He puts his breakfast tray to one side and considers her, his eyes moving in far too close. 'You see, you and I got a date with each other. I ain't gonna do nothing to upset my Harriet, way things are, but you're going to learn a few lessons from your master after that baby is born. Them eyes of yours, sassy and wild. Mmm, I like that, and I'll enjoy removing that sass like I'm enjoying telling you this right now. Coming to getcha. Huh. Indentured fuckin' servant in-deed.'

His right arm is moving rhythmically beneath the sheets, pumping up and down, but his glare remains constant. Still, Conté gives him nothing. He grunts, shunts around the bed and sighs. 'Real good. Better.'

'Yessir.'

'Bring me up a towel.'

'Yessir.'

'And a day suit, the herringbone. Then draw me a bath. Looks like I got business across town. Wars to win.'

'Yessir.'

'Yessir indeed. Three bags full, dammit,' he mutters, 'Now, get.' Conté steps out. 'Ha.'

The house closes in on her, as if she has taken some Mexican tincture of peyote or her morning tea has been spiked with some ancient and occult Haitian medicine. Not much of either in Liverpool, though. Her heart thumps in her chest, demanding restitution. Maintaining focus with a murderous rage boiling up inside – like a lake of brimstone – is not easy. She paces around the U-shaped landing, the ornate, domed skylight fanning out all the colours of the rainbow, the sun diffusing through stained glass. Going to be another warm day, or warm by Liverpool standards. Easing the door open, it seems like the occupant is still asleep, but this can't wait.

Harriet has been as sick as a dog since yesterday evening. Nothing has been mentioned in the local press about the terror on Lime Street, but Conté is beside herself in the need to parlay what Grace and Dudley have in store, alongside this other news about the Union delegation. Why in hell couldn't Butler have sent prior warning? Just what is wrong with that slug of a man?

Harriet is bedridden now and unable to hold down anything. Conté can't get a moment with her without some physician ordered by Banastre fussing about her, or rather making sure that the baby is doing well. All clear at the moment, though.

Conté checks her for any evidence of smallpox, typhus or tuberculosis, a trio of modern plagues, each likely to kill or maim her severely in her current condition. Her skin is clear and her temperature is in the normal range, so it must be fatigue or a simple ague.

Maybe she could go herself to the Cotton Exchange, attached as Banastre's retinue, but then he'll parade her as his property in front of his hobble-de-hoy cronies and, of course, the Union delegation. What will Butler think? Why should she care? Any sort of victory has disappeared over the horizon. Perhaps they are better off out of sight, but that is how men like women to be.

'Harry. Sorry. I have to wake you.' Harriet stirs. Conté checks her forehead again and then strokes it. 'Harriet Farrell, come now.'

'We were back by the river,' murmurs Harriet, 'with the whole tribe. The War was over, or maybe it hadn't even begun. Either way, it felt sweet. It felt free.'

Conté continues to caress her brow. 'And here you are. I've returned you to this dirty old world. Damn this mouth and these prodding fingers.'

Wakefulness finally takes hold of Harriet and she focuses upon Conté. 'What confounds you, Conté?'

'I've just watched him eat his breakfast.'

'Oh. Watching him eat is always an ordeal.'

'Butler is pending. He'll arrive at the landing stage presently. Then he'll take his party straight to the Cotton Exchange.'

Harriet moves to get out of bed.

'What magnificent timing our great leader has. Then we must join my lovely husband and accompany him. Why didn't Butler tell us that he was coming?'

Conté mutters, 'Same reason he keeps us in the dark about everything. We don't exist, remember. I'm not so sure that we should see him, Harry. It may complicate things.'

'It's an opportunity. He will be here for us. At last.'

'I'm not so sure, Harry.'

Harriet stops in her tracks. 'What's the problem?' she asks.

'I might kill him myself. For what he has done to you. To us.'

'Conté, we must soldier on. How many times have I said it?'

'How many times must he piss me off?'

'Well, we'll just have to remind him that we exist.'

'Why must I always be second fiddle in my own life? Why must my instincts – instincts which are always good – be continually dismissed? Why can't I do what my grandfather did?'

'Because you are an agent of the United States Government, Conté. As am I. And you are not in Haiti.'

Harriet forces herself up, grunting and heaving. 'You're not at all well, Harry,' says Conté. 'I'll go; I'll handle Butler and Banastre.'

'You know the deal. This is The Blob we're talking about, and we are his agents.'

'He'll hit the roof if he finds out about-'

'-We'll handle it and him. Is showing initiative such a crime? Let's get ready.'

For the first time ever, Conté feels like Harriet's servant for real. 'Yes, Miss Harriet.'

Harriet recognises this and checks herself. She squeezes Conté's hand.

This is the busiest it has been here in weeks, and there is a very good reason for that.

A huge mob has assembled in the open square of the Cotton Exchange, directly behind the Town Hall. A place of enterprise, a place where a sharp fellow can make a name for himself and a fortune in short order. A place teeming this afternoon with angry men looking for recompense, stoked up by the voices planted within their ranks by Banastre and Mayor Harrison.

These men, who bustle and fight for their place at the top table, do so with pride in their elite membership of the Liverpool Cotton Traders Association. The American Dream began here, leagues and fathoms and knots away from the virgin soil. It has been a vastly profitable arrangement for decades now. Until recently, until that damned blockade.

Which is exactly the kind of horseshit that Harriet and Conté find themselves having to listen to every time the exchange is opened up to the lesser mortals of the city and the world, ergo women. Wives and daughters are permitted here on such a ceremonial day, when Liverpool gets to bluster about its own fame and bloated wealth. These two women know, as they step out of the carriage and onto Water Street, that it is the base infliction of suffering upon fellow humans that props up this vast mountain of money, more than anything else. More than the clever machinery in the mills, the smokestacks or the wheeler-dealering in this place. More than the ornate, Ionic columns or neo-classical splendour. More than the lazy platitudes of spoilt, angry white men and their self-entitlement.

Slavery was abolished several decades ago in Great Britain, yet it underpins an entire economy right here and now, in plain sight on this cinder floor, a place above the law, a place that makes its own rules that supersede anything or anyone else. Behold again, those carved stone African faces staring down from the ornate creation of the Town Hall next door; their silent, permanent submission etched in the relief of the stonework like gargoyles. This place and all these fortunes are carried on their backs, trampling on their souls, but there are no tributes to that. This is what two women of the Mississippi must fight, in the heart of darkness. Amongst everything else in a war that grows more savage, desperate and complex daily, this open square is the very centre of the Battle of Liverpool, and today it is a gladiatorial pit.

Conté squeezes Harriet's hand as they follow Banastre in full swagger down a narrow lane that leads to the back of the Town Hall and to where the magic happens. Red, white and blue banners greet them, with a gantry and platform holding a selection of dignitaries that include Ginger and most of his Athenaeum chums, esteemed members of the Chamber of Commerce, Lord and Lady Derby, and just about every monied big shot in this city. A brass band plays patriotic favourites, military tunes and anthems. No Irish jigs here. Here are all the old money and new money gathered in one place. Conté wishes she still had that Welsh dynamite, as it could be put to very good use right now.

They climb up the wooden steps to the scaffold, lifting skirts and petticoats. It occurs to Harriet that this is not unlike a public hanging, with the feeling of dread welling up within her, exacerbated by the eyes of one Maj. Gen. Benjamin Butler scanning her person like a disapproving headmaster. Banastre makes a beeline for him and Butler rises to his feet. Ginger senses the tension and potential embarrassment, tearing himself away from Lord Derby and following his Confederate chum in his wake.

'Welcome to Liverpool, Benjamin. You're sure a long way from The Crescent.'

Butler emits his trademark grimace, or smile, whichever is anyone's guess. He shakes Banastre's hand. The temporary truce produces a weird electricity that Harriet and Conté can feel from a few paces behind. If The Blob thinks this is neutral ground, he is sorely mistaken.

'I'm surprised that you're not decked out in your grey and gold this morning, Banastre. I speculated with my delegation that you'd be fair ready to take a gunboat out into the Mersey and let our steamer have it.'

Banastre laughs. 'That wouldn't be very sporting now, would it, Benny? I wouldn't want to embarrass you on your big day. I'm sure you'll do a great job of embarrassing yourself.'

'And when's your big day coming then, Dixie?'

'That would be telling. But you ain't stopping it.'

Butler's retinue stare through Banastre as the men spar. Banastre drinks it in. The only exception is Consul Thomas Haines Dudley, who wears an impassive smile and perches on his seat with a straight back, in the company of his equally stiff wife. He emits a tiny nod in the direction of Harriet and Conté.

Butler admires Harriet's bump. 'This is your new bride, I take it? I can see that you haven't wasted any time in producing the next line of Dunwoody?' The Blob takes her hand, kisses it and claps his heels together. He doesn't even register Conté.

'Nice to meet you, Major General.'

'Ma'am, will the baby be British? American? Rebel?'

Banastre intervenes, as she expects: 'Liverpolitan, sir.'

Ginger guffaws like a plump bird. 'Good answer, Banastre. Bravo.'

Stood next to each other, the American General makes the Mayor look positively slimline. In the United States, big means huge. Ginger scoffs and waddles back to his seat.

Butler smiles, keeping his cordiality up in plain sight. 'Yes indeed, Mayor. Good answer.'

The two rivals shake hands again, knuckles whitening. The crowd of company men and traders below has swelled, all interested to see the powerplay taking place up above. Harriet takes her place next to Banastre and Ginger. All sit.

Banastre grunts into Harriet's ear as Butler approaches the podium behind Ginger. 'Now watch him fall right smack on his wide Yankee ass. You watching?'

'Yes.'

'Yes what?'

'Yes, darling.'

'Yes sirree.'

Conté scans the crowd as Ginger stands and holds his palms up, bidding for quiet among the boisterous throng. Many of them look like they've been at the booze already this afternoon and she notes the presence of Peelers on the outskirts of the square in case it gets less than gentlemanly, which it often does here.

Ginger waves his arms about the air. 'Now then, members! Ladies are present, and I bid you to be on your best behaviour for our guests.'

Out comes a heckle. 'Thought this was the Cotton Exchange, not the Pie Exchange.'

Ginger presses a finger to his lips. Banastre chuckles. Conté notices a Peeler watching her intently, a man she has not seen before but who she cannot miss due to his huge stature and quintessentially sharp Igbo jawline and build. He remains stone-still in his body and eyes, hidden in plain sight. But she sees him.

Butler takes the podium. 'Mayor Harrison, I thank you kindly. Lord and Lady Derby, esteemed guests, gentlemen of the Cotton Exchange.' A fragile hush descends, and not for the first time today, Harriet wonders why Butler wanted to come all this way for such a bum steer. Just how desperate are they? 'Now then, many of you know that I hail from Boston and not New Orleans, but the Crescent City has come under my auspices owing to the actions of war. I am here to present a unique opportunity for the businesses of Liverpool to engage directly with the city, which remains by some distance the biggest port in the South. It is the present and future gateway for all commerce in the region. Of course, the passage of the war may concern you, and I am sure that you all feel that you are backing what you perceive as the fittest pony, but I know that this is not about deciding who wins, but rather who pays. I know your bottom line.'

Harriet steals a glance at Conté. *Nice try, sir.*

A heckler interjects. 'And they pay more, so piss off home, you Yankee porker.'

From another side of the square, more heckles. 'If he stays for much longer, he'll eat all the fucking Mayor's pies.'

Ginger is moved to get to the top of his lungs. 'Gentlemen! Manners! Language! Ladies present!'

Butler announces himself again, ramping up the theatrical projection. He's used to sitting in courts and the hubbub of assemblies. 'That's alright, Mayor. You men remind me of Bostonians and New Yorkers in your gruff, direct tones, and I understand your cynicism, I really do. But consider this, we have vastly superior naval power, control of the entire Mississippi basin and, therefore, the Gulf and Eastern Seaboard. If you choose to trade with us, we will suspend all export duties and provide free warehousing stateside for all your goods. We will guarantee a lower price on all cotton exported from areas within Union lines than the other side, and we will freeze these prices beyond the conclusion of our conflict for a year. If I may cut to the chase, you need to back the winner here and for all the bluster and chicanery of the Confederacy – their mercantile allure and their Rebel Yell – the facts about our position have a direct bearing on your existence right here in Liverpool and upon our entire network. I beg you to look forwards, not backwards. This is about your profits and your trade; I know it would be churlish to broach any other subject in this square.'

At the first opportunity, another heckler pipes up. 'And are you going to pick the cotton yourself then, fatso?'

Ginger is on his feet, waving a paper like the Speaker of the House of Commons. 'Oi! Less of it, sir! I'll bar you, I say, sir!'

Banastre raps his cane against the platform and snorts. Harriet rubs her bump.

Butler holds up a hand, playing the diplomat. 'Future agriculture and industry will not require slave labour, sir. Or the labour of big-boned Bostonians like me.'

The play on words runs flat among the crowd. He's not in some Massachusetts courtroom trading quips with an educated audience; he's in the pit. An egg hurtles over and strikes Butler square upon his bulbous forehead with a resounding splat, to the intense amusement of the throng. Peelers carve their way into the crowd, dispersing the trouble and collaring the culprit, who is removed from the floor, grinning and laughing. Butler smiles and wipes yellow goo off his bald pate with a napkin.

Ginger screams, 'Order! I really must apologise on behalf of the city and the Exchange for this unruly behaviour. Are you men savages? What's the matter with you, I say! Order!'

Banastre seethes under his breath, more into Harriet's ear. 'Don't lay it on thick, Ginger. There's a good chap.'

Dudley rises and grips Butler by the elbow, whispering into his ear. For a moment, Harriet can see rage etched into what is normally a gentle, rational countenance. Butler eases the Consul back, smiling at him all the way. Banastre continues to rap the tip of his cane against the platform, revelling in the mess he saw coming from across the Atlantic in the morning news.

Ginger raises himself higher on the gantry, bidding to be heard over the raised disquiet. 'We shall retire for the civic reception and lunch. Gentlemen, you are an embarrassment! A bloody shower you are! The lot of yer! A disgrace.'

'Put a cork in it, Ginger.'

'Whose side are you on, Mayor?'

'Yanks out! Yanks out! Yanks out! Yanks out!'

A chant rises of Yanks Out, undiminished by the Peelers' meek attempts to break up the disorder. Butler relents and he beckons his delegation to follow him as he removes himself from the platform. Conté uses the distraction to get to Harriet's ear. 'Well, that went well.'

Right on cue, a peal of thunder announces another lightning flash and torrential shower of rain. This does a better job of dispersing the sneering traders than the Peelers ever could, and they retire to the hostelries surrounding Exchange Flags in order to pump themselves up with more beer and bluster, rejoicing in their easy victory. It's what their Confederate cousins call a turkey shoot.

The statue of Admiral Nelson, another slaver, is impassive in the hubbub, as is the figure of Mr Ake standing to attention on the edge, not joining in with his fellow Peelers in their redundant attempts to control uncontrollable men way above their station, pumped and righteous in their new wealth. Mr Ake watches Conté, Mr Ake watches Harriet, Mr Ake watches Commander Dunwoody. Then Mr Ake pencils a note in his pocket book, and he removes himself from the square with his customary, preternatural élan.

Heading home at last. Not like him to refuse food, Butler absconded from the reception before the main course was served. No one missed him. Dudley and his wife stuck it out. Harriet cited the usual pains and left Banastre in the company of his favourite boozing buddy to drink up their moral victory, safe in the knowledge that the real version is pending. He doesn't even acknowledge her as she leaves.

Conté and Harriet say nothing on the trip home, even though the carriage is a safe space. It is as if there is no plot, as if Harriet really is the demure Southern Belle doting over her perfect gentleman of a husband and glowing in the prospect of their imminent arrival, with her childhood servant forever at her side, a little bit of the antebellum exported into a hansom cab.

On arrival at 101 Canning, they retire to the kitchen and Conté makes black tea on the stove, which they enjoy with freshly-baked digestive cookies to settle Harriet's belly.

Promptly, there is a stiff, firm knock on the basement door to the staff quarters. Who could this be on a rainy early evening? Banastre wouldn't be expected home until much later, especially in a moment that allows him to showboat in such close proximity to the enemy, albeit only Dudley whom he roundly abuses thrice daily anyway. If Harriet was feeling more like talking, she'd tell Conté that this is the real reason for her wanting to duck out early, but like most things, this doesn't need to be said.

It can only be one person, and both of them were hoping that it would not be so. Conté answers and there stands Butler, without a trace of his retinue or security detail, a portly gentleman out for a late evening stroll. As to be expected, he has left the niceties in his first-class cabin.

'Get your coats and shoes. I want you two to come for a walk with me. Right now, if you please.'

They walk at a fast pace uphill towards Catharine Street, at a quick enough march to challenge the Major General's breath. Butler emits verbal barbs in between paces, ten times more alert and furtive than the act he performed at the Cotton Exchange.

'You knew about the Confederate gambit with the British Government, and yet you failed to inform me. Why?'

Conté is stunned. 'How did you…?'

'I am paying Mr Rollo of Martin's Bank for a special service too, from the same budget pot you have been using. I should strike the pair of you off. Court martial you, toss you both in a hole.'

'*You* have been lying to *us*,' grunts Harriet, no longer the diplomat. 'Someone got the word out about the Banshee plot. What's your game, sir?'

'Do not challenge me, you cocky Irish bitch. I've traipsed over here to sort out your mess.'

Conté seethes. 'Thank you for your unstinting support, Major General. While we fight The War for you.'

'And what a sterling job you are making of that, my dears. Bravo.'

The pair have picked up where they left off back in Louisiana, but this time Harriet is done with trusting her commanding officer. She should have listened to Conté, the only person she's ever been able to completely give herself over to. They arrive at their destination. 'This is why you made the crossing? I knew it had to be something else.'

John Frank's house is a few steps away. Harriet had a feeling that this was where they were going. Butler smooths his greasy beard. 'Of course. I didn't come here to humiliate myself in front of those pea-brained hyenas in the Cotton Exchange, Missy.'

Conté stalks him at the rear. 'But that's exactly what you did.'

'It was all for Commander Dunwoody's benefit. Come on, catch up. You're better than that.'

Harriet finds a way in between them. It has reached 9pm and it is still full daylight, something she still isn't used to, among the litany of things about this strange city. In the tropics, night would have long fallen. How she wishes she was there, right now. 'Are we allowed to ask what we are doing at this address, then?'

Butler raps the brass knocker three times. 'One last attempt to save our collective asses.'

To their surprise, John Frank answers the door himself.

'Surprised to see me, Johnny? Did you not think that I would bother myself coming all this way? Um?'

The Captain smiles and opens the door for his impromptu visitors.

'Captain Frank, are we not paying you enough? Or is it the cut of our jib? Please tell me as I have a boat to catch.'

Butler sits by the unlit fire in the reception room, sipping tea. Harriet opts to stand by the wall with Conté, conscious of being in hostile territory, alert to any danger from this apparent kitten of a man who she knows from reputation rather than experience to be a lion.

Frank chuffs on his pipe and strokes his Siamese cat. 'Shuttle diplomacy doesn't work in this city, sir. You have to put time into building relationships. You have to be present, to make the right assignations.' His narrow, lynx eyes dart in the direction of Harriet and Conté. 'Not everything is solved by throwing money at it.'

Butler's corpulent frame squirms in his seat. Conté knows that The Blob likes to keep a tight circle, with information the main currency of diplomacy, but Frank is right. Butler has spread himself and his agents too thin. They are losing this war, and altogether grander, bolder gestures are required, lest the Confederacy will outbid and outcharm him every time.

Butler thinks that the wave of a palm will sufficiently dismiss this very immediate problem. 'New Orleans is enough of a handful. And we had an agreement, did we not?'

Frank nods. 'You need to feed such alliances with success. Not much of that is coming your way, I hear.'

Butler says, 'We have New Orleans, Johnny.'

Frank extends his bottom lip. 'The square root of nothing. You are encircled. Sitting ducks.'

'So you are now in the Mayor's pocket, then? Or worse still, Dunwoody's? And there is nothing we can do?'

Frank strokes his chatty cat, feeding it treats, impassive. 'Save the baiting, sir. We make our own decisions and we serve the public. This decision is all to do with the changing of the tide. Their money is as good as yours. Soon it will be better.'

Conté can't help herself. 'Their money is drenched in blood.'

'Did I ask you to speak? Did I?' growls Butler, suddenly feral, black-eyed. Even Conté recoils.

In a moment, Butler calms and tries another tack. 'We have full control of the Mississippi. The Eastern Seaboard. The Confederacy cannot win. It is more intricate than you think, with respect.'

Frank takes a deep chuff and knocks out his pipe before giving his feline a fishy treat. 'The same line you feed to everyone. And what chance do you have against the Royal Navy, then? I know a thing or two about my former employer and I don't fancy your prospects in a straight fight on the open ocean. They have twice as much firepower as every other navy combined. You'll be scuttled and scattered to driftwood in days. Nothing intricate about that.'

Butler's face enters a deeper shade of red and violet. Conté can feel the two heartbeats within Harriet quicken alongside her own. Where is this going?

'So you know.'

'Of course I know, man. Nothing happens in this town without my knowing. Seymour is wheeling Palmerston to Liverpool to sign up to it, just as the Confederates plan to mount a fresh attack upon Pennsylvania, thereupon to pincer and destroy Washington. Rather timely, eh? A Prime Minister whose marbles have fallen down the shitter and an opportunist First Lord who would bring back slavery if he could. They've seized the moment under your noses. The dissenters in Parliament have been bought up with promises of land and titles in the North, once we've annexed you back into Canada. Well, the ones that matter have. It'll sail through both houses on a bogus ticket of protecting British trading interests from hostile Union vessels, and those MPs who protest on the neutrality ticket will be defeated. Then, of course, your fleet will be annihilated, and you know this, so why am I even giving you my time? Pah, you must think we Peelers are thick as two short planks. It is my business to know things, and I know that you are yesterday's man. Is that plain enough, sir? Did you come all the way from America to hear this, sir?'

Frank stands tiredly and faces the two women. He gazes into Harriet's eyes and strokes her bump. She lets him, unnerved by his forwardness. It dawns upon her that Butler has led them here, and they are now known to Frank in plain sight. Why?

Butler interrupts the moment. 'We'll put up a fight, like you've never seen.'

Frank continues to stroke her belly, his perfectly coiffured beard twitching with his steady smile, his eyes like blue chips of ice. 'Doubtless, but pointless too. You have Lincoln's ear, do you not?'

Butler shakes his head, his droopy eyes even droopier now. 'No, Johnny. That is complicated.'

Frank's eyebrows lift. 'No? Goodness me, this is exactly what I'm talking about. Dear, oh dear. Well, just save yourself then. If you know the ball will land on red rather than black, bet on red and get out. Take all the money you can grab and run. The Indies, the Antilles, Barbados, a thousand or so nice spots out there. Leave the fight; it's what I've done. If you want an answer to why I've turned, look no further than what is coming to you.'

Harriet feels his breath on her face. She twitches, her senses alive to the abject situation of distant and close-at-hand dangers. These two men are controlling the conversation, and she can't stand for it any longer. 'And where can *we* run to, Johnny?'

Frank turns and smiles, welcoming another interlocutor. 'You can tow the line and be a good wife before I have to tell Commander Dunwoody exactly what you've been up to. I may anyway, not for devilment you understand, as I'm not that type of fellow. Rather that when I commit my services, I prefer to go all in. So, perhaps you two troublemakers should jump on that boat home with the Major General here? Um? That would be the cogent, sensible course. Now, I'm all out of advice for one evening, so it is high time you all left.'

He continues to stroke her bump, confident in his assertions, completely unaware of the short but incredibly sharp army-issue blade that is about to sever his jugular. The slit is quick, neat and immediately deadly.

Captain Frank drops to his Persian rug, unable to shout out, clutching his throat as it spits and spews thick, viscous crimson. Butler wipes his blade on Frank's immaculate gold-leaf waistcoat as the Chief Constable stops twitching.

'Johnny, Johnny, Johnny…' Harriet and Conté stare down at Frank, then, in unison, back at Butler. 'What? One less smart ass. No loss to the world. Come on; this damned house is giving me the collywobbles.'

The Blob has surpassed himself this time.

Butler isn't quick enough on his feet for their liking. Yes, Frank seemed to be at home alone this evening – which might be explained by the typhus spread across this end of the city quarantining staff – but who knows who saw what?

Conté keeps glancing behind them as they bound down the pavement. 'Dammit, sir. You don't have to live here.'

Harriet keeps up with Butler. Where do they go from here? The shock of the murder only abates enough for the realisation of what has been going on all along. Harriet blinks and gasps. 'It was you who wanted Banastre dead. That makes no sense, sir.'

Butler walks and nods. 'Of course I did.'

'What about us?'

'You became Plan B. Expediency.'

'Plan B? This is…'

'It's the way of the world, young lady. Our world. Sorry you weren't number one. It was a calculation. A probability index. Espionage is a science, a game of numbers and best bets. Your numbers were weaker. I can't blame you for that.'

'But you wanted us to destroy his ship? Wreck the infrastructure.'

'Yes. A great idea. Dynamite, what an invention.'

Harriet wants to stop him in his tracks to make him account for his actions, but this is the best she can do. She just hopes Conté doesn't try something rash. 'You sabotaged us. Why?'

'Expediency. Am I a cuckoo, forever repeating myself? Dunwoody had to believe that his ships were being compromised. It gave us leverage in negotiations, between enemy lines.'

'But you… you're suing for peace? The President would never agree to that.'

'That's what changed,' grunts Conté, probably way ahead of her. 'That's what got us skittled.'

Butler sniffs like he's just been told a dirty joke. 'I know, dear girls, I know. Don't look at me like that. I had high hopes for you both, but the longer it went on, the more Banastre could damage us. And don't think it was just about him, even though he'd like us to. Richmond and London have been talking for a while. The British just wanted to see a representative in person and on their terms. See? Bigger than him, bigger than you. Unfortunately, that means we've probably lost the war, so someone on our side had to see sense and talk about a settlement while the going was good. You were victims of timing, is all.'

'Fucking traitor,' mutters Harriet.

Conté grunts, neck still craning behind and around, frantically scanning the street. 'Bigger than us. Bigger than you?'

'Ha. Perhaps yes.'

This is all too much. Butler is backing a horse and cart over them, while telling them how he did it in the same sentence. Harriet still needs answers, but none of them are the ones she wants. 'We could have assassinated him for you. We would have done the job well. Untraceable, even.'

'Sweet Harriet, I am convinced you could. But I needed you on the ground. Best not to muddy the missions. Frank seemed to be a willing partner until I discovered the extent of his strangeness. Did you see that conservatory? Phoo-wee.'

'Years of training. For this? A surrender.'

'An armistice but, well, we're just too late for even that, alas. Rebel units are assembling for a run at Virginia and with an unstoppable Navy, well you know the rest, I'm sure.'

'You betrayed us. You betrayed your country.'

'Don't be harsh on yourself, Ms Farrell. That leads to true ruin.'

'What the hell? No…'

'We like to think that we can change the world in this service, but others have their hands on the tiller. Take that self-righteous asshole Lincoln. No, in fact, don't take him.'

'You came four thousand miles to cut a man's throat and stand us down? Out of what? Spite? Do you even care any more?' seethes Harriet, her steps finally in synch with him now.

'If you have to ask, you'll never know.'

'Bastard.'

Butler settles into a faster pace, preferring the downhill experience. 'Retire to bed, the pair of you. The less you know, the better. Play ignorant and let it become your normal order. You'll both be safe in this city. Await further instructions, if they ever come.'

Conté blocks his path. 'And what about you?'

'As your commanding officer, I don't have to answer that.'

Harriet joins Conté. 'Is Banastre next? You got a score to settle?'

Butler chuckles again, his gruff countenance dissolving since he took Frank's life. How well a spot of killing seems to augment his mood. 'No, dear. Now please, shift.'

Conté stands firm. 'Do not be flippant with us. You have no idea. Well, maybe you do, but you don't care, and that is worse.'

Harriet tries to pull her back. 'Conté no…'

But Conté gets into Butler's face. Of course, it doesn't faze The Blob, who is only further amused. 'No yourself, Harry. Just what have you done to us, Butler? Signed our death warrants is what. I ought to stick a blade in you for that alone.'

Butler shows his palms in mock submission. 'Ooh. Like to see you try, mamacita.'

Conté screams and punches the garden wall outside 101. She winces in pain, her hand throbbing.

Harriet grabs her side. 'Conté, are you alright?'

Butler shakes his head, glancing at his pocket watch. 'Of course she's alright. Tough as teak, this one. Like all those legendary Louvertures. I know her bloodline better than she knows herself. It's in the selection criteria. Did you know we chose her first? Yes, Miss Farrell. You were the real second fiddle. Delicious that, isn't it?'

It's Harriet's turn to seethe, not at his barb but at his interruption. 'I didn't ask you, did I? You're as bad as *him*.'

Butler shrugs. 'That's war for you. Righto. I shall be on my way, then.'

Harriet steels herself and steps up to Butler. 'Just, just wait a moment. We'll have to pay the consequences of your action this evening. In our own blood.'

'Really? How? Unless…' He glances sideways and smirks. 'Unless there is something else that you are not telling me, my two precious dears.'

'Just know that we cannot leave this city now,' replies Harriet, fatigue and pain suddenly all over her.

'Who says? On the contrary, I rather think I saved you from the oncoming train. All three of you. I cannot comment on the state of the Union, but that's something, isn't it?'

'So you take off back to New Orleans and leave us with this mess?'

Conté mumbles, still immersed in loathing and chagrin. 'Unless that is what he came here to do. And then he goes off and plays cards with the enemy.'

Butler throws his hands up and claps them together. 'Just being civil is all.'

Conté pushes herself to stand up straight, fighting back her anger. 'What about the British? The Cotton Exchange? Goddamn Banastre?'

Butler looks up to the sky as it starts to drizzle. 'Maybe I shall ask them what *they* think. Worth more than a tight alibi, do you not reckon? Que sera.'

Harriet can't stop that choking feeling, the one she usually gets in the presence of her husband. 'I'm about to give birth and the British are about to send the Navy across the pond to wipe you out. Oh, and you've just murdered the only man who could help us stop this from happening. Any more havoc you want to wreak while you're over here, boss? What's the bigger picture?'

Butler's eyes darken and he adopts a straighter countenance. 'The bigger picture? Lincoln will have to sort out the mess he created, but even if he sees sense, it will be too late. Be grateful for small mercies; that bent bastard Sheriff is dead. You saw it;

he wasn't for turning back. Now go home, be obedient women and Godspeed.'

Butler straightens his back and his cane as he strides away. He tips his top hat to them and lollops downhill, a spring now in his step. Conté and Harriet don't bother themselves to follow him.

Conté helps Harriet down the path and to the front door of 101, hopeful but far from certain that Harriet will get the good night's sleep that she needs when Banastre comes home, roaring drunk and still bloated with his small wins and pending huge victory. And then there is Conté's underlying, gnawing anxiety, only heightened by the noiseless street and the nagging feeling that they are being tracked, a forest river sprite she learned to trust since she was a child when she channelled the movements of white scavengers in the long reeds of the Bayou. The Choctaw senses – nurtured into both of them – makes her look this way and that, scanning every alley, every cranny, every crack. She is, as ever, completely right to do so.

For watching on, under cover of darkness and embedded into the one recess she misses, Mr Ake has now abandoned his note-taking for the evening. His book is screwed up in his hand and his pencil snaps in his balled fist. A lone tear traverses his mighty jawline, brow furrowed by the aftermath of what he has just seen after he observed the three Americans leaving John's residence. He was too late. He could have stopped it, but John had him watching Dunwoody, to protect the investment in the light of their new accord. Upon returning to resume his detail about the wife, he discovered the horror.

It was a struggle, but in order to go and trail the culprits, he had to leave Captain Frank prone on his rug, cats circling. The servants will find him upon their return with Elspeth and children, who are staying at their other residence in North Wales this evening. Bless them for what they will have to witness, and a lifetime to follow without a husband and father, but John's endowment will keep them well.

As for Mr Ake, what will he do now? Where will his endowment be? What does this leave for him and his family but malcontent and destitution without The Captain's patronage?

Everything changes now, except for the inevitability that blood will follow blood.

#24 THE LAST SUPPER

June 24th, 1863

They dine on oysters wrapped in bacon, roast duck and plum sauce, followed by charlotte pudding in creme anglaise and a nice bottle of claret from the cellar, albeit one that Banastre enjoys alone as it repeats on Harriet. In the aftermath of dinner, they gaze at each other from either end of the long table. Banastre picks out bits of meat from between his teeth with the tip of his short knife while she watches on with as much serenity as she can muster.

Tonight, Banastre is as calm as she has ever seen him. Positively serene, even. 'So where's your girl, tonight? You two are normally inseparable.'

'On horse business.'

He nods and sips more wine, adjusting his midriff. 'We'll have our own stables soon, sweetness. Then you won't have to go hiring ponies like the hoi polloi. And we'll get a proper staff too. Ones without miserable faces.'

She nods and smiles, knowing that time is limited and soon his little barbs won't affect her any longer, one way or the other. 'That's lovely, dear. I am excited at the prospect entirely.'

'Speaking of hoi polloi, you and I are going to have a talk soon.'

'About what, darling?'

'Your duties as a wife and mother.'

'Oh.'

One way or another, she hopes and prays that conversation will never have to happen.

'But not now. Tonight, I just want to enjoy you and junior there, in your belly. A pleasure that I have seldom had these past weeks and months.'

Oh Banastre, you romantic fool, you. 'Yes. That's lovely, darling.'

'You look beautiful tonight. I might join you in our bed later, if it pleases you?'

Nothing would please her less. 'Of course, dear.'

'Settled it is. And we'll rise real early tomorrow. Get ourselves bathed and in our finery and over to Ginger in good time to meet the train.'

She nods. Yes, and yes again. Yes to anything. She rubs her belly.

Banastre nods at her midriff. 'How is my son doing? Is he content? Does he look forward to inheriting his Daddy's world?'

'Couldn't be better.'

Creaking floorboards in the vestibule. Conté is home.

Banastre sups and studies her, then the bottle. 'Not bad this plonk. Not bad at all. I think we can have another? One more before bed? What do you think?'

'Of course, dear. Yes.'

'I do like your style, ma'am. You look brighter this evening. Keep that up.'

'I will, sir. Keep it up.'

He nods, and his man attends to the wine errand, leaving them in the room alone. He wipes his mouth, gets up and saunters over to Harriet, bending the knee at her feet and taking her hand as if he is about to propose properly this time.

'Oh Harriet, the things you must tolerate from me.'

'You are my husband, and it is my duty to entertain your every whim.' The dutiful wife and mistress of the house speaks again in that disembodied voice.

'My belle,' mews Banastre, kissing her hand and leaving a print of spittle. Then he grips it, hard enough to hurt. 'Just you remember to be on your best behaviour tomorrow, um? Use all of that Frenchie charm. Then, who knows, we might return as heroes and reclaim that family pile of yours for good. How do you like the sound of that? Money will be no object once I'm through. We'll buy the whole of Baton Rouge. Hang it, Louisiana, the moon.'

Harriet gets a flashing image of slaves being moved and sold as Banastre supervises the sale of Les Cyprès to one of his nouveau riche New Orleans chums, counting the cash in front of her nose whilst chewing on a stinking cheroot. The only thing missing was a whore on his knee. Another unforgiveable consequence of Butler's strategies. The pain from his grip is nothing to this memory, and it is all that she can do to return herself to the moment and her pressing task.

She needs to be bold. She has to counter him. 'I am close, darling husband.'

Banastre nods. 'Mighty so.'

'I fear that I will be an impediment. Should the moment occur while you are about your business.'

His face drops and she worries that he'll snap again, but then he emits a slow nod. 'Good point. And wise. Looking after that horse's ass of a Mayor is enough trouble.'

Harriet grips his hand, allowing her eyes to pitch around, hamming it up just for Banastre. 'I am vexed so, sir. You will not tell me what you are doing tomorrow, but I know it to be momentous. I am so disappointed in myself that I cannot be there for you. Will you forgive me?'

He takes this in and shrugs. 'Yessiree. Suppose I will, if you make sure he comes out good and clean.'

'Oh, I will, sir. Surely I shall promise you that.'

'Good then. All good, better than good.' Banastre rubs her belly. She can feel her baby recoil. 'So, do you have a plan?'

A slither of ice runs up her spine, and she gets the irrational urge to run and run as far away as she can from this place, to fetch up Conté and take her baby to safety. Then she forces herself to settle again, planting her feet into the carpet. The tumult inside her will be too much for the infant if she carries on in that fashion.

'A plan for what, dear?'

'For bed, you sweet idiot.'

The claret arrives. His cold eyes burn into her. It will bring up the nausea if she lets the moment mature.

'Oh, of course. Well, I'll join you in a small glass and you finish the bottle and we'll hatch these plans along the way. How does that sound?'

Banastre shrugs and chuckles. 'Dandy.'

Dear God, save us. The demon inside her laughs. She hopes the filthy liquid doesn't make her vomit as she needs to sleep tonight, even though she knows that there will be no sleep, only the pretence of it.

Tomorrow, tomorrow. All day they've complained about not having enough time, about how Butler has abandoned them in their hour of need. Now it all can't come soon enough.

They toast glasses.

Conté knows that Harriet is in the dining room with Banastre as soon as she arrives at the rear entrance downstairs. The kitchen is alive with activity as staff clean up after a grand, impromptu meal for two. She makes a point of walking past the door and eavesdrops for a moment, but with staff coming and going, she retreats to her quarters downstairs. Poor Harriet won't sleep tonight, but she can't let that worry her.

Who is she fooling? Of course it will worry her.

She opens the door to her cramped quarters, beckoning for her straw mattress to swallow her up. Before she can get that far, a strong scent overcomes her; Sandalwood. She looks behind the door, following the source.

Mr Ake regards her, but he doesn't let a moment pass. The rabbit punch catches Conté square on the jaw and he breaks her fall by catching her in his other arm. She is out cold.

#25 ST JAMES' CEMETERY
AT MIDNIGHT

June 24th, 1863

She wakes up in what – at first – appears to be a fresh grave, the peaty smell of earth and dewy foliage strong in her nostrils. Above, the moonlight dances through the fluffy blossom on a chestnut tree and she is aware of a giant, solid shadow standing over her, like an obsidian cathedral. Is this a mirage or phantom of her long-dead father? Is it the ghost of Toussaint Louverture even, come to offer her succour and strength? No, alas. This spirit carries malevolence rather than salvation in every sense, not least with that infernal sandalwood reek about him.

Saline water dribbles from her nostrils and it dawns on her that this devil has probably just administered smelling salts in order to rouse her. She feels the damp soil in her palms and runs it through her fingers, now aware that she isn't in a grave at all. Rather, she is beside one.

Conté struggles to her feet, head still dazed from his punch and some weird intoxication that he has given her, but she must look her assailant in the eye. Even though she is exceptionally tall herself, she has to crane her neck back to meet his black eyes, the whites seeming to give off their own light in contrast. Her jaw aches.

'Why?'

A raven pecks at the dirt beneath Mr Ake's feet, prospecting for worms. With a flick of a hobnail boot, Mr Ake shoos it away and it squawks in derision before alighting and landing on the next grave. As Conté reaches full awareness of her aching jaw, she spots a mound of earth beside the open pit and a shovel balanced against the chestnut tree. She feels motivated to repeat herself.

'Why?'

She looks around the ethereal site. There are still many places within a short radius of 101 Canning Street that Conté has not yet visited, and this is one of them. Grand mausoleums share the yard with simple plots, a reminder of how death is the great leveller above all great levellers. This grand forever bed overlooks the long drag of Duke Street that leads down to the Customs House, Goree Piazza, the Pier Head and Landing Stage, with the full expanse of the docks in a rolling tapestry of the life of this city, gaslights twinkling like grounded constellations. Up here is the very death of this city, from cholera victims to slaves and slavers, from clergy to politicians, from aristocrats to paupers, from the murdered to murderers, some sharing most or even all of these descriptions. Nowhere else does the city of a million faces become more illustrated than here in the necropolis of the metropolis, with names from every corner of the earth resting about the ground.

Mr Ake knows this site rather better than Conté. His wife is buried here with his youngest child, but he has also put people in this place and they are getting too numerous to recall, save from his meticulous records that now only serve his own memory, not the greater good of Captain Frank's detail. Who knows what will happen to the ledgers? Into whose hands will they fall? Should he burn them? Why is he worrying about that now?

Conté registers that this is a warm summer night, but she trembles nonetheless, fully aware of Mr Ake's seriousness and of his status in the distinct, navy blue Peeler uniform. His very appearance answers most of her questions for her. He pulls some leather gloves on.

She has to speak, for all the shock and horror. 'Sir, if you were firm in your conviction, you wouldn't have needed to rouse me. You could have just gotten it over with, and dumped me in that hole. So I figure that we can talk. Am I right?' Mr Ake shrugs. 'Come now, Mister. You are able to understand me. Do I at least not deserve some sort of reasoning to take with me to God?'

He studies Conté and nods. 'Yes. But you won't be going to God, and we don't always get what we deserve, child.'

Conté flinches and squirms. 'That is not yours to judge, sir. Officer.'

'Perhaps. Not important right now, though. Well, maybe to you, but not to me.'

'It fits you to be so casual. Did Captain Frank give you these jobs regularly?'

'Yes.'

'Then should you be surprised that he came to such a sticky end?' Mr Ake shrugs an encore. She's smart, for sure. Too smart and too ambitious. 'What's your reasoning now? Seeing that your boss is no longer around to do the thinking for you?'

Mr Ake smiles. That one got him. Not that it matters.

Conté persists with the line, her only line. 'Is this just force of habit, then? The standard response? Kill.'

Mr Ake offers a quick puff of the cheeks. 'You're not talking your way out of this, ma'am.'

'I feel so strange. What did you do to me?'

'I used a tincture of surgical ether to keep you under. So you would be too docile to try to fight your way out of it. For your own good and for your mercy.'

Another reason Conté feels like being sick. 'You know Butler did it. You have the wrong culprit.'

Mr Ake's smile evolves into a wide grin. 'The Butler did it?'

Oh, so he has a sense of humour! How can a man that has such a genial side to his countenance be so ready to perform this action? That makes it even worse. 'No, sir. Is this the moment to tease me? Major General Butler. From the Union delegation? I'm sure you know who he is. That same man is on the Atlantic swell right now. He murdered Frank, in front of my eyes, may God strike me down if I lie.'

Mr Ake nods. 'I know, child, I know. Rest easy on that. Butler is your master.'

'Not my master. Never my master.'

'Where is your loyalty, child? That you would readily shift the blame, um? He is your superior and you should know your place. He *is* your master, and you don't get to choose such things.'

This does rouse her and her eyes widen, attempting to rabbit punch Ake in the solar plexus, but he parries her fist, as quick as he is strong. The ether has made her slow and woozy, as much as she wants to fight him, make a last stand. She can barely stay on her feet.

'Answer me, child. Where is your loyalty?'

Conté bristles to retort. 'My loyalty is elsewhere. With good people.'

'Ah. Again, more information than you should have told me. So, you do value your own neck?'

'Only if it means your joining the right side, sergeant. We need all the help we can get.' Mr Ake's eyes smile, as if he is considering her proposition, but it is fleeting. He steps up to her, close enough for that aroma of sandalwood to drift about her face again, this time at even closer quarters. Her stomach quakes, all-consuming terror not too far away now. 'Save me, and you will save millions more. Can you not remember Africa? You wear it on your skin and there is no denying it. You can do this, sir. Don't be like all the other bogeymen. The ones who turn you against their own. This is how they control us. Don't you understand, Officer? I implore you.'

Mr Ake has listened, but he is all but done here. 'We are not the same, ma'am. Not even close.'

'To them we are, and to them we must take the fight. We have the chance right here and now. This is where they have all their money, their trade, their ships. We hit them here, we hurt them. Your uniform can help us. Be a leader. Join us. You are free now.'

'Fine speech.'

Conté ignores him, impassioned. 'Yes, right here in this godforsaken city that neither of us should have to call home. You have children?'

'Six living.'

'Then they will know what you did for their future, and so will their children. Please join us. Please. If you need money, we have it…'

Mr Ake gently closes his hand around her neck. She checks for blades hidden around her body, anything to shank him. He removed them.

'Heaven help me, then.'

'A familiar conceit, ma'am. I'll say a prayer when it's done.'

'Thank you for that much. And spare Harriet. I beg you.'

Mr Ake shakes his head slowly. 'Only until the baby is born. Then the debt will have to be completed.'

'What about Butler? I implore you, *he* is the murderer!'

Mr Ake places a finger over her mouth and shakes his head. 'If he ever sets foot on these shores again, which he will, this reckoning will visit him too.' His huge fingers tighten steadily, each as powerful as strong arms.

Conté is unaware that she is foaming at the mouth, her bladder weakening. 'See what they're doing, brother? On all sides? All countries, all wars, all of them? Pitting you against me, African on African. We collect their slaves for them in exchange for trinkets and fancy goods. We enslave our brothers and sisters for them. We act as executioners. For them. They lie and tell themselves that we are the savages, but we were building cities when they were living in caves.'

Mr Ake moves his thumb across her lips. All done now. Conté shuts her eyes, knowing that they will not open again. Then Mr Ake closes his hands.

Watching on, from up above, on Gambier Terrace. Pat puffs on his corn pipe like a steam engine, staring down between iron railings at the tableau as Ake pushes poor Conté into the grave before grabbing a shovel full of dirt. He was on his way up the hill to see Miss Conté and Miss Harriet, but this something in the corner of his eye stopped him dead in his tracks. Some godawful thing like this.

'Oh, great fuckin' decision that was, Padraig. No dear, I want to stay. No dear, don't get on that boat, my friends need me. I beg you, Sarah. We can make this work, Sarah. Fuck me, fuckin' sterling idea that was. Next time, get on the fuckin' boat. Next time listen to your fuckin' wife.'

He continues wittering and whining to himself and skittles off in the direction of Canning Street, with more urgency to his mission than he ever could have anticipated.

Back on the cobbles of Canning Street, Banastre stands tall in formal Confederate Navy Regalia, replete with sword and medals. An ornate, ceremonial carriage pulls up; Ginger is in the passenger compartment, donning his full civic chain and regalia. He swings open the door.

'Don't you look the part, old boy.'

'Have you not learned to quit the soft soak, yet?'

Ginger's face straightens. 'And your lovely wife, will she be joining us?'

'No.'

Banastre shoves past him and boards the carriage. It trundles off.

Pat watches from the shadows. He scales the stable wall with spring-heeled ease.

#26 RECKONING

June 25th, 1863

In her chamber, Harriet wakes in a cold sweat. She's aware that a pillow has replaced Banastre's iron arm. She feels, she *knows*, something is awfully awry.

'Conté. No.' A knock on the window startles her. 'Pat? I thought you'd...'
She gets out of bed and pulls up the sash.

'I am so sorry, love.'
Something snaps in her mind. She dashes out of the bedroom.

And into Conte's room. No-one home. Pat follows in her wake.

'So sorry.'

'Where? How? Who?'

'That grock of a Constable. He took her down to the cemetery. I couldn't stop it. I'm so sorry.'

'So you keep saying.'

Harriet balls up in sudden agony, screaming. Pat nods.

'Right so. Seen that too many times. Awful timing above all else, isn't it.' Sobbing and screaming from Harriet, physical agony joining emotional agony. Pat grabs Conté's straw-filled pillow and blanket and supports her head. 'Help! Someone! Mistress is having her baby! Oi!' Penny cranes her neck around the door. 'Be a love and go get us a physician. This wee fucker's not hanging around.'

She nods and scarpers out again.

Harriet screams, 'Conté! Come back!'

'There love. It's all going to be fine. Trust Pat here. He's a dad. He knows.'

The only thing Pat can be is gentle. What else is there? He's seen the death of brothers, sisters, daughters and sons. To consumption, to starvation, to typhus, to murder. He knows its icy, uncaring, ruthless reach, and it is a more callous thief than he could ever be. It has just visited upon this lady in the cruellest way, and he now knows the terrible reason why he was summoned by God to turn back at that Landing Stage.

'Conté. Conté please God no…'

'There love. Just think about yourself and the child. That's all.'

In the midst of her agony, Harriet grips his arm so hard that it feels like she might snap the bone. Her bloodshot eyes are wide and furious. Pat will never know that she has visited this pain before, far away and long ago in that raid on her wagon train in a Louisiana clearing.

'I will not. I will not, sir. I will have satisfaction. I will!'

'Ah, Jesus. Yes, you will, you will. Wow, that's some strength you've got there, Miss.'

Lime Street Station, another marvel of the city, the first urban railway entrepôt in the world. Liverpool is *always* first, and how Ginger likes to crow about it. Another thing that Banastre won't miss when they finally get to blow this town. Gentlemen of the press, local and national, line up in an orderly corridor as a distant steam engine gets progressively closer, the shooping and hissing coming this way. What a magnificent machine.

Ginger is stiff-backed and eager. Horses bristle as Banastre leans against the golden coach like a lazy, miscreant youth, chuffing away on his Virginia blend. It is all part of the act for the press, naturally. His insides are currently dancing a jig, but keeping up appearances to himself, as much as to others, is a habit he got into a long time past.

Ah, here it is. The train draws into sight, pumping along.

'Gentlemen of the press, this day will go down in history.' The Press Men look at each other, wary of the Mayor's notorious hyperbole. 'I mean it, sirs. Buck up and note the arrival. This is history to behold right here.'

Banastre finally straightens up as the train comes to a stop.

The doors to the mail van slide open and a small troupe of burly adjutants emerge. They struggle to lower Pammy to the platform in his huge wheelchair. Seymour, replete with his own entourage, hops down onto the platform.

'History,' mutters Banastre.

Ginger approaches, arms open, all smiles. Palmerston froths at the mouth. Seymour looks like he's smelling shit.

'Pammy, Eddie!'

Banastre slaloms around Ginger, pushing himself to the front of the reception committee. This is his show now, however Ginger wants to play it to his press corps.

'Prime Minister. I relay cordial wishes from President Jackson and await your visit for some Southern hospitality, upon formal diplomatic ties.'

Banastre goes to shake Palmerston's hand but is cut off by Seymour.

'You'll have no joy there, sonny. He's had another stroke. Can't wipe his own arse.'

He turns his attention to Seymour, who is the true architect of this event. 'Your Grace. It is an honour to see you here.'

'Let's get on with this, chaps. This infernal city gives me the heebie-jeebies.'

Ginger is determined to be seen, so much so that he goes in feet first. 'Must have been the crabs you caught last time you were up, what ho Eddie.'

Seymour's eyes sear into Ginger. The Mayor is jumpy, too damned jumpy. 'Do you see me laughing, Harrison?' The First Lord strides to the carriage as the porters and the rest of the aides scamper to keep up.

Banastre wants Ginger to disappear. The Mayor is altogether more sober and nervous today, perhaps because the press attend. He's far easier to handle when he's three sheets to the wind. Their relationship has soured to the point of hostility, and only mutual interest keeps it intact. 'What's the matter with you?'

'Harrow boys can't take a joke.'

'I know you're excited, but keep it shut, man. You have nothing else to do than that.'

The porters struggle to fit the chair into the carriage, and the Press Men look nonplussed. Banastre shakes his head.

Town is quiet now, like it's holding its breath.

The assortment of carriages emerges from the station concourse and heads down the hill towards St George's Plateau. Not a soul strolls or works today.

They are joined by a cavalcade of Peelers on horseback, the same gang Banastre recruited to take care of that Irish rabble. To a man, they will be made rich if today goes well, on the promise of Dixie dollars. They're alert to any signs of trouble, but this is easy pickings.

Banastre settles back in his seat. Yes, now this city really does belong to him, but he's not here for Liverpool. He's here for Dixie and for victory.

They trundle and galumph up to the entrance of the Town Hall and then roll to a halt.

Palmerston's wheelchair is strapped awkwardly to the back of the vehicle with bridle swatches. Adjutants scramble off the accompanying charabanc, and they struggle to pull it down and set it upon the pavement.

Banastre, Ginger and Seymour alight the compartment. Palmerston sleeps in the back.

'Wouldn't His Excellency be more comfortable if he remained in the carriage?' says Banastre, eager not to let the old buzzard slow things down.

Seymour blows his nose into a handkerchief and hands it to one of his advisers. 'And who's going to sign your declaration?'

'He could sign it out here. Then we could complete formalities upstairs without him.'

'You were better when you had less to say for yourself. Let's do this properly, Commander.'

Ginger shuffles on his feet, wary of the waiting press corps. 'Not how things are done in this country, old boy. No, sir, what what.'

Banastre is tempted to slap the Mayor there and then, his pecker up and heart pumping, but that won't do. Footmen rouse Palmerston and lift him out of the carriage and into his chair. Today has to be perfect, no hitches.

Seymour casts his eyes over the impressive limestone building. His shaggy eyebrows drop.

'Always something to prove in Liverpool, haven't you?'

Ginger is still preoccupied with his own local top-dog status. 'We can buy anything, sir.' He glances at Banastre. 'Or anyone.'

'Braggadocio,' grunts Seymour. 'Perhaps we should have done this in London.'

'This is for the Cotton Exchange. For the press. Think about it, Eddie.'

Seymour waggles his cane at the entrance. He's thought about it, alright. 'Let's just get it over with.'

They head inside. The Footmen push Palmerston into the magnificent atrium as Seymour strides up ahead, bounding up the staircase. Carrying the Prime Minister up a flight of steps is proving to be a challenge.

Banastre matches Seymour stride for stride. This competition with Ginger is getting irksome.

'I'm impressed how you swung the lobbies.'

Seymour already looks like he has a train South to catch. 'There is work to be done yet. Just wait for the stink that will follow this accord.'

'I gather, sir. But it is all going to be worth Britain's while.'

'I hope so, my lad.'

Seymour doesn't look as cocksure as he did within the safe confines of 10 Downing Street, but in his own way, he is organising something of a coup. Small wonder there are some heebie-jeebies, even for a man with so much lead to swing. Their window is tight and it's getting tighter. High Command in Richmond must have promised him the Earth, but sometimes even that isn't enough for such men. Banastre again feels the rush of blood to get this signed and sealed right here and now, lest knives come out. The twitching is enough to make him want to shoot something, or someone.

'Your unstinting support has swung this entire issue, sir. I cannot thank you enough.'

'I merely follow the establishment. The best interests of the Queen and Her subjects. I am merely a public servant.'

Now that Seymour is a captive audience, Banastre is quickened to be bolder, but Ginger gets his riposte in first, coming up the rear between them. 'You *are* the establishment, Eddie.'

Banastre gives the Mayor another admonishing look, but it merely bounces off him. They reach the top of the stairs and head towards a sumptuous-looking office. Ginger inserts his thumbs into his waistcoat pockets, asserting his domain with inimitably ridiculous pomp.

'Welcome to my humble Liverpolitan garret, my Lords.'

Laid out on the mahogany table is a neat stack of papers with two quills and a red wax approval stamp, the Prime Ministerial seal of office. The Queen herself will ratify this formally, but this is the moment that matters. Now that they are at the business end of the proceedings, the adjutants are dismissed and Seymour takes over, wheeling Palmerston over to the table. He holds smelling salts under Pammy's nose. The Prime Minister wakes up with a start.

'Good-oh, Pammy. Got a little bit of work for you, old chum. Just a minor codicil.' Seymour hands Pammy the inked quill and guides his shaking hand over to the document, helping him draw his signature. 'There, old boy.'

'I trust you'll be making a speech from the balcony to the waiting press, sir?'

Seymour leers at Ginger, singularly unimpressed with him. 'What do you think, you oaf?'

Banastre mutters, 'Should have done this in goddamn London, sure as apples.' He steps in front of Ginger, blocking the Mayor's line of vision, all smiles. 'He *means* in your capacity as First Lord of the Admiralty, Your Grace. It's your Navy that'll be doing the dirty work, after all.' He glances at Palmerston, passed out. 'You'll agree, as the *next* Prime Minister?'

Seymour grunts. That impresses him. 'Yes, I suppose. I'll have to think of something, won't I?' He pulls out a ready-prepared speech from the inside pocket of his frock coat. It seems that someone has done the thinking for him.

Banastre grins and takes his quill. He leans down to sign. 'Oi. You. Shithouse.'

Pat McCartney emerges from the balcony, dusting his hands off.

Seymour jumps like a scalded cat. 'How did *he* get up here?'

Banastre's stomach flips and his jaw grinds. He pulls his Smith & Wesson. 'You after some revenge for your thumbs, boy? You certainly pick your moments.'

Seymour's bushy eyebrows fold with distemper and the Mayor is first in the line of fire. 'This is highly irregular. Harrison. What is this? The Prime Minister is present, for fuck's sake. Where is your security? This is a snit!'

Ginger's lower jaw wobbles, but nothing comes out.

Pat ducks behind Pammy as Banastre trains his gun on him, unable to get a clean shot. 'I'll tell youse, since you fucks are all turned out. Eighteen hundred and forty-eight I came here, forced out of me own country by you bastards so that you could steal all the land. Make yourselves a little England. Just like youse are doing now, with your quills and laws.'

Banastre is incredulous. Pat looks him in the eye, fearless. He stands up straight, sticking his chest out, aware of another presence in the room.

'What varmint bullshit is…'

'Oh, you'll wanna hear the rest, darling.'

Harriet's husband frowns, cranes his neck and sees his wife standing next to the open servants' entrance. She is gaunt and half-dead, blood seeping out through her lower garments. Her elbows are tucked tight against her. Banastre leers at Pat, who matches his glare.

'Don't look at me like that, bollocks,' says Pat. 'She insisted.'

Banastre redirects his ire to Harriet, fuse already burning to the powder keg. 'It was you. And that throwback, funky flunky of a maid. All along. The saboteurs. Was it not?'

'Yes. Before you and I even met.'

Banastre gets closer to Harriet, ready to unload. Seymour grips the handles to Pammy's chair, eyes darting between Banastre and the exit.

'A bit unseemly this, old chap.'

Banastre has lost all of his appetite for diplomacy. 'So this is all Butler's doing? Conniving, slimy prick. I should have popped him as soon as he showed his face in town.'

'Don't you dare give him all the credit. *He* sabotaged *us* in the end. I just wanted to end your little game with your little friends.' Seymour is ashen. He twitches the wheelchair handles, as if he is about to take part in a race. Harriet glances down at Banastre's gun, her eyes still full of vitriol and fight, even as her body threatens collapse. It is in this moment that Banastre realises who he really married, and how this woman just doesn't care for him or his precious Dixie. 'So what are you waiting for, dear?' says Harriet, stepping slightly to her right.

A slow, rictus grin spreads across his perfect jawline as Banastre considers how he has been so artfully duped. It amounts to the same old shit though, just another assassin hiding behind a curtain. She's close enough to see every muscle, every twitch in his body language, reading him like the latest Victor Hugo. Banastre wins, men like him always win. He knows it and the last thing that is going to go through her head before his slug is that she'll know it too.

Banastre Xavier Dunwoody's finger squeezes the trigger, but he is slow to adjust to Harriet's new posture. In a lightning flash, Harriet's twitching fingers snap into her petticoat and she draws the pistol tucked by her side, shooting low and true. Straight in the balls.

Yeah, sure, she knows it alright, but what he *didn't* know was that his wife could outshoot just about any man, even doubled over from labour pains and loss of blood. He gasps in shock and sudden horror, then gurns, looking down to where his manhood used to be. How did she do that? How in hell can a woman shoot like that?

'It was a girl, by the way. Thanks for asking.'

Banastre thuds to his knees. Harriet shuffles over. She looks him in the eye and raises her Colt .45 to his face. It is the same piece that he gifted her back in Les Cyprès, and he knows it.

'My baby is safe and resting. Her momma needs to get back to her. You know she's got Creole blood in her? And Irish. Not one bit of her is a Dunwoody. How about that? Her real daddy died a hero only last night, but that ain't none of your business, husband.'

'Bitch.' Banastre is in a frantic mess, blood pissing out now. He is unable to fathom what has just happened, bested in a gunfight by his own wife. There's a tune playing on tin whistles floating up from outside and through the open patio.

'The Battle Cry of Freedom,' explains Harriet. 'Our troops have arrived to escort your soul back to hell.'

He grits his teeth and snaps into a hard, tombstone grin, suddenly aware that his pistol remains in his grip. 'I'll see you lynched like a n-'

Harriet Farrell unloads into his head. Banastre rocks and slumps.

The song lilts and tilts towards being a pretty little Erse ditty rather than a Union battle anthem, but the message is sufficient. Seymour glances outside and his jaw drops. He shakes with shock and disbelief.

Several hundred Irish men have assembled up the Water Street and Castle Street intersection. Dudley stands tall at the apex next to the ceremonial cannon, which takes aim at the Town Hall, right at Seymour himself, it would seem.

The press, below, are bewildered but nowhere near as much as Seymour is. 'This is an act of war.'

Harriet waggles her smoking gun and shuffles over to the First Lord. 'Why don't we tell the waiting gentlemen of the press all about it, then? Right now?'

Seymour shuffles, trying to think on his feet. 'That fucking oaf Harrison has brought half of Fleet Street up here, Madam. I cannot countenance the scandal. No, lay down your gun and I will take care of this mess. What grievance you had with Dunwoody, you do not have with Her Majesty's Government. I'll vouch for leniency. They might even just deport you.'

Fucking weasel. Harriet winces again, hot knives in her abdomen, but stays focused. 'How about I get to be the lenient one, if you will permit me.' Pat grins, loving the devilment. 'You can see from the presence of our boys outside that we would like you to make the right decision. Your proposition is not the right decision, so try again.'

'A bally show. British troops would skittle them in seconds.'

'I see no British troops. Your second biggest mistake…
besides coming here in the first place.'

Seymour flaps his arms. 'This city. This *fucking* city, I swear
blind. Paddywhacks and American troops on sovereign soil,
lording it. What next? Infernal province.'

'You were ready to send in the Royal Navy to attack our fleet,
milord.'

'I still fucking well am ready,' he grunts, with no attempt to
hide the threat in his voice.

'And there it is. That's what is on the negotiating table. Right
here, right now.'

More than shooting Banastre, it is just this that puts the wind
up Seymour. 'Balls, madam. Balls, I say. Surrender, I say.
Immediately, I say.'

Harriet nods in the direction of Banastre and twitches her gun
hand. Restraint is difficult, but a bullet for Seymour would mean
the rope for both of them, so she has to be smart. She whistles
along with the tune of her Irish Volunteers. 'You sure about that
tack you're taking, sailor boy?'

Ginger hides underneath his grand desk, gibbering nonsense.
Palmerston drools on the expensive carpet. Seymour wipes the
Prime Minister's mouth with his pocket square. 'The Prime
Minister demands that you relent.'

A thin smile crosses Harriet's lips and she nods to the
wheelchair. 'You're keeping him alive just to push this deal
through, aren't you? Doubtless, you would push him off a cliff if
it furthered your cause and extended your portfolio.'

Seymour's face turns to granite. Busted. 'What of it?'

Now, they're getting somewhere. He won't even deny it. 'I'm
here to tell you that you've failed, milord. Miserably, irreversibly.
So, it is you that should surrender to me.'

'Poppycock.' His huge shagpile eyebrows drop in derision.
'This is sovereign territory; this is England. Put down your
weapon and yield.' He glances outside to the cavalry. 'Or we will
crush this charade like the mutiny of savages that it is. Last
warning.'

'Now, milord, come on.' She picks up Banastre's fateful
document with her spare hands. Seymour looks like he wants to
make a grab for it. 'You don't want lil ol' me telling those

gangplank willies down there how you came to be making such an agreement. With all the codicils and addendums promising vast tracts of American land to Members of Parliament? There just ain't time for your army to get here and stop that, is there?'

'What? How did you know about…'

'Yes, I've proof of all of it; every dirty deal, done dirt cheap, every coded message that my beloved husband sent back to Dixie. I've still got the key to my Commander Dunwoody's safe, if not his heart. Enough transcripts and papers to embarrass the whole of your little old boys' club to death, were they to become public domain. Those press boys out there will lap it up, every sweet drop of it. Care to have a wager on the outcome?'

Banastre twitches. She shoots him again for good measure. Ginger bunnyhops on all fours, thumping his pate against the underneath of his desk. Harriet winces and wobbles on her feet, dizzy and failing. Pat props her up. Not much longer now. Must hold firm.

Seymour winces for different reasons, flailing for a different tack. 'Madam, you are clearly a woman of intellect and substance, but in pain, deranged and…'

'Fella, look, I am not surrendering to you or anyone. You got that? I have nothing to lose and everything to gain for the world that my child will grow up in. Your game is up.'

'Damned straight,' grunts Pat. 'But we gots to go, Mrs Dunwoody.'

Harriet swats this away like an imaginary fly, not quite finished yet. This deal needs to be done, here and now, now or never. 'Suppose you won't get to buy that island in the Indies now, milord. You and your cronies will have to make do with what you've got.' She nods to Palmerston. 'He'll die soon enough and you'll never be Prime Minister, but I'm offering you a way out of being disgraced, for the expediency of both our great nations. Now we have conditions, and I want your agreement, on pain of my releasing my intelligence to the Great British public.'

He looks about ready to burst, spluttering and sneering, right where she wants him. 'Spit it out.'

'Maintain neutrality. Enshrine it *permanently* in law.' Harriet knows that she has to spell it out for him, but that's just fine. She just needs to get it over with before her legs give way from underneath her. 'Nothing has been signed, right?'

Seymour thinks about it. 'It isn't ratified. But the lobbies have agreed to…'

'Ah, your secret lobbies. Your little old boys' clubs *again*. Well, they'll just have to know when they're beaten, won't they? Every abolitionist in England will come after you in the courts if the true nature of this filthy accord gets out. Every corrupt little offering to every corrupt little man. Do it my way and you get to scurry back under your stone. Do it his way…' she nods to Banastre's corpse, 'and I will fucking ruin you all to penury and the workhouse, starting with you personally. Consul Dudley has the writs drawn up already, efficient fellow.'

Seymour licks his dry lips. 'Very well.'

'No, not very well. You need to hear me out. You need to take this exact narrative back to London with you.'

'I'm listening,' rasps Seymour. If she put her gun between his legs to see which side he dressed on, she couldn't have any more control over him than she does now. Hell hath no fury, even if fury is the only thing keeping her upright.

'There is no story, sir. Apart from a ceremonial demonstration of solidarity from the City of Liverpool with the United States of America. That's how you'll explain all the blue uniforms out there when you go out and talk to the press. Within the bounds of Britain's neutrality, *naturellement*. So, First Lord, do we have an accord?'

Seymour raises his hands and edges towards the door, puce and defeated, the scurrying rat. 'I think we should be going.'

Harriet looks him in the eye, keen to know that her message has been absorbed. Not Butler's message or even Lincoln's, but *her* message. Conté's message.

'Always trouble, this city,' he grunts before shunting Palmerston briskly out of Ginger's office. 'Footmen! I say! Where can I get some assistance around here! Footmen! Adjutants, I say! Infernal incompetents!'

'Mrs Dunwoody,' whispers Pat in her ear. 'We must…'

'One last order of business, my friend. Mayor?' Ginger squeals. Does he fear a bullet too? 'Your job is to make that corpse disappear. I'm sure you have enough influence to arrange that. Discreetly, like he was never here, got it?' She points at Banastre with her gun, pleased that this is her last sight of him. 'Got it?'

Ginger nods vigorously, still on his hands and knees, prone like a stuck pig. 'Yes ma'am,' he rasps.

'Good show, old boy.'

Ginger dwells on the body as Pat props up Harriet. Banastre's deal is as dead as he is.

'Risky game, Mrs Dunwoody,' says Pat.

'It worked, didn't it? And it's Farrell. Harriet Farrell. No Missus or Miss or Ms.'

'Good Irish name, so.'

Pat helps her out of the office, leaving the quivering shambles that is Liverpool's Mayor to contemplate how to dispose of a high-profile corpse. It will probably involve a hemp sack, a few hundredweight of ballast, some of his favourite local ruffians and a short trip to the river, but she's sure that he'll make a proper job of it. They pass the wheelchair of Prime Minister Palmerston on the staircase and First Lord of the Admiralty Seymour, who won't even acknowledge them.

They head outside to a huge, thunderous cheer from the throng. Peelers twitch, but the press are watching every move.

Harriet grips Pat's arm and pulls them to a stop. The press eye her but are quickly distracted by the oncoming Prime Minister and his twitching First Lord.

Boom, the Napoleonic cannon fires a blank volley. Seymour sweats and jumps. 'Gentlemen, the Prime Minister has come to this fine city to underscore directly Britain's neutrality in the American War. Mayor Harrison has agreed to address the unequivocal issue in his Chamber of Commerce in relation to the illegal funding of Confederate vessels…'

Conté should have been here to witness this.

Pat says, 'It'll make for good folklore. No sane person will ever believe it, though, Harriet Farrell.'

'The desired effect.' Harriet offers a fading smile. 'Please call me Harry, would you? I need to hear someone say it. Someone good.'

'Fella's name.'

'A good name. You said it.'

'I did so, Harry.'

'Thank you, kind man.'

Pat holds her arm up in victory but quickly realises his mistake as she passes out. 'Bollocks.' He emits a brief, loud whistle, and Grace attends with Rosalinda.

'Oh my, Miss Harriet.'

'Better get her to a quack fast like, I reckon.'

#27 CONTÉ-MARIE FARRELL

July 1st, 1863

Pat smokes his corn pipe by the wall of the stable, keeping a lookout as ever. From an open window, above, a baby cries. 'There, there. Little sausage.'

Upstairs, in her chamber, Harriet Farrell's face is flushed with colour, her movements have renewed vim. She is dressed for outside, rocking her howling baby, whose powerful little one week-old lungs belie her tough start in life. The servants stand to attention.

She nods to them in passing. 'You take good care of Mr McCartney and his family, yes? I'll see to it that your wages are paid promptly every week.'

They bow. She heads out with the baby.

Harriet emerges from the front door with a pram. She approaches Pat and passes him some keys.

'I don't like this. I never got nothing for nothing from no one, Harry.'

'There is a *something* involved.' Harriet flattens a palm against his heart. 'You turned back. That took some courage.'

'To go against my Sarah, you bet.'

Harriet laughs. 'For sure.'

He doffs his cap. 'The big fella's still at large. Working his bridewell, happy as Larry.'

'Nothing happy about him. He'll come looking. Sooner or later.' She glances up and down the street. 'Sooner, I'll vouch.'

'What will you do? Run? You should run.'

'I won't be far away, but I won't run. You didn't, did you? Plenty of work left, Padraig. The War ain't won yet.'

Pat hugs her and she carries on with the pram down the hill, heading towards St James' Cemetery.

He looks up at the grand, white edifice and jiggles the keys in his hand, still not quite believing his luck. He walks inside, through the wide entrance and vestibule, the long hallway big enough to fit all of his hovel he has called home with extra space by itself, then into the parlour, where some special people are waiting for him.

Pat's family sit huddled in one corner of the room, not quite able to fathom where they are.

'Would you look at the state of youse. It's a big house and it's all ours, so. Spread out a bit will yers. Enjoy. Jesus.'

Sarah approaches him and they embrace, home at last.

A rainbow crests over St James' Necropolis as Harriet approaches Conté's resting place. A gravestone has appeared, freshly inscribed.

Conté Marie-Louise Louverture, 9th May 1841 to 24th June 1863. Eternal Rest Grant Upon Her o Lord and Let Perpetual Light Shine Upon Her - Her Friend, Harriet.

'Hello again.' Harriet caresses the stone and places a fresh posy down. 'Look who I've brought to see her namesake. Baby Conté. I know, maybe I should have called her something Irish, eh?' Harriet takes a breath and spots the rainbow. 'No way, you'd spin in that grave and make a right mess.'

She takes it in, the colours washing over the sky. It's a fresh day and the city's stink seems to have dissipated from the air. Either that or she has finally gotten used to it. Harriet twitches her fingers and cracks her knuckles.

'We're winning this war, Conté. I should tell you all about what is happening in Pennsylvania. Dudley is so rapt. And I gave the house away. Guess who to? You'll laugh your ass off.'

Harriet wipes away tears that she permits to flow now. 'Oh give me a sign, Conté. Something, anything. You can't just go and leave me like that. She needs her other Mommy. She needs her Daddy. She needs you, my love.'

The rush of a breeze rattles around the trees. Like a spectre, Mr Ake has appeared behind her clutching a Browning pistol, proving his uncanny stealth again. Harriet doesn't turn, but she knows he's there. Of course, where else to do business?

'You had to choose this place to do this, didn't you? Poor taste, sir.'

'You could have come and found me. I don't hide, ma'am.'

'In that fortress of yours?'

'Not for much longer. They're not too keen on my kind in the Watch, never have been.'

Harriet keeps her back to him. 'Don't harm the child.'

Ake glances at the pram and looks almost insulted. 'I would never.'

'I wouldn't harm yours. I promise to see that they are well-cared for.'

Ake frowns and adjusts his leather gloves. 'As I will yours.'

'Good, then.'

Harriet pulls a string cord attached to her foot and the pram detonates, sending Ake reeling. Her ears ring, but that was just the right amount of gunpowder for the effect.

Ake levers up, making a half step, but his other foot dangles in the air, hanging off a shattered bone sticking out of his destroyed lower leg. Harriet turns and aims. The shot rings out across the cemetery, scaring away a murder of crows. She faces him, her Colt .45 smoking. Ake clutches his throat and collapses backwards, hitting the ground with a resonant thump.

'You'll have one, big, happy family. I promise you, sir. Why you had to do what you did, I'll never know, but that ain't your kids' problem, I suppose.'

He fits for a moment, then remains still. Harriet checks; no others around. She studies the slain giant, then rolls his corpse over with her foot. Gravity takes care of the rest as he falls six feet down into a heap. She rides up her sleeves and grabs a shovel.

Baby Conté coos from behind her namesake's gravestone. 'Momma will be with you in a little moment, sweetheart. Everything will be fine. Hush, my angel face.'

Harriet shovels dirt over Ake's body and, in a beat, everything is disembodied, like a spirit watching from above, higher and higher. Perhaps it is the forest river spirit, to which her friend now belongs, or another spirit somewhat closer to this place, but it brings peace.

Up, up, up where the rainbow now straddles the city, framing the heavy industry and the Welsh Mountains on the horizon. Smokestacks in the docks and thousands of vessels flow in and out of the Mersey.

These entries are fragments of time, a snippet of how a place gets its character, which is imbued just as much as any person. It is a gateway to the world, an enigma to even itself, and it will grow and decline and grow again. Its love and its hate, sadness and shame, are still to play out.

It is a city that always looks to the West. It is Liverpool.

The spirit slips off to the heavens and we plummet back to earth.

Harriet Farrell finishes shovelling dirt and resets herself, cracking her neck. She dusts off her hands and checks on her sleeping baby before carrying her away down the cinder path, whistling a pretty little Irish ditty.

EPILOGUE – THE BLOB

November 19th, 1863

'Four score and seven years ago, our fathers brought forth on this continent a new nation, conceived in Liberty, and dedicated to the proposition that all men are created equal.

Now we are engaged in a great Civil War, testing whether that nation or any nation so conceived and so dedicated, can long endure. We are met on a great battlefield of that war. We have come to dedicate a portion of that field, as a final resting place for those who here gave their lives that this nation might live. It is altogether fitting and proper that we should do this.

But, in a larger sense, we can not dedicate—we cannot consecrate—we cannot hallow—this ground. The brave men, living and dead, who struggled here, have **consecrated** *it, far above our poor power to add or detract. The world will little note, nor long remember what we say here, but it can never forget what they did here. It is for us the living, rather, to be dedicated here to the unfinished work which they who fought here have thus far so nobly advanced. It is rather for us to be here dedicated to the great task remaining before us—that from these honoured dead we take increased devotion to that cause for which they here gave the last full measure of devotion—that we here highly resolve that these dead shall not have died in vain—that this nation, under God, shall have a new birth of freedom—and that government of the people, by the people, for the people, shall not perish from the earth.'*

The Soldiers' National Cemetery at Gettysburg, on the solemn occasion of the dedication. The human detritus and dreadful carnage has been long cleared, and now all that remains are thousands of graves, monuments and fine words. Gentlemen of the press clamber around President Abraham Lincoln as Butler watches on from the side of the gantry, but several yards away.

Yes, such *fine* words, Mr President.

Two young, handsome men emerge from the shadows, dressed in fetching civilian attire. Both are journeymen actors, the kind that Maj. Gen. Butler likes to employ from time to time, when he's looking to stir the pot. They are Mr Surratt and Mr Wilkes Booth and their very presence here is an act of treason on the part of their paymaster.

'Take a good look at him, gentlemen. I've got a job for you.'

Milton Keynes UK
Ingram Content Group UK Ltd.
UKHW012116240124
436635UK00006B/452